The Dogwood Tree

Mary Allen Redd

Cascade Books

Grateful acknowledgment is made to the
following for permission to use material
from their unpublished essays in an edited form:
Geoffrey Watson, "Why Me?" Patty Madert,
"Love Your Cat, Annoy Your Husband"
Eun-Young La, "My Hometown."

Library of Congress Catalog Card Number: 2003090906

ISBN: 0-9636548-4-5

Manufactured in the United States of America

Cascade Books
4271 Vintage Drive
Provo, Utah 84604
cascadebooks@madmac.com

To Robert

then, now, always

Also by Mary Allen Redd

Fiction

The World of Holly Prickle

Nonfiction (Mary Allen)

*The Necessary Blankness: Women in Major
American Fiction of the Sixties*

Animals in American Literature

Contents

Part Two: After

The Dogwood Tree

.

Part One: Before

1 *Stan*

The day her husband left, the sun was shining. It was the first morning of spring in Virginia. Buds were bursting out on dark limbs before the green. Leaves unfolded pink. The air was soft again.

Time to play tennis outside. Let the sun get in your eyes, the wind blow the ball. The ceiling is high, you're running—alive—

Abby went out on the patio. The concrete was warm on her bare feet. She breathed. Yes.

They had a lucky life. Stan said one time, "How is it that we found what everyone is looking for?" They were thirty when they got married, both for the first time. That was six years ago already.

She met him on the tennis court. He was a short person who ran all-out for every ball. His stocky legs appeared misshapen at first. Soon they seemed just right. He hit the most beautiful backhand she had ever seen. It went straight down the line.

His name was Stan Swan. A fine name, and it fit. He was unpretentious but full of grace. No one physical feature was perfect, although together they were more than handsome.

3

His front teeth extended slightly, offering a soft upper lip that was voluptuous. Eyes that were gray in a certain light became blue with a blue shirt. When he smiled his whole face went into it, making creases around his mouth that stayed. He saw these things, accepted them, and liked himself.

Stan was a person who could fix anything. When their stove wouldn't work, he dismantled it and found the little wire at fault. He installed a new patio door, knocking out the old one with small panes and peeling paint, putting in smooth-sliding glass to give more light. And he fixed things so cheerfully, jumping up to do it, that it would have been cruel to mention this to women who lived with leaky faucets. Certainly not her sister Elizabeth, whose husband Jack never did anything right.

Abby stepped off the warm cement onto the narrow strip of lawn inside their condo wall, which Stan kept meticulously trimmed with a Weed Eater, wearing goggles to protect himself from flying rocks. He'd cut it this morning, and pieces of the warm, wet grass clung to her feet. They hadn't done other planting here since both of them would rather play tennis than do yard work.

She went back inside, downstairs to where Stan did his stretching exercises before going out to the court. He was in the bathroom shaving as she passed, his face a mask of foam. She watched as the razor made a path that showed his clean, smooth skin. He shaved on weekends even when they weren't going anywhere. Sometimes Stan shaved before he came to bed, always smelling good.

She touched his back as she passed, going on to put

4

clothes in the dryer, wads of white tennis socks of nearly the same size, his and hers.

As she came out of the laundry room, they met in the hall with a familiar embrace. Abby liked being his height, or maybe she was an inch taller at five foot eight. It's nice to hug someone your size. Stan's new moustache still gave her a start. The bristles felt exotic on her mouth, as though she were kissing a stranger. Yet those were his soft lips, only his. She could not remember anyone else's lips. When he kissed the back of her neck, the moustache felt delicious.

Stan went in the recreation room, which they had made into their bedroom down here in the basement where it was cool and dark. He stood with his feet apart, reaching to touch his palms on the floor, doing it so easily. Her fingertips barely touched. Just because you play tennis doesn't mean that you are limber. And Stan was strong. He could carry a big TV without panting, or lift her onto the bed with ease.

Abby stretched out on the bed, not made yet. She rather liked seeing the sheets pulled out from last night. They were a jungle pattern of Stan's favorite green colors. From inside the sheets you could see yellow eyes looking down at you through vines.

OK. Time to go play tennis with Marge.

When Abby looked back on that moment, as she got up off the bed she was remembering to get her water bottle out of the freezer to take to the court. The bottle was naturally frozen solid when she thought of it again three days later.

5

Stan finished stretching and stood up with a warm face. "Can we talk about something?"

"Of course." She sank back on the bed. The cat leaped up beside her, a big tabby named Dwayne. Stan sat on her other side, his hand on her bare knee. She would know that hand if she were a blind person. The callous where he held his racket, hard with a sharp edge of skin, tickled her leg now.

He smoothed his hand out on her thigh. "I don't know if I want to continue in this relationship."

Her foot kept rotating on her ankle, her version of warming up. "What relationship?"

"This is the longest I've been with anyone," he said.

Abby watched her foot slow down, stop, the toes sitting up stiff. "It's the longest for me too. You mean us?"

"I guess I'm just not good at this."

This. This?

His eyes were gray, with an emptiness in them she had never seen. "What is it, love?" She turned to him, a terrified tightness coming into her, unable to register. "Tell me. What's the matter?"

"It has nothing to do with you." Stan tied his shoelaces, the long ones that come with Nikes for extra support, she supposed, although she tripped over them. "I need to figure out my life."

She thought of scenes in movies where the characters say such things. Those people weren't real. This was Stan. Her husband. Dearer to her than anything.

"Speak to me. Explain." He did not meet her eyes. She

looked past him to the wood paneling of the wall, here in this room where they had been so happy. Maybe it wasn't real wood. "We should be able to discuss the problem," she said, using her teacher's voice, trying to sound rational, fair. "Let's work on it together. We aren't stupid."

Stan double-tied his laces and pulled them tight. He sat up and planted his hands on his thighs. "I have to decide if I'd be happier by myself or with another person."

The purring in the room stuttered, grew faint.

Hold tight. This was one of those bad moments that come in every marriage. All couples have them. Could be a mood swing. Temporary insanity.

Stan went to his closet and got his tennis bag. It was black with the red word *Prince* on the side, although he no longer played with a Prince racket. He now used a Wilson Sledge Hammer. Stan held his bag by the grip, never one to sling it over his shoulder carelessly. The bag was equipped with sweatbands, new Penn balls, Band-Aids, everything he needed. "It must be this midlife crisis thing."

Dwayne dropped to the floor and started coughing. Hunched, neck extended, he gagged a few times and spit up a pale pellet of fur.

Abby let it lie there on the rug. "You're only thirty-six."

"I don't feel excited about my life" was his answer.

So a person leaves home? Still, she could not deny the dead look in his eyes. How could she not have noticed? How could she be married to someone and not know?

Stan's face crumpled then, and he came to her and held

7

her tight. "This will make us better, Abby. It's just temporary. I'll come to my senses."

They held each other for a long time, their tears commingling.

"We need to think of ways to make our life better," she said. "We should travel for fun. You always go for your job. We could even do yard work." That brought a smile from him, although it didn't stay. "And there's always—" she said in her gentlest voice. However, this wasn't the time to talk about children, was it.

"I'll come to my senses," Stan said again, stroking her hair, which she wore long and straight the way she had in college. It was light brown hair, which under certain conditions could be called blond. "I just need some time to figure things out."

"I understand," she said, which was to be the first of many lies.

He kissed her, deeply and well, their bodies meeting through their clothes, hearts beating frightfully from their scare, until the sweetness came up in them that had always been theirs. Maybe Stan was being brave by trying to improve their marriage this way. Most men won't take the initiative. Meanwhile, she had gone along contentedly, not knowing anything was wrong. Sure, he had seemed a little distant at times. So what? People have a right to their private thoughts.

"My things are in the car."

Things? What things?

She watched him go up the stairs, his sturdy legs taking

the steps lightly, wearing white tennis shorts, the soft wave in the back of his hair familiar, dear to her. At the top of the stairs he turned to say, "There's no need to mention this to our parents, Abby. I would appreciate that."

"No. No need," she said in a voice from a distant place. Indeed, that's the last thing she would want to do, call her parents long distance to tell them this.

His steps sounded sharply on the wood floor of the dining room, then they muted as he went on to the living-room rug. The door up there clicked shut.

She stood for a long time. Who knows how long it would have been if a cat hadn't brushed against her leg, again and again. She sank down to his soft body, to the cool linoleum of the floor. Through his fur she could feel the rapid beating of his heart.

So they sat, a woman and a cat, in the dim light of a basement. She stared over at the carpet of the bedroom, with a dark thread in it to camouflage the dirt. The rug didn't show a footprint. Nothing.

It was quiet here in their neighborhood, far enough from King Street so that you couldn't hear the traffic. Just an occasional siren, or the faint rattle of a helicopter out over the beltway looking for wrecks.

Now the only sound was the clothes in the dryer going around, thump, thump.

"It has nothing to do with you," he had said. But if that were true, why would he need to leave?

Her throat tightened with the next question. When did Stan decide to go? Did he plan his departure in the winter, counting the days until the weather was good? Perhaps he had tried to leave in other springs, faltering as he took his things to the car, disappointed with himself for not having the nerve to go.

He might have known from the beginning that this day would come.

"I'll come to my senses." He had said that too. "This will make us better." A person wouldn't say that unless he meant it.

Abby got up off the floor. The fragrance of the Irish Spring soap in Stan's bathroom made her feel faint as she passed. She stepped in and leaned on the towel rack. Look. He'd put out a new bar of soap. So of course he was coming back. In the cabinet he'd left aspirin, which he took every day without fail to keep from getting a heart attack. However, the faucet was polished so brightly you would think that the house was up for sale.

Slowly she went to his walk-in closet, reached into the dark, and pulled on the light. Stan often drew her in here, ever so tenderly, when he was getting undressed. He did that just the other night.

Plenty of his shirts were left. Pin-striped, blue, white ones, all in immaculate condition. If a collar of his got stained, he threw the shirt away. Abby calculated the space left on the rod, enough for a dozen shirts. Not that he necessarily had taken that many, or that he would use them. He might have wanted extras to be safe.

She was holding the crisp terry cloth of his bathrobe when she heard a car drive up.

He'd come back already! Of course Stan would come back, this conscientious man. He didn't hurt people. He was good to everyone, never failing to visit his parents, calling if he would be ten minutes late. They liked to tell the story of young Stan's loyalty to his dog, how he slept on the floor by that German shepherd the whole summer before she died. A dog named Jackie.

Stan succeeded at things. He got promoted in the government even when there was a freeze.

The car driving into their parking lot was not Stan's Cherokee. Of course it wasn't. He was out on the tennis court. You don't just run off and leave your partner standing there.

And she had to go meet Marge. If she ran, she still could make it. Try to keep the ball in play somehow. From the far end of the court, Marge couldn't see her face. She would never need to know.

Abby stepped out in the glaring sun, into the half-deserted parking lot on this sunny Saturday. Stan liked to park down by the bus stop so he could wait in the car when it rained. They had enjoyed the Grand Cherokee, feeling secure in a four-wheel drive when it snowed here in the Washington, D.C., area, where cars slide off the road with the first flake.

His parking place was empty. Not even a grease spot left on the ground.

A bus wheezed up to the curb, letting off a single dark figure moving down the aisle. She watched, waited. Could it

11

be? But the man hopping to the ground was too tall to be Stan. Most men were. The man walked briskly down the street with his key in his hand, eager to get home to someone.

Abby held to her tennis bag and ran, past the oak tree out front with its excellent posture against the wind, azaleas ready with color in their skinny arms. She ran to the wooded area at the end of the street, where in the shade of bigger trees the dogwood soon would spread white petals on the air.

Breathe in, breathe out.

She hugged her racket and ran until she could see the tennis court back in the trees, that oblong of green with its clean white lines.

2 *A Cat*

I watch for my lady. Where is she?

Some bad thing has happened. Her tears fell into my fur, many tears, making my coat wet. She filled my bowl with tuna, not a mere spoonful.

You may wonder at my vocabulary. We live here with books, books, everywhere. I've been known to sleep on the dictionary. On top of the couch, I watch her read. I touch my whiskers on her neck, and she will give me anything.

I hear a car. My ears stand up. When she comes she'll wave to me at the window. Walk over and tap the glass.

It's getting dark, and I am lonely. Where is my lady out in the night? I have known the terrifying wheels of the highway. I remember them.

I once lived with children who tormented me. My claws were taken out. They dressed me in a bonnet. One awful day they took me for a ride—

I lived on the street for a time, eating out of garbage cans. I went looking for a home with no nasty children. In one place they threw me out when I ate a chicken. The big bird was sitting on the counter. What did they expect? In another house a man made me sit on his lap. I ran away.

One chilly day as I was stepping through dead leaves, I came to a stairway going down to an open door. It was no mansion with a fishpond out back. This was a building. Scrawny grass in front. A dirty sidewalk. Comfy looking though.

She was coming in then too. I trotted alongside as if I owned the place, just following my nature.

She let me stay. No big deal. Not that she fawned over me (not then, although I have since trained her as to my preferences). It was just a basement room. But she let me sleep on the bed. The blanket grew warm under me. I knew I had found my place.

A cat has to be careful though. People can be nice at first, petting and saying soft words. Then for no reason they change. I tried this person out, leaping on the counter and licking butter off a plate. She didn't knock me off the way most people do. She laughed and threw me meat. It was wonderful.

She was my lady. I was her cat.

Where is my lady tonight? I listen for her. My ears are ready.

The phone rings. I leap down and dash across the room. A cat does not like noise. The clanking of a dishwasher. A garbage disposal chewing on steel.

It's quiet again, and I soar back to my windowsill. I watch the car lights going by. The light on our porch isn't on tonight.

Surely she will come soon. She always does come home.

3 Teacher

Abby sat in her car outside the community college where she taught English, watching the students going in. They come from everywhere. A Hispanic family arrived in a van, delivering the daughter who would not have gone to college in her country. That's how the students say it, "my country," in reverent tones, with no need to mention the name. A gentleman from El Salvador strode up the walk, proud with a big moustache. The day he left his country, human heads were stuck on the fence posts there. Still, he wanted to go back. It was his dream to go back home.

A convertible swerved up, driven by an Iranian with swarthy good looks and manners to please his teachers and prove to his classmates that he wasn't a terrorist. A girl in a sari glided by with a red dot on her forehead, stamped and sealed for the man she would marry in the summer, a man she had never met. They might even be happy together. You hear stories like that.

Many Asians come to school here, working together in the library, bringing fat dictionaries to class and staying until the last moment of a test. Cambodians, Chinese, Koreans, but mostly Vietnamese, incredibly learning the English language after speaking tongues that don't sound like words. Yet despite the errors, their writing is often beautiful.

They tell of families leaving Vietnam, getting in the little boat at night with nothing but a map from a high school text as a guide. How could an inch of the South China Sea be so far? They set out on the dark water, never knowing where it will take them.

People come to the community college from down the street, some who have never traveled farther than Maryland. Dropouts who have hated school ever since that first insult, rejection, failure. Then for some reason they give school another chance. A dead-end job might bring them back. Or they meet a new love who likes to go to class. That makes all the difference.

They come out of work. Out of rehab. Out of jail. Parents register to keep up with their kids, wearing the same running shoes, bearing the same backpacks. The happiest are mothers who had given up their schooling to have children. They are thrilled to be back.

Anyone can come. And many vanish. Some don't drop the class. They just go. A teacher doesn't know why. Is it something you did or did not do? More likely, it has nothing to do with you. Nothing to do with you at all.

In every class at least one person is falling apart. A boss might bring on the craziness. It could be an illness in the family. A breakup. A breakup of any kind. Yet in her ten years of teaching, Abby had never learned to tell from the faces who would disappear. You can't tell from the smiles.

OK. Time to go to class.

She got out of the car, gripped her briefcase, and strode toward the building to her composition class. Go in and be a teacher. But one look at her, and they'd know something had happened. You can't fool the students. Not for long. About suffering they knew far more than she did. Hey, she'd had a happy childhood. She wasn't cut out for pain.

A car stopped in front of the building, and the driver kissed the girl getting out. She could not have been called pretty. Yet she glowed as she came up the steps. The fellow watched until she got inside before he drove away.

How did these people do it? How did they know how to be happy?

Abby stopped in the restroom. Whoa, did she look bad. She applied more Erase to the dark pockets under her eyes. The person next to her had purple hair, piled up and fastened with chopsticks. It takes nerve to do that. Any change to your hair. Maybe she should lighten hers. Become a different person.

As she approached the classroom, hearing the hum of the students inside, for a moment the old glad feeling of things as they had been returned. Maybe when she went in here everything would be all right.

"How was your weekend, Mrs. Swan?" Denise sat in her usual place on the front row. Her dark eyes saw everything.

Abby set her briefcase down. It was an old-fashioned, square-edged, tan case with scratches on it. The handle wobbled. "My weekend was—dreadful."

Denise gave that look of not knowing if the teacher was kidding, but she was too polite to ask more.

Abby looked around the familiar room, the bulletin board with its tattered messages: people seeking roommates, rides, a buyer for an outdated car or computer. Colorful announcements inviting students to travel to exotic places. Yet here they were, sitting in their seats as usual.

Except for one empty chair in the middle. Phuong. Where was Phuong? She never missed.

On the podium in front were handouts left from last Friday's class, way back then. Directions Abby had typed with such certainty, requiring that all essays have a main idea. "Come right out and state your point," she proclaimed to the students. "That's what everybody wants." What other lies had she told them?

Who was she to stand here and tell them anything?

A thin fellow named Todd took his seat in the back. He was really skinny, and he always wore a baseball cap. Why hadn't she thought of it before? Chemotherapy. Or he might be hiding the scabs from AIDS.

A woman named Sue came heavily into the room and dropped into a chair. She put her head down, pushing her fingers back through her hair, tight against her scalp. What had made her late today? More bad news about her boy Jesse, waiting in prison for his parole?

The man sitting next to Sue was the healthiest-looking person you ever saw. Harry's cheeks were pink. His eyes were bright. He wore a crisp white shirt with red suspenders. Under his shirt beat a heart lucky to be alive. Three times they had cut into his chest looking for the cancer.

Harry smiled at her now.

Abby smiled back.

Time to start. But she'd forgotten what they were doing today. She had forgotten to look at the syllabus.

All right. She swung around to the blackboard (if anything, a teacher knows how to fake it) and wrote WRITING TIPS. She kept the words in an even line, not writing downhill this time. Number one. "Tell the truth." She had always been so sure of that.

"What else?" she called, gripping the chalk, the size of a pea. "Help me out here."

"Surprise the reader," someone said. She had taught them well. Except that she hated surprises. A car wreck is a surprise. An earthquake is.

"Avoid cliches," came another excellent suggestion. She liked to tell them that a cliche was a zit on the page. "Don't write cliches and don't be one. Be more than a statistic." She was full of this stuff.

"Should we hand in our essays?" Denise asked as Abby swung around to face the class. Damn. Here she was giving directions when the assignment was due today.

"Certainly." Busily she went down the aisles collecting the compositions, exclaiming about the titles, and holding the papers close to her. Grading these tonight would give her something to do. "So, I hope you followed the tips," she added brightly, with a dismissive wave at the items on the board, not that she was fooling anyone about her little blunder here.

After class she held office hours in her cubicle, in a pen of offices she had considered collegial. Now she crouched

19

behind her desk, hoping that no colleague would drop by. Especially not Marge. Abby might be able to fool her on the tennis court, even when she was hitting those balls *way out* on Saturday. Anybody can have a bad day on the court. But fool Marge across this desk? Never.

So where were the students coming in with problems when you needed them?

Instead, here came Marge. Abby grabbed a pencil and pulled over the pile of essays.

"You're looking serious," Marge said.

"All these papers to grade."

Marge sat down anyway, this smart little woman who went to the heart of things. She counseled students by the hour, and they loved her. A person should learn to do that. Abby had always been in such a hurry to get home.

She saw Phuong waiting outside and jumped up to get her. "Come in. Sit down." Abby shooed Marge out of the chair. "Catch you later."

Phuong sat carefully on the edge of the chair, slim in a white blouse, her dark bangs cut straight above her glasses.

"Sorry I miss class, Mrs. Swan."

"We missed you."

"My car stop while I am driving. Going along beltway, it suddenly stop. Cars are honking all around." Phuong's eyes blinked rapidly, but her face stayed smooth.

"I'm glad you're all right."

"Nice man help me roll car off to side. When tow truck came, I call taxi on cell phone so I get here. I never want to miss class."

20

"Oh, Phuong." Tears stung in Abby's eyes.

"You nice to care for me, Mrs. Swan." Phuong turned politely from the sight.

"Actually, it's for myself."

"I not bother you." She stood to go.

"No bother. We could talk about your paper. Anything."

Phuong produced her essay in a clear plastic folder. The title was "The Other Vietnam," and her main point clearly followed: "Vietnam is not just a place of war; it is beautiful." Wonderful student.

"I would like to visit your land."

Phuong nodded. "Now I go." The phone rang, and she darted out.

No doubt somebody calling with a complication, an excuse. But Abby was glad for the distraction today.

"You're there. I haven't been able to reach you at the house," Stan said in his everyday, magnificent voice.

The darkness fell away. "Oh, love. It's been hell. Where are you?"

"Listen, we're still having dinner with my parents on Saturday, right?"

"Sure." The pencil in her fingers, which had been poised to record a message of distress, spun wildly on the desk.

"I'll pick you up at six. Abby, I can't wait to see you."

4 *Edna*

Stan's mother stirred her pie filling, breathing the sweet smell. She was making the family's favorite, a black-bottom pie. It's a layer of creamy custard on top with bittersweet chocolate underneath.

The mixture was starting to boil. A bubble lifted like a little mouth, saying something, then it was gone. Another and another. She stirred faster, keeping the bottom of the pan smooth. If you stop stirring, you get lumps. She did make a good pie, even if she wasn't the smartest woman, something her husband liked to remind her of.

It was a Saturday night, and her son and his wife were coming. Just for fun. The ladies in the bridge club didn't have grown children who did that when it wasn't a holiday. Naturally, Edna wished she'd had a daughter too. Yet she got one anyway, didn't she. And Abby was probably nicer than her own daughter would have been.

She and Fred thought that Stan would never get married. But when he was thirty, he found the right girl. There still might be grandchildren. Fred wouldn't let her pester them about that though. Edna did secretly hope that one of these nights Stan would have an announcement to make.

He had always been a good son. It was nothing she did.

Stan liked doing chores, going on his paper route in the dark, in the cold, never once asking her to drive him. Ellie Naylor's boy down the street had made her take him when it rained, Nelson, who later got a girl pregnant. Stan would never do a dumb thing like that. He was decent with girls and people. And he took perfect care of his pets.

Edna inhaled the fragrant custard, fogging up her glasses as she pulled the pan off the stove. In a fog. That was her. That's what Fred thought anyway. So she went along and told stories about the crazy things she did, such as hemming his same pant leg twice (which actually happened). Edna didn't care if she looked silly if it made the family laugh.

Except for being mean, Fred was a good husband. He just had to prove he was smarter, reading out of the newspaper about places like Rwanda that she didn't know on the map, not that he cared for those poor people looking like black sticks. The only suffering Edna knew about was the pain of marriage, if that counts. It's probably nothing compared to houses being blown away in hurricanes or children with holes in their arms.

Fred probably suffered too, thinking that his marriage would be a grander thing, with smart conversations over the dinner table. Except that he needed to be superior, didn't he, so he got what he wanted after all.

The pie filling had cooled enough to pour. Here it came, falling in golden ripples over the dark chocolate, covering it entirely.

"What's for dinner?" Fred came up behind her. He tasted the pie filling with his finger. "You are good." They

23

did get along well in the kitchen, as she liked to cook, and Fred liked to eat.

Edna pretended to push him away, but he knew it pleased her when he complimented the food. That was one thing Fred knew, so he did it all the time.

"When are they coming?"

"Seven. Same as always."

"Can't wait."

Edna handed him the bowl of whipped cream. She knew she was evil, making these rich foods and getting him to take seconds. Then she nagged Fred about being fat, after the way he made fun of her.

Stan would never make fun of his wife. He was nice.

The phone rang at the end of the counter, the way it does in scary movies when the stalker is calling. She hollered for Fred to get it, but he had disappeared. Sometimes Edna let the phone ring when her hands were full. But this was the time when people call to say they'll be late. Stan was usually on time though. He and Abby never canceled.

The man on the phone was selling lifetime light bulbs, when who on earth buys those things at dinnertime? But he said he was blind, so she charged a dozen bulbs on Fred's Visa card. You don't have to go to some hot country to be decent. We have handicapped people right here.

Edna didn't like to fly, and those awful airline meals —which they don't give you anymore. Just a bun in a plastic sack. Not even peanuts. Tiny little pretzels.

Tonight she was making crab imperial. It's sounds fancy, but it's easy to make. You just mix mayonnaise and melted butter with the sweet chunks of crab, each one picked out of the shell by someone's hands. Those people deserve what you have to pay. She put the crab mixture in individual dishes, sprinkling on paprika for color, knowing how delicious it would be. This recipe never failed.

She set the table, feeling so glad. This is all she had ever wanted, to be a housewife and have her family here. If she had been born in a later time, she'd be forced to have a career. Going out in rush-hour traffic—and she didn't even like computers. Not that she didn't admire women who had jobs, such as her daughter-in-law, the teacher, standing up in front of her classes and knowing what to say.

Edna set out her Waterford wine glasses. Her friends would never use theirs except for special occasions. Well, to Edna these Saturday nights were the most special of all. She was serving red wine because it looked pretty in the glasses even if doesn't go with fish. Her family didn't care about such things. If Fred wanted a piece of lemon stuck on his wine glass (he was that tacky), he could have it. She just wanted everyone to have a good time.

She turned down the dimmer switch so the candles would stand out, although the daylight was staying longer, now that it was spring.

Everything was ready. They would be here soon.

5 *First Date*

Stan would be here in minutes. He was always on time.

This felt like a first date. Or worse, the prom. "You feel sick but in a good way," as a student described it.

Actually, the first date with Stan had been easy. He was just someone Abby met playing tennis, the short guy on the next court, hitting that beautiful backhand down the line.

The air had been soft and warm that night, a perfect southern evening. They started out up at the net stroking volleys so they could talk. Already something wonderful was happening. They didn't play games. They just hit for the joy of it. From the baseline she watched Stan run in his white clothes. She saw the control of his shots, topspin sending the ball with a jaunty bounce deep, or slice to keep it low. Her own strokes went out easy. She could have hit any shot that night.

With other men their flaws emerged in time. With Stan his virtues did. He was smart. He always caught the joke. And he understood her well. More than anyone, Stan knew what truly mattered to her and what did not.

They never had a parting.

So one bad week in seven years together wasn't much.

All couples have tough times, surviving worse than this.

Stan had said he would come to his senses. Now he had. He'd said on the phone that he was excited to see her.

Abby wore a red silk blouse with no bra for the occasion. According to *Cosmopolitan* magazine, men like to see your nipples. She did look perky. And the touch of silk on her bare skin was making her feel precocious.

But what if Stan were coming to ask for a divorce? Maybe he was excited because he'd solved his problem. Damn him. How could he decide about their marriage by himself, and pretending all along to be happy. She slid off the silk blouse and yanked on a T-shirt.

When he came, they would talk. She would demand to know what was going on. Give her the truth. She could handle it. Well, after rehearsing in front of the mirror she thought she could, practicing until her voice no longer quivered and her lips did not twitch. They would make a list of problem areas and possible solutions. That's what Stan did at work, coming up with answers for the federal government. They would see a marriage counselor. She got out the yellow pages and plopped them on the coffee table, ready.

She wasn't cut out for this misery shit. She'd been a happy kid.

The rain had stopped as she looked out the window for Stan's white Cherokee. The puddles in the parking lot were smooth, reflecting new growth on the oak tree above. A patch of sunlight was moving up the street, coming this way.

Would Stan step out of his vehicle as usual, whistling as he came? He was a good whistler. He used vibrato. He could whistle "Tonight" from *West Side Story*.

Dwayne darted away. He knew something was up. Abby was down talking to her cat under the bed in the guest room when she heard the front door opening. For a minute she thought somebody was breaking in. Stan did have his key though, didn't he. He did still live here.

She got up stiffly and went in the other room.

Stan stood just inside, holding out a flower, one red rose.

There he was, that dear, dear man. Not an angry or a mean person out to hurt another, just someone going through a bad time. A short and lonely-looking fellow, holding out a flower to his wife. His eyes were blue, so very blue, with her favorite blue shirt.

"It's beautiful. Thank you."

Abby went to put the rose in water, up on a chair in the kitchen, groping along the top shelf for the slim little vase pushed to the back. There it was. Her fingers touched the cool glass throat.

She felt Stan waiting as she stepped down. Gently he encompassed her in his arms, as he knew so well how to do. Stan knew how to touch a woman, and how to wait. He held her close, and she knew that he was afraid too.

They kissed lightly, as beginning fingers might test the keys to make sure the notes are right before striking them. And they were. They were.

The afternoon light in the guest room came through the shutters in gold slices on the bed where they lay down together, hearts going like mad, as if they were teenagers trying this out for the first time. She and Stan kissed wildly,

28

like starved people. They touched as if the terrain were new. Gradually they became themselves again, moving to familiar music, the most beautiful of all.

All was well. All was well again.

Better! Stan had been right. He had said his departure would make them better, and it had. O sweet reunion. O the joy of second chances.

Their nightmare week was over, barely to be remembered, like the wreck you almost had on the highway that leaves you shaky for a few miles. Then you change the station on the radio and hum along. There was no need to make Stan explain, to rub his nose in his brief excursion. He had come back. Some people would stay away out of pride. She thanked him with her heart for not being one of them.

Stan had asked so little of her in their marriage. One week away was a small thing.

"I've missed you, Abby."

She nodded, and her eyes were full.

They went out in the washed world, where the sun sparkled through the dripping leaves, and the grass was green, so green. They waved to their neighbors, the Dawsons, a couple who never touched in public. Stan's arm came closer around her waist.

They were laughing high in their Grand Cherokee as they drove around the beltway, the road around Washington that people hate, where tractor-trailers spill and back you up all day. Today as a driver maneuvered a delivery truck with an Oreo cookie on the side, Abby waved up to him. He tooted his horn back. Who wouldn't feel good on this Saturday evening in spring?

Ahead of them the glittering traffic slowed on the Woodrow Wilson Bridge, an old drawbridge with the potential to slap up in your face and strand you there. But it didn't do that. This was just an ordinary slowdown, nothing to be bothered about. It gave a chance to look down on the Potomac River, riding high after the week's rain. Sailboats tilted at amazing angles but kept moving merrily along. Across the water rose the Washington Monument into a clearing sky, that pencil of white marking this underloved city, a most beautiful city of trees.

Stan spoke with animation about his job, the commodities under his care at the Department of Agriculture—coffee, bananas, and a new one, jute, that fiber produced in Bangladesh for making rope. Stan had become a skilled negotiator, dealing with the various national groups: the eloquent Brits, the aloof French, tardy Third World delegates, who arrived at meetings hours late. By nature a patient man, Stan used his gift to keep communications going until international trade agreements were reached. He had reason to be proud.

Traffic spurted forward, and they crossed the rutted part of the bridge over to the Maryland side, on to Riverdale, where Stan's parents lived in a neighborhood of one-story brick houses, yellow and brown. There the trash receptacles with their big black shoulders stayed out by the curb beyond their day, and garage doors were left open to show off leaf blowers, used cans of paint, tangled Christmas lights piled by the family van. Yet when the azaleas were in bloom, this street, like a hundred others in the area, was transformed into a glory of pink, purple, white to make visitors, even residents who saw the sight each year, gasp with delight.

They turned on Oleander Avenue, the street where Stan grew up. On this very sidewalk he had learned to ride his bike. Here he first drove the family car over to his high school pep rally, where he was a cheerleader because he was too small to make the team.

From these beginnings, however it happens, a most excellent man came into being.

Fred's yard was easy to spot. It was the one with the pink flamingos. If somebody had told Abby that she would be related to people who actually like those stick birds, she would not have believed it. Now she felt a flood of tenderness for the ridiculed creatures stooping to pick their awkward lunch out of the grass, swallowing uphill.

Stan took her hand as they went up the walk. They with the glow of a couple coming from bed. Her body still tingled. Stan was smiling too.

The door opened before their touch, and Fred came out with his arms wide. He was a handsome man who looked like Stan. They had the same thick wavy hair, the same smile lines engraved in the smooth tan of their faces.

Edna came to Fred's shoulder, a tiny little woman with bright capped teeth and eyes that grew big behind her glasses. She gave the quick smile of a mother seeing her child. It extended to Abby too.

"You're here," she beamed. "Dinner's ready."

31

6 The After-Bottom

Abby woke the next morning to the sound of Stan's footsteps in the living room upstairs. The red numbers on the clock said 6:30. They didn't blink. He often played early-bird tennis. There was nothing unusual in that. She heard him leave. Outside the Cherokee started up and drove away. It was quiet in the neighborhood on a Sunday morning.

Sleep, just sleep. But for every sleep there would be a waking, to know again that he had gone.

And—he came back. Last night Stan brought a flower. Not lilies for a funeral but one red rose. He had never been more tender and loving, this sexy, sexy man. Their reunion was thrilling, joyful, sweet, the beginning of a new life for them. At dinner when Edna suggested that they all take a trip together, Stan agreed enthusiastically, in a way he never would have before. A weekend in Hershey, Pennsylvania, might be just the thing, where the streetlights are shaped like kisses, and they give out free candy in the stores.

Yet the sound of him leaving fell on her like lead. A weight pressed against her head, her aching, throbbing head.

The lump on her forehead began to purr. A paw slapped her cheek. Whack. Again. Get up.

The phone rang, sending Dwayne soaring off the bed, a jarring sound at this hour, which one day would be a call from a hospital saying a parent was gone. It was somebody wanting to play tennis with Stan. *Well,* she wanted to snarl, *he doesn't live here anymore. Get him to explain.* Instead, she gave out Stan's work number and said that he was on the tennis court. She always said that. Even Edna believed it when she called at 11:00 at night, although her son was known for going to bed early.

Later today Abby's parents would call as they did every Sunday. She would chat about what she and Stan were doing, giving more details than ever before, including scraps of truth. This time she would recount the dinner at the Swans' last night, describing Edna's crab imperial, her delicious black-bottom pie. Abby was so ready with her story that she would have called her parents now to get this over with, but it was too early in the west to do that.

She dragged in the *Washington Post,* heavy in its plastic bag. Looking through it could take half the day, although she chucked the travel section featuring romantic island getaways. She did secure the TV schedule, that little bible which gets you through the week, noting that tonight's movie was a rerun of *The Burning Bed.*

Dwayne was perched in the window, looking out. Was he miserable trapped in here too? Never again to creep through the grass, pounce on a bird, trot across a moonlit street to a cat's tryst. Another bowl of tuna, one last nap, and that would be it.

Abby opened the door, where a hall led to the outside entrance, propped open on this lovely day. Dwayne dropped to the floor and crept through the carpet in a jungle mode. The times she had let him outside he ate grass and threw up, which supposedly is good for a cat to prevent hair balls, but it didn't look like fun. She told herself that Dwayne liked living indoors. Well, at least it was safer.

Paw by paw Dwayne edged toward the open door, sniffing his freedom, that precious something. It was the myth she discussed in American literature classes, epitomized by Huckleberry Finn, the boy every man wants to be, escaping barefoot through the grass. The Lone Ranger riding off into the sunset.

Dwayne's tail lifted, a nice fat striped tail. It brushed the sides of the door frame as he took his first cautious step out. Then like a snake floating on air, the tail was gone.

She didn't watch him out the window. Nor would she wander in the neighborhood moaning her cat's name, crawling under bushes to look for him. He would come back if he wanted to. Pets do that, cats as well as dogs, incredibly finding their way across the miles when they want to come home.

Later she called her folks out in Utah. No answer. What? Parents aren't supposed to have a life.

But she was ready with her fabrications. She would call her sister then. If she could fool Elizabeth, she could fool anyone.

"Abby? It's you. What's up?"

"Nothing has to be up. I'm just calling to say hello."

"Well, I had a rotten night because of Jack's snoring. You wouldn't know about that, would you. I'm sure Stan doesn't snore. He's perfect."

"Whoever said that?" Abby peeled a banana. Stay serene.

"What I don't understand is how anybody can make that racket without waking himself. But no. Jack gets his sleep. I want to snuff him with the pillow."

"Right. He should die for snoring."

"Since when are you standing up for Jack?"

Abby bit the banana. "He's a good man."

"Well, you might be sympathetic once in your life. And you're eating, aren't you, while we talk. Let me say hello to Stan."

"He's playing tennis."

"On a Sunday, without you?"

"He's an excellent men's singles player. Later we'll go for a nice dinner, take in a museum."

"Abby, you hate museums."

"Maybe I've changed. Stan goes to museums all the time overseas." She aimed the banana peel at the trash, missed, and it slapped the cat's water bowl. She watched the ripples die away. Dwayne might never drink from that bowl again.

"You should travel with Stan."

"I teach."

"Get a sub."

"They don't do that in college."

"The almighty college teacher never gets sick?"

"Well, I'm *not* sick."

"At least take the summer off, Abby. What's the point of being a teacher if you work all year? And Mom and Dad are coming to visit you."

"To Virginia? This summer?" She halted. "But it's so hot, humid."

"Abby, you're acting weird."

"So, tell me about the boys." She really should get to know her nephews, although by now Tucker was a teenager. Too late to talk to him. Roy, the surprise child, was too young to be interesting. Yet he would be six by now, wouldn't he, born the year that she and Stan got married.

"Tuck works at Blockbuster. Thinking about college, he says. I've raised a son with no ambition. Of course Jack thinks everything is great."

"Listen to yourself, Elizabeth. You never say anything good about Jack."

"All right. He's a good father, if that means he'd rather play computer games with his kids than—"

"See. You should appreciate that he likes to stay home, that he enjoys your company."

"Excuse me for not getting gushy the way you do. OK, Jack is my friend. He's a good man. I've just never had that gaga feeling you have—you, the rational one. At least if you would once admit that Stan isn't perfect—"

"Listen, I need to go. Papers to grade."

She saved Paul's essay for last. It was about a girl who hurt him, no doubt one of those adolescent breakups that seem like the end of the world to a college student. Paul was a dark-eyed, handsome boy with a tragic look who left the room while the others were writing, agitated as if he were on drugs. She thought he had gone, but at the break he was outside, smoking a cigarette.

"I can't do it," Paul said, pacing on the walk. "My whole life is, like, falling apart."

"Something you could write about?" Abby suggested greedily.

"Her?" Paul sank down on the step. His jeans had a ragged hole big enough for a fist. "I *hate* Maria." He bit his cuticle. "Ouch."

"There's your main idea." She crouched beside him. "I want to know what happened."

Paul stared past her. His eyes looked old.

"Can I do it out here?" Paul flipped his cigarette to the walk, watching it burn down.

"Yes. Sure."

After class Paul was still sitting cross-legged on the step writing furiously, lost in his words, a sight dear to an English teacher.

Here is what he wrote.

Maria

Her name is Maria. To this day I can't rid myself of the pain she has caused me. I went from being a person who thought of love as something good to one with a twisted view of it as the most negative thing ever.

I was visiting my dad in Brazil. There on the beach I saw a girl with blue eyes and light brown hair blending in with the crystal soft sand. I had no will but to approach her and ask her name. We talked for eight hours straight that day, and all I could hear was her cute laugh. The chemistry between us was on fire.

At the age of eighteen I was cast into a blind spell of deep passion for her. I guess it was love at first sight. Still, I was sure it would last, and we were married three weeks later. I had always promised myself that I would be at least thirty and stable before I got married. Then I met Maria.

I returned to Virginia ahead of her to continue my university studies. But I couldn't concentrate as I waited. I quit school and got a full-time job. All I could think of was being side-to-side in each other's arms.

Maria soon arrived and began her new life with me as her husband. She had never been to the United States and had no contacts or friends. I thought what a difficult decision it must have been to leave her homeland to be married to me.

But we got along great. Maria made new friends almost instantaneously. She was definitely the most innocent creature I had ever met. She came from a poor family, and I felt I was saving her from a miserable future.

I taught her everything I knew about politics and computers, even the livestock on the farm where I grew up, now rented out after my parents' divorce. I introduced Maria to American football, fast foods, and the multiplex theater. She absorbed everything, and we were inseparable. At least that's what I thought.

I had always heard jokes here in the states about a

38

man's wife being a burden to him. This was certainly not the case with Maria, who was anything but a nag. I trusted Maria with my innermost secrets, and she told me hers, which I never doubted. Not until one day when I did some house cleaning.

Abby put Paul's paper down, immersed in his dread, that fear of the lethal item left behind by a loved one.

At the time Maria was visiting Brazil, I was cleaning the closet when I found a brown dusty bible. I took a peek. There in that disastrous book was something that would change my life forever. Between the tissuey pages I discovered the wedding certificate of Maria and Juan Rodriguez. I flipped through the endless pages and discovered pictures, letters, and other dreadful documents. I felt sharp internal pains. Could Maria really have been married to someone else besides me? I called her long distance in Brazil to see how she was doing. She could tell something was bothering me, but I had decided not to question her until she returned.

When she got back home, I feared to face her with my findings. Yet I found the strength within me to ask about the documents. She raged about the findings and sat there with no remorse. Then the deadly truth spilled out of her. She confessed she was still married to Juan and that he was her true lover. I shivered in disbelief.

Maria told me she could no longer fake a love for me. She continued to proclaim that I was the nicest and best man she had ever known. But she married me for an American citizenship and a better life. I saw a side of Maria I had never known. She was downright a disgusting liar.

I do not have the words to describe how ugly I felt inside. Maria had stripped away three years of meaningful companionship to nothing in five minutes. She had felt nothing but friendship toward me the whole time we were together. On the contrary, my love for her had grown constantly. For the next few days, the pain grew slowly inside me until I had no choice but to say good-bye to Maria forever.

I see life in a dim light now. Love is not a dying passion that leaves no tracks upon the person it has touched. I am filled with despair and horror for my future, and I don't know where to turn or who to trust. Things are supposed to get better after you hit bottom. But for me the after-bottom grows worse as I try to grasp how such a thing could have happened.

The love of my life has become a nightmare of reality, and I am doomed to personal anguish because of the one I loved so dearly. I was betrayed and used, and this is why I will hate Maria forever.

Who was this Maria, in all the earth?

And which is worse then? Being married to someone who never loved you or someone who did and changed?

Abby wept for herself and for Paul, looking with horror to the future, as he did, years in which to grow bitter, hard. If only everything could end now. Just stop the breath, isn't that it? Let the poor little pump inside shut down. Take an early retirement.

Stan would be sorry then. But no, he probably wouldn't. Embarrassed, maybe. Or relieved that he would never have to admit that he'd left his wife.

The air gushed out of her. Actually, she did want to return these papers, to give Paul his *A*. At least he would have that.

A tongue licked her hand, the gravelly tongue of a cat, cleaning off the salt.

He was back. Dwayne had come back home. Excellent cat.

7 *Hiss*

Someone is coming. My body goes stiff. A thud outside. Steps in the hall. The door here clicks open.

It's him. I hop down and meander over. He doesn't look my way.

He never has liked me. Not that he's mean, kicking or throwing things. Mostly he ignores me. This guy doesn't pet a cat. If you lick his fingers, he moves his hand away.

He has a suitcase and hurries down the stairs. I gallop after him, entangling myself in his legs. He doesn't stumble or slow down. His feet quickly step over me, as if I'm not there.

Meow. *Meow.*

Downstairs he drops his bag on the bed. He does this when he's been on his trips, bringing chocolate candy for her. Never anything for me.

He's putting clothes in the suitcase.

I race around the room, stopping at the wall. I crawl under the bed and sneeze from the dust. He used to vacuum here, coming at me with that sucking machine. *Bzzzzzz.* My ears prefer soft compliments. Or the squeak of a can opener.

There's a ball under the bed. He threw it to me. A cat

should fetch? I pat the ball, and it rolls. Stops.

His feet come by the bed. It makes a creaking sound. I crawl out to see, careful through the strings hanging on the spread. I got tangled there once and almost choked myself.

His leg is next to me. I give it a whack. Again. He doesn't push me away, acting like I'm not here.

I bound out and run back and forth across the room. I'm here, I'm here. He responds with laughter. Doesn't say a word. He never has been one to call my name.

I trot away with a cat's nonchalance, although I am trembling.

He goes in the closet. I hop up in the suitcase on the bed, settling into the soft clothes. Here I am. He comes bringing socks. I look and yawn, opening my throat the whole way, sticking out my tongue. But he doesn't grab me like a normal person would and toss me out. Slowly he reaches in and clamps his hands around me, placing me on the floor as if I were a potted plant.

I smolder. I fume. I stroll away.

I learned to hiss because of him. Now I hiss at children, strangers going by, anybody who ticks me off. Life was good in the basement where we lived before this man came (making my lady dance around like a crazy person). The window was up high with tall grass outside. A cat came to visit me. She came stepping through the grass in the sunshine. Her coat was gold.

This guy was always there. Then we moved. I *hate* moving. Weird smells. Not knowing the good places to hide. But now I like where we live. I can race up and down the stairs. My front window is big.

He's putting more stuff in the suitcase. I warm up my hiss, starting with the little hiccupy ones. Now here comes the kicker from down deep, *khhhhhhsssssss* . . .

He goes in the closet. I charge in ahead of him and crouch behind some shoes. I chew on the laces. He reaches up to the shelf, and I rub against his pant leg. He shakes it like a burr is stuck on him. I roll off to the side. Everything goes dark. He's gone out and shut me in.

I charge to the door and paw it. I whine. Let me out of here! I was only trying to be friendly.

I wait. He doesn't come back. I hear sounds upstairs.

Then it's quiet all around. I sit in a dignified manner in my dark enclosure. A cat doesn't need a lot of space. However, I do not appreciate being locked up. I howl. Let me out. Let me out.

I wear down and doze off.

When I wake up I'm in urgent need of my litter box. I am proficient at holding back. I don't have accidents on the carpet or a person's lap. And I have *never* peed intentionally to soil a fabric. I may not be a nice cat, but I am a gentleman.

The humiliating moment comes when my body can't wait. The warm stream flows out of me onto the rug.

I soil my paws stepping in the wet and feel ashamed.

When I'm done I sniff the spot. Oh well, it's mine. I will be back.

I cry out for all that is happening. I piss on this man for dissing me. Here's to you, mister.

8 *Tennis*

Before Stan, there was tennis. And there would be tennis still. She had gone to the court when she was happy. Now Abby went when she was sad. The very sight of a tennis court lifted her, that oblong of green with its clean white lines, the net fastened just so. The net seems to get in the way. But if you've ever hit in the street, you know the beauty of the game is gone.

It had been so ever since the first public court where she had learned to play out in the Utah sun. With its bleached baseline, weeds hiding the balls, which as kids they hit until they were brown, lobbing them into the purple evening sky as long as there was light to see. They played in the rain, smacking the ball to make it spray, chasing across the slippery court with no fear of falling then.

In any town Abby drove through, a tennis court called. She could spot a court from the air, thrilling to that rectangle of green on the concrete earth, or a pair of red courts next to a golf course. The island of Bermuda, though it might have inspired Shakespeare's *Tempest*, was to be honored for bringing tennis to the United States. Past the portraits of the queen, the pastel houses and pink sand, she and Stan followed viny paths into backyards with their own tennis courts, a tall chair waiting for the game to start.

To pass an empty court spoke of the unlived life; approaching one to play was life itself. Whether it be indoors with its rubbery smell on a winter day or outdoors with trees, mountains for walls, each one had a soul. Even when she went out to practice by herself, as she got near the court, her heart did a little dance.

Then one day your game goes bad. Feet don't work. Eyes don't see. Your arm becomes cement. A life event might weaken every sinew. Yet you must go out. To stop playing would be worse. A little death, or a great one perhaps.

She played scared these days. Shots that used to land gloriously inside the line went further than "just out." They flew. When she got careful, the ball thudded into the net. "Mine" was not a word she used in doubles as a lob hung in the air. Her fingers on the racket handle no longer told her where the ball would go. She had lost her grip.

She lost to people she used to beat, and that's a nasty feeling. Still, she had to go out, to run, to sweat, and for a short time, forget.

It was a breathless night in June, and Marge was coming over to The Commons where there were six lighted courts. It was a reason that Stan, Abby too, had chosen to live here. What could be finer than a soft summer evening in your own neighborhood? Always somebody to hit with or watch. Non-playing neighbors ensconced in their rooms were to be

46

pitied. Those who came out were buddies. They knew each other well. From a distance you could tell who was hitting by the person's strokes. Everyone knew who had the nerve to go to the net and who would double fault when the game got tight.

The day had looked like rain. The sky in the north turned black, though to the south it stayed a steady gray, and no drops had fallen yet. Abby watched the leaves to see if they trembled. She scoured the ground for the first dark spots.

The sky held, and she went out. Maybe tonight her game would return. It shouldn't be so hard to hit a tennis ball. She practiced swinging until the air coming through the strings made the right swishing sound. She followed through on her forehand, wrapping her arm around her neck.

While it is never pleasant to lose to someone you used to beat, Marge was the most gracious of winners, acting as if luck played into her success, whereas certain people insist on analyzing the game afterward and explaining how they beat you. "My topspin was on today." "This new racket is great." Marge compassionately changed the subject as they came off the court.

Here she came now, this gem of a friend. Marge got out of her Ford Escort, a little person with red permed hair, head down, trudging through the parking lot with a big tennis bag slung on her back. She brought everything for an emergency. An extra racket for when a string pops. Her cell phone. Bandages.

Fortunately, there was no time to talk. A court opened

47

up, and they hustled out to get it, stopping only to set the clock nailed to the wire wall, fixing the stiff hands to show when they started, and when their time would be up.

Marge pulled on her headband, and Abby opened a new can of balls. A snap of the lid, and the rubbery air hissed out. She inhaled. She poured out a crisp yellow Penn ball with a number eight on it. Maybe it was lucky.

Love the ball. Stay with it.

As they hit a few practice strokes, Abby felt her old game come up in her, its rhythm and its song. The excellent geometry of tennis, the ball arcing deep and then angling back to a sideline. She was ready at the net, wrist firm, and volleyed crisply into the open court. She could do this.

That was in the warm-up.

"Ready?" Marge called.

Abby nodded and took a breath. The serve came to her backhand, her favorite side. She returned it deep, close to the line, possibly out. Marge missed it. "Good shot," she called. Excellent person.

The sky was getting darker. They ran harder, rallied longer, dripping, having a good set.

The score was 4-4. Abby's serve. She sliced it to the outside corner. Just wide. Better than in the net. Her toss went up for the second serve, a yellow ball on a black sky, when she heard a laugh she knew on a far court, a wonderful sound on a summer night.

Fault.

Why did he have to come play here if he insisted on living somewhere else?

Marge won the set. "Isn't that your husband?" she asked as they stood at the net, looking over at him. She had met Stan once, some time ago.

Abby drank from her water jug and nodded. They watched as he ran back for an overhead, turning sideways, running smoothly, not staggering backward the way she did. There he went, a little guy leaping high, smashing the ball. "He is good," Abby said, wiping her mouth with her knuckles. His game hadn't faltered a bit. Stan changed ends after his win and waved at her. She waved back.

Thunder groaned in the distance, but no drops yet. "We better play."

All right. At least hit the damn ball. She should be able to do that.

A short one came. Go. Go to the net now, or maybe she never would.

She got down with the ball, staying with it. She watched and saw the seams. She released. *Yes.* A good approach shot. See, her game wasn't ruined. Stan was not all the world. Onward she charged, up to the net, ready to show off her volleying expertise. But her new shoe must have stuck to the ground, and down she went, her racket clattering across the court. "I'm OK," she called to Marge, who hurried over. "Nothing's broken." Abby had learned to fall, after all, having tried it several times recently. You just let yourself go. "No problem." She leaped up, as the rain came now, before friend or acquaintance might wonder at the husband who did not come over to inquire about his wife's fall.

By the time she and Marge got to the house, the rain

had stopped. So they took their beer out on the patio. Abby did not turn on the light. You couldn't see faces, just pale tennis clothes.

"Will I get to say hello to Stan?"

"Dunno."

"You two are certainly independent."

"Yup."

"You were smart, waiting to get married," Marge said.

Abby laughed and drank her Budweiser. "Tell me about your marriage."

"Big mistake." Marge finished her beer and squeezed the can until it folded. "Marty told me in the first year that he'd never loved me. Can you believe, we stayed together fourteen more years."

"Ouch. So why did you stay?"

"Both waiting for the other to leave, I guess. He finally did. What a relief, that divorce."

"Really." Abby sat there disliking Marge more by the minute, someone she had thought would understand. "You celebrated a divorce. It wasn't tragic at all."

"After a bad marriage, not really. I remember driving around the beltway so relaxed without Marty criticizing me. My computer didn't freeze when he wasn't hollering directions. When I first met him, I thought it was great that he knew so much. Later, I couldn't stand him because he knew everything."

Abby went in the kitchen to get another beer, standing in the dark with her head against the wall, feeling so lonely. The lurid light of the refrigerator showed a red row of

Classic Coke cans, Stan's favorite, which she kept stocked for him. If she had any character at all, she would throw them out.

She got a couple more Budweisers, glad that she hadn't bothered with the frosted mug in the freezer for Marge. She went out and handed her a can, gripping her own chilly one as she sat in the silence, watching two fireflies stumble toward each other. They floated, sank, then one went out. That's the way it is with couples. One always cares more than the other.

"What do you think is worse: if your husband never loved you, or if he did and changed?"

Marge took a minute. "Isn't love always better?"

"I always thought so." Abby thought of Marge in her loveless marriage. Fourteen years. What would that do to you? "But what if, say, two people truly love each other. Then one stops. Isn't that the most terrible? What can you believe in then?"

Or maybe Stan had never loved her. He just had a talent for pretending.

"Everything changes," Marge said, in that casual tone people use when they utter cliches.

"Not everything fails. That just isn't true," Abby snapped. "Some people stay loving each other. Would you ever stop caring about your kids? Is there anything in this world that could make you stop loving them?"

"Motherhood is different."

"Well, not everybody is a mother." Abby swung her feet off the table, letting her tennis shoes land with a thud.

"You could still have a child. Any reason why not?"

"No reason," Abby said quietly. "No reason."

For a long time they sat in the dark. Nothing but the wail of a siren in the distance. Then it too was gone. No rain. No wind. Just the night. "Stan left."

"Your husband. The one out there on the court."

"Yup. He got up one Saturday morning and left. He said he had to find out if he would be happier by himself or with another person."

Marge scraped her chair on the concrete. "He said what? Then he just walked out? You two are separated?"

The word hit like a stone. It was not a term Stan used. He referred to their "situation," the way you might describe an office problem. Abby hadn't used the word either, not even to herself. "Yes. We are separated," she said, making it true. "Stan didn't want me to tell anyone. You're the first."

Marge leaned across the table and took her hand. "Oh, Abby. How are you doing?"

The kind words brought up tears, as a reproach cannot do. "Not too well."

"Stan wants a divorce?"

"Oh no. He's never said anything about that. This is just temporary. He keeps saying he will 'come to his senses.' We go out every weekend. He's very sweet, and so sexy."

"Sweet? He's not sweet." Marge's fingers let go. "The man is torturing you. He's like one of those creatures that paralyzes its prey and slowly devours it. How long ago?"

"April."

"You've been playing this game since *April*? Abby, do

something. Give him an ultimatum. Surely you've changed the locks. There must be another woman. There always is."

Abby's face burned with the thought, not that she hadn't considered it. "I don't think so. Why would he be with me on weekends and be such a lover?"

After that she did monitor Stan's closet for more than the number of remaining shirts. She checked pockets for the scrap of paper with a phone number on it, a receipt from Victoria's Secret for a gift she never saw. Clues you find in stories. But Stan's clothes bore no new fragrance. The only unusual scent in his closet was from Dwayne peeing there when he got locked in. She had scrubbed the spot with the potion they swear by in the pet store. But you can never quite get rid of that smell.

One day she was in the closet counting suit jackets when she spied a Nike box on the shelf. If there were shoes inside, why was it tied? So—here was the evidence Stan had set out for her, just as Maria left her marriage certificate in the pages of the bible for Paul to find.

Abby wished she could call Paul on the phone and see how he was doing.

She tugged at the knotted string, feeling deceptive and dark. She had no reason to think that Stan had lied to her. If he were going to lie, he could have said nicer things when he left. He told her the tough truth then. He rather liked the truth.

The string slid away. Inside were letters. Folded type-written letters.

She slapped the lid back on the box. Why was she torturing herself with this? Stan should be the one tortured, forced to confess to her in person, not take this cowardly way.

But it was too late, wasn't it. Too late for many things perhaps.

All right, then. She would get this whole mess over with. See who the little sneak was sending letters to her husband, which he obviously wanted her to find. If Stan was that rotten, so be it. She had no need to stay with a man who cheated. And thinking he could fool her with their sexy Saturday night "dates." They were obviously meant to cover up his affair.

She snatched out a letter. So, the bimbo thought she might look smart by typing it, did she?

"Oh, Stan." Oh please. "I dreamed of you, my love." Bad writing. Really bad. "The stadium was full of people. In the middle was a grass tennis court so it must have been Wimbledon." How could Stan do that, find someone else who liked tennis as much as she did? "I looked out into that crowd of faces, but all I saw was you."

Something was familiar here. The bimbo was also a plagiarist. She couldn't even come up with her own material for a so-called love letter.

Then as the picture became clearer, Abby saw again the dream she'd had. The masses of people in the stands. The grass tennis court worn to dirt, the way it gets at the end of the tournament at Wimbledon. She did not see the players. No duchess with high white hair. Just Stan in all that crowd.

She turned to the second typewritten page. Sure enough. "All my love, Abby."

Idiot. This separation shit was making her lose her mind. At least Stan wasn't a liar. She grabbed her cat up in her arms and danced around the room. "He saved my letters"—he who threw things away—just as she had saved every word Stan had written to her, from the hotels of Europe where he went for his job, postcards from every place. "Stan didn't lie to us," she sang. "He's just going through a bad time that we don't understand. He needs a friend." Dwayne swatted her face, but she didn't mind. "We'll be his friends. Surely he'll want to come home, just like he says."

9 Yellow Memos

Stan started leaving notes. He put them under the fruit bowl on the dining-room table while she was teaching a Saturday morning class. The first time Abby came in and saw his handwriting on the yellow memo, she hurried over and grabbed it. You expect good news when you've had a happy childhood.

Only as she unfolded the legal-size paper did she feel slightly ill. What if? What if right here in her hand was the end? But Stan wouldn't do that in writing. She did not think he would. He had told her in person when he left. Some people just leave a note and go.

Yes. It was a friendly message. An odd way to communicate perhaps. But surely this new attempt showed progress.

My Love,

I just wanted to check in and say I miss you, even though I will be seeing you in a few hours for our Saturday night date. I thought we might get an early start this time, say around 5:00 instead of our usual 6:00 time. I'll call later to see if this is acceptable.

Let's have a fun evening. We could crack crabs if you

like, maybe drive out to Robertson's on the water. I know it's a favorite place of yours. Or if you want to pick some other romantic spot, please do.

I'm really looking forward to this evening, Abby. You might wonder at my saying this, after the way I have been acting. But you are the only thing that gives meaning to my life.

Love always, Stan

Life is good. It is. It is.

Every week after that Stan left one of these notes. He also mentioned that he didn't know what was happening to him.

Then one Saturday after a good class, Abby took her yellow memo out on the patio where she could stretch and enjoy.

Love,

I am struggling to understand what is happening to me and to make sense of my existence. Yet I don't seem to be any closer to a resolution.

I realized there was trouble in the marriage (for me) from the beginning. This isn't something rational I can explain. But as I have said, it has nothing to do with you.

Something that must be said is that there is no other woman. I have not had an affair or even a one-time lapse. My feelings do not come from a desire to be with someone else. Maybe if they did, I could explain them more easily.

Perhaps the problem is a failure on my part to bond

with another human being. I am embarrassed by this and hope to remedy the situation. I want us to be happy always, Abby. That is my greatest wish. This may not seem to be the case from my recent behavior. But I felt I should remove myself from the situation rather than burden you with my problem. I am trying to work things out. Please believe that.

I look forward to seeing you tonight, as always. I will call later this afternoon to confirm the time. We could go to your favorite Mexican restaurant, or any place you wish.

You needn't worry that I will bring up the problems stated here. Let's just relax and enjoy ourselves. One of the things I like most about us is that we are always able to have a good time.

Please bear with me. I know this isn't easy for you either. I still don't see any point in bringing our parents into this (as it is a difficult situation to explain), so I would appreciate it if you wouldn't discuss this with them yet.

I really need to be with you.

All my love, Stan

Her heart went stiff with the words, *trouble in the marriage . . . from the beginning.* So that was it.

Stan had been unhappy from the start. Did that mean their wedding day? It was sub-zero weather on that New Year's Day. What could you expect? Pretty icicles in the windows were daggers to him. His smile at the ceremony was merely stoic. It was too late to back out. That wouldn't be polite. Stan was very polite.

Or did he first detect trouble on the honeymoon, there

on the lovely island of St. Thomas? They had stayed in a place called Blackbeard's Castle, calling up images of bloody pirates slicing up their women and sailing away free. Maybe that's what Stan was thinking about, all those hours they spent in their room. Surely his sense of doom couldn't have come as they strolled on the white sand beside that turquoise sea. It was even bluer than the brochure promised.

Stan hadn't seemed nervous the night they got engaged. It was the Fourth of July on the capitol lawn, there where they spread a blanket by a magnolia tree. Yet maybe he chose that occasion so he could hide his uneasiness with the crowds and the noise. Duty made him say, "I want us to be married," not desire. Yet when she answered *yes*, the sky exploded in a fountain of red, white, blue, and the band played "The Stars and Stripes Forever."

The music sang on in their blood as they lay together that night, too excited to sleep. Or so she had thought. "I know we'll always be happy," Stan had said. He must have been talking to himself, trying to convince himself. If she could have looked in his eyes at that moment, she might have known the truth. Probably not though. She probably would not have recognized that look at all.

Had he felt something was wrong on the first rapturous (can you use a word like that in modern times?) night that they made love? They had hiked the C&O trail that day, talking of many things. The sky was soft and gray, the leaves brilliant yellow, orange, red, reflected in the quiet water of the canal. All around them it was gold. "Abby, there's a rightness of fit with us" Stan said that night, which

59

she had taken to mean more than sex, but maybe that's all it was.

I realized there was trouble in the marriage (for me) from the beginning. Sometimes if you stare at words long enough, they lose their power. She tried that now. It didn't work. Again, again, they took her down into the dark.

But that wasn't all that Stan's note said. Look. Here. *I hope to remedy the situation.* Stan was good at solving problems. He fixed many things. Why not this? *I want us to be happy always, Abby. That is my greatest wish.* You couldn't ask more from anyone.

Still, after getting this message Abby dreaded going home on Saturdays to the yellow memos under the fruit bowl. Certainly, she could ask Stan to stop leaving them. A word would do it. But cutting off any communication did not seem wise. Or maybe it was the English teacher in her. There was something wrong in asking anyone not to write.

She could destroy the damn memos. That would be more satisfying anyway. Stuff them in the trash without reading a word he said. Shred them. That would show him.

She did leave the bananas in the fruit bowl until they grew black spots.

After class on Saturdays Abby took to driving around, anywhere, usually arriving at the library, planning to escape into some gory tale that would make her problems seem like nothing. Instead, she ended up at the marriage racks, checking one more how-to book for the tip that would save her. They all said to compromise, to communicate. Crap.

She went to the mall at Tyson's Corner, testing perfumes that promised intimacy and fingering the lacy undies. She had tried a new black bra recently, but Stan still left the next morning.

What the hell. She headed for Sports Authority, that cathedral to hope for the athletically inclined. Somewhere among its vast supplies was the equipment to turn your game around (and thus your life). Rows of golf clubs, propped up like cobras, promised longer drives, more perfect putts. Boxes of the little white dented balls awaited purchase, though they might be struck into the water or the rough.

She wandered down the canyons of shoes that Sports Authority offers for every manner of walking, running, leaping. Nike's swoosh mark reminded, "Just do it."

But she did not know what to do. Nothing that would make things better.

There were crossover shoes for those who change their minds and shoes with lights in their soles that blinked when you stepped on them. Pairs of shoes tucked neatly in boxes and others with their tongues hanging out. Here and there a shoe was tossed onto the carpet without a mate.

That's what she would do. When she got home, she would burn Stan's memos. She was sick of all the *I*'s he used. Sick of waiting for him to decide about *his* life.

That thought perked her up as she strode into the house. She grabbed the stupid message under the black bananas, snatched a box of matches, and marched to the disposal.

Through the yellow paper Abby could see that the message was short. This one was shaped like a poem. All right, all right. She would see for herself just what type of cruelty he had managed to put into verse.

My love,

Take a long breath, relax.

Go to the freezer and sip the gin and tonic for you there
  (with plenty of gin so it won't freeze).

I will be there soon.

Together we will draw a bath, get undressed,

Sink into the suds with our drinks in hand.

While there we will have thoughts of the loving that will follow.

Know that someone is imagining you now in that tub.

Dress in clothes that won't be hard to remove.

You won't have long to wait.

10 *Waiting*

We wait for buses.

We wait for seasons to begin and end.

We wait on the phone on hold.

We wait for *other people.*

How long?

Some folks leave after waiting fifteen minutes. Half an hour, tops. Some slap down the phone when the canned music begins. Others stay on the line, paralyzed with waiting, yet believing that at any second the torture will end. When you give up you throw away your investment.

Even with her happy past whispering that all would be well, Abby couldn't wait forever.

What to do?

She could decide on a day, an hour, when Stan must announce whether he would go or stay.

She could tell him to go to hell now.

Get mad.

She might make a joke of their clandestine arrangement, the "situation" as Stan referred to it.

Call in a priest.

She even thought of getting pregnant. Stan would bond

with the little mini me, or maybe a daughter, and want to stay home then.

OK, bad idea. One more child in this world waiting a lifetime to know the father.

Damn the waiting.

And so, we wait.

11 Off the Radar

The phone rang late one night, that hour when her family called from the west. Or it could be Stan's parents, although he was good at heading them off, checking in from his office often. It wouldn't be Stan calling from the basement where he had returned, after coming home to stay for a week this time. He went to bed early.

When he came bringing a suitcase instead of an overnight bag, Abby turned up the gas on the stove and cooked a real meal. No, Stan had not been to a therapist yet (his alternative to marriage counseling), although he had made an appointment. Meanwhile, he wanted to spend time here at the house. Stan felt comfortable with her, he said. Abby had not heard of separations ending in a graduated manner such as this. Yet any step toward reconciliation was cause for celebration.

But when Stan's work holiday was over, he left.

What a loathsome creature she was putting up with this. Never again would she berate the battered woman on TV, smiling through her bruises as she stands by her man. "He can be so nice."

Your man's good traits are a bitch.

What would give her the strength to end all this, Abby did not know. Still, maybe she wouldn't have to. Maybe not. She went on hoping, as people do.

The voice on the phone was a whisper. "Mrs. Swan? This is Brenda from your English class."

"We've missed you." So what was the excuse this time? The flu? Brenda's car wouldn't start? She had to take her dog to the vet—again—which doesn't require three weeks?

"I have a problem." OK, OK. Obviously Brenda hadn't learned the first thing in her English class about getting to the point.

"Lawyers are camped in my yard. I can't go anywhere." Visions of straight-talking Brenda entangled with the law caused Abby to sit up in bed. "It's my mother. She was on that TWA Flight 800. Families of the victims are now supposedly celebrities. We're supposed to sue the airlines and go on the talk shows. I don't want to be famous, Mrs. Swan. I just want my life back."

Abby turned the TV down, Jay Leno making fun of the president, and told Brenda how sorry she was.

"I just want to come back to class, Mrs. Swan. I really do."

"Then come."

"The Lockerbee people visited us as if we're in some sort of cult thing together, supposedly in mourning for the rest of our lives. We go to vigils on the beach with candles, looking for the exact spot where the plane went down. They're reconstructing the aircraft, putting back every little

66

piece of metal so you can see the seat where the person was sitting. It's sick.

"Everybody has an opinion about how it happened. It was a missile. It was the airline's fault for using an old plane. Mostly people want it to be a terrorist. Why is that? I guess they need somebody to hate. It's this closure thing the counselors talk to us about—like I'm going to have closure losing my mother this way? You don't get over the shock. You just don't. As they say, the plane went off the runway at 8:19. It went off the radar at 8:48. But it never goes out of your mind.

"These people wear T-shirts saying, 'Forever in Our Hearts.' I'm sorry, but that doesn't do it for me. I want my life back, Mrs. Swan. I want to come back to school."

"And your mother would want that," Abby told her.

"Her? Nah. She liked to travel. She never could understand why a grown-up would want to go back to school and study books."

"How's your father doing?"

"Oh, they're divorced. He hates travel. So now my mother goes everywhere. Or she did. She'd never been to Paris though. This was her first time. That's why I haven't been to class, Mrs. Swan. I had to go to New York to identify the body. Naturally, I had to be the one, as my sister Sondra lives out in Michigan, and she has a job. It's not easy identifying someone who's been underwater for three weeks."

"Was that really necessary?"

"You don't want your mother down there being eaten by

fish. When that Valujet crashed in the Everglades, the families had to worry about alligators chewing on their loved ones. That's right. This is the stuff we talk about. So you can see my mind is messed up for my school assignments."

"You could write a paper on aviation—or alligators. That sometimes helps," Abby suggested.

"Her body was so puffed up at the funeral I wanted to stick a pin in it to let the water out."

"Did you recognize her?"

"Sort of. But positive ID was her nail polish. Cranberry Ripple. I will say, that stuff is good. Her nails were still dark red on her blue fingers. But I shouldn't bore you with these details, Mrs. Swan, and calling you this late. I guess I needed to talk."

"No problem. If there's anything I can do—"

"The worst is the lawyers hovering around. Well, not the real worst. The real worst is getting a call from your travel agent in the middle of the night. 'You better turn on the TV, Brenda,' she says. 'I think your mother is on TWA Flight 800.'

"It's horrible enough losing someone in your life. But the shock of this, Mrs. Swan. You don't get over it."

When Stan arrived the next day with his overnight bag, a nasty little carry-on type Abby had never seen, looking like a doctor's satchel back when they made house calls, she told him to stuff it in the closet. He wasn't staying this time. She sat on the floor winding a new grip on her tennis racket, ultra thin black leather, smooth as skin. It lets you feel the bevels of the handle so you can know where the ball will go.

Stan seemed surprised, but he moved the bag out of sight. "Remind me, when are your parents coming?"

"On Saturday. Don't forget, you said you would show them around."

"I may have to go to Geneva."

"What? It was your idea. You told them on the phone."

"I want to see them, Abby. You know I like your parents. But I have to cover trade negotiations in Geneva for a guy in my office."

Negotiations, poof. All right, then demonstrate your negotiating prowess, Stan. Let's see how you do it. "What commodity is it?"

"Jute."

Ah, for making rope. "Well, you call my folks and explain. Why not tell them everything?" Abby gestured to the phone, an old one she had brought from her previous life. It still worked. No answering machine or call waiting. You just pick up the receiver and talk. "How can you keep on deceiving your parents? These lies are killing us."

She could spill the story to Edna. That would get him.

Stan looked scared. The blue had drained from his eyes, leaving them a cement gray. "I don't see any need to disturb our folks unnecessarily. I still haven't resolved this," he said, using one of his many vague pronouns. "But if it's what you want, of course go ahead and tell your folks."

"You know it isn't what I want. This is the last thing I ever wanted." Abby wadded the tattered racket grip and threw it to Dwayne to bat around. She watched her cat battling silently. The only sound was a running toilet, which she was too proud to ask Stan to fix, and he pretended not to hear. "I hate the lying," she said (meanwhile wondering how she would deceive her parents when they came).

"I didn't choose this either," Stan said, stuffing his hands in the pockets of his jeans. He went to the window and looked out at the wet parking lot. No tennis today. "I love you, Abby. I've never stopped loving you. It's just—"

"What?"

"I guess I don't like being responsible for someone else's happiness."

"But I have been happy. Surely you know." What if he didn't? Abby rose and went to him. "Of all the people I ever met, I got to be with my favorite one." She stood beside him, looking out at the sprinkling rain. "This is about your unhappiness, not mine."

"I've never thought of myself as unhappy." He stared out the window.

"I haven't either. You never complained." He was such a positive person when they met. That was one of the things she had liked best. "Maybe you should have."

So how did this marriage take him down? And everyone knows there are two sides to it, no matter what Stan said. Which of her bad habits bugged him? The slovenly housework? Attention to her cat? Or was it something in her nature, an inclination to silence that made him feel alone? Other worse things.

Stan was too polite to say. Maybe that was the thread he

hung to now, knowing that he would always be a gentleman.

"I don't like to lay my troubles on anyone."

"I'm your wife. Lay your troubles on me. Do it to me, Stan." Abby collapsed to the floor and sprawled out there, spread-eagled. "Go ahead."

He smiled, but he didn't laugh. "I know I haven't given you everything you wanted." He sat on the edge of the couch. Not coming, not going. "I know how much you wanted, well, you know—" His hands were bunched together, and he put his head down, unable to say the word *children*, like so many other words eliminated from his speech— *separation, counseling, divorce.*

"Yes, I wanted a child." Abby blinked up at the ceiling, where a hairline crack was starting from a puffy place in the paint. "I would have loved to have a son like you. A daughter. But that wasn't the most important thing. We were."

She sat up. "But, heck, we might have raised a drug addict. A deadbeat who wouldn't leave home. We'd never have the privacy you like. Or maybe our kid would hate us and run away. Never call. How embarrassing."

She got up and went to Stan, sitting close to him. "Or we might have had a wonderful child. We still could. Imagine someone getting the best of both of us." She looked at him. He didn't turn away. "Surely there's something we can do here. You are always suggesting there is. You who are so good at fixing things. We are healthy folk, still with half a brain. Fatal diseases separate some couples. Cancer cuts them down. Nothing they can do. Plane crashes wipe out

71

families. Tragedies like that. We are the lucky ones. Come up with a plan!"

Stan put his hand on hers. "I better get going. Of course tell your parents whatever you want. But since the situation isn't resolved—" He stood, started for the door then paused, looking around at his place. "Do you think I want to give all this up?" He looked over at the sliding glass door he had installed so carefully, the pictures he had hung meticulously. A blurry Monet she used to like. You couldn't tell if the sun was coming up or going down. "Just a little more time, please," Stan said, his voice breaking now.

He came and put his arms around her. "I know it's asking a lot. But maybe on this trip I'll be able to focus. I'll try, I really will, to come up with something, as you say. And it will be easier with your parents if I'm not here. You won't be lying when you say I'm in Geneva for my job."

He was right about that. She could fool them better without him here. Besides, why tell them now and spoil their vacation to Virginia?

And so, reprieve. A little time yet before she would have to see her mother's stricken face when she heard the news, or hear her father's cheerful voice not knowing what to say when he learned that his daughter's marriage had failed. He had always been so proud of Stan, the way he could fix things, his steady temperament. Before her parents met Stan they thought that Washington bureaucrats were laggards who picked up a government check. Stan showed how passionate and dedicated a federal employee can be.

All right, then. When her folks came, she would keep them so busy sightseeing that they'd be too tired to talk. If they ran out of monuments to visit here in Washington, they could drive up to Gettysburg.

Perhaps in view of the losses there, the breakdown of a single marriage wouldn't seem so huge.

12   The Dogwood Tree

The access road to Dulles Airport, reserved only for those traveling there, allows you to focus on the journey. There is no other choice once you take this route. Anyone driving out to the terminal just to turn around will be severely fined.

It is a spacious road with little traffic, a comfortable grass median, and a protective wall softened by vines that grow out of concrete here in the south. Trees that once were twigs marked by colorful flags now offered the buffer of green you find along the highways here. The beltway, dreaded for its costly backups, is ringed with green along both sides. Taken at a lightly traveled hour, it is a pleasant ride going around into Maryland, where the blue-veined spires of the Mormon temple rise out of the trees, and the angel on top turns his trumpet to follow you.

Abby was in no hurry to meet her parents, and she slowed to let a taxi pass. It was one of those wavering D.C. taxicabs that become disoriented when they cross the Potomac River. A soft back tire meandered along the yellow line, and the driver looked lost even here where the road only went one place. A stretch limo swished by with its important person tucked away behind tinted windows. Why the rush? A diplomat eager to get out of town?

Then the road was empty, and all she could think about was Stan, the many times they had driven here when he was going overseas. The power of their good-bye intensified the closer they got to the terminal. Here at the five-mile marker, Stan would pull her close and kiss her in the speeding car. He could keep it smooth driving with one hand. He could keep a car steady steering with his knees if he needed to.

She accelerated past their final marker, a glass building propped on its corner, an immense green cube poised on a golf tee. The sun flared gold off the windows, catching fire in her mirror as she passed. Ahead of her the terminal rose up with its long concave roof, as if the building were holding its breath at the momentousness of the arrivals and departures within.

Get ready to look cheerful, girl. Show your parents the well-adjusted child they raised. Cars slowed going into the parking lot. Abby didn't mind. Then somebody honked, and she spurted forward to pluck the ticket hanging out of the box like a tongue.

The next morning she announced to her parents, "We'll visit the monuments."

Her mother soothingly said, "But you've always complained about driving visitors around. Let's just relax."

No way. Abby raved about the value of memorials, the significance of tombs. All business and helpfulness, she ushered her parents to the car, glad for a chance to be in charge.

Her mother sat in the back seat so Abby could chat with her father even though they'd always gotten along great by not talking, and this was no time to start. Because of him she felt it was fine to be silent with a man, whereas in high school the idea of a successful date was no lulls in the conversation.

"I'm sorry Stan isn't here," her mother said from behind, one more time, a motif she had taken up before she got her luggage.

"And he's sorry. He had to cover negotiations in Geneva for a colleague in his office," Abby answered, swerving onto the George Washington Parkway, where the elegant views might be diverting.

"Getting to be an important fellow in the government, is he," her father said, peering down at the Potomac River, so calm along here you would never guess that a few miles up it became Great Falls, churning with rapids that overturn small boats.

First stop, the new FDR memorial, disguised by foliage along the Tidal Basin. Back in the trees, statues of folks line up for food and huddle around a radio. Voila, Franklin appears in his cape, with those smiling eyes that belie the numb limbs under him.

Down the path in her own portico stands Eleanor.

Abby discussed all she knew about the Depression, which didn't take long. Then they took the trail around the Tidal Basin to see Thomas Jefferson, following along under the dark knotted branches of the cherry trees, where once again she was with Stan, holding his hand as they strolled beneath the white bloom there.

Up in the rotunda she didn't look to the words carved on the walls today. It was the man standing alone she saw —this great person with his many books, his wines, his plantation, friends, a man who played the violin, yet who was forever lonely for the young wife he lost. That was the one grief he could not reconcile.

She looked out where Jefferson faced, a path carved through the trees over to the White House. And how were Bill and Hillary doing?

Next stop, the Holocaust Museum. But her parents didn't want to go. They were tired. All right, then. She would describe the museum to them as they drove to some pretty place. She told of the thick gray walls with slits of light to give the illusion of freedom, the photo ID you get so you can follow the fate of a Jewish person. Down the narrow halls you go, past the sound of burning books, bins of scorched shoes, a display of calipers used to calculate the length of a nose and thus determine whether the person deserved to live or die.

"I had no idea you'd become so interested in these things," her mother said.

"It's a part of history," Abby answered curtly.

She could easily have driven into the lovely Virginia countryside then. But the call of death was too great, even if it tipped off her parents that something was wrong in their daughter's life. She parked at Arlington Cemetery, finding a certain comfort in those miles of cloned, white headstones, reminding that human misery is but a moment, and soon we will all be similar bones in the earth.

After the cemetery, her parents insisted on going home. Whoa. This meant hours of afternoon to kill. Abby showed them around the house, pointing out Stan's home improvements—the sliding door to the patio, permanent shelves over the kitchen sink. Her father did notice the leaky faucet in the basement, observing that it must have been dripping for a while. "Really? Well, Stan has been traveling, you know."

It was a hot afternoon, but her mother wanted to sit outside. So while her father fixed the faucet, the two of them pulled chairs into the strip of shade from the adjoining condo and sat.

"Stan must be doing well at his job with all these trips he takes." Why must a mother constantly refer to her daughter's husband? Once you get married, that's all she wants to talk about. "He and your father are so much alike. They would both rather work than play."

"They aren't *that* much alike."

"But, Abby, you mention it often. You always did go with nice, reliable fellows. We never had to worry. Elizabeth, she looked for trouble. If the boy was wild, a dropout, that's the one she picked. I guess you've heard that Jack wants to operate his own painting business from home. He quit that nice fellow he worked for."

"I like Jack."

"We all like him. We just worry about him. Working on his own, he'll have to rummage up customers. Where's the security in that? But he has been a good father to those boys. Roy is such a smart little tyke. And imagine Tucker graduating from high school next year. You and Stan should come. Elizabeth would be so pleased if you did. Tucker would."

"I'll go check on Daddy."

The three of them sat on the patio, facing the meager grass around the edge. It was turning brown. There are periods in Virginia when that happens. Out here they don't use sprinklers; they just wait for rain, and the green comes back. Abby hadn't thought to water the lawn for her parents' visit. However, she had defrosted the refrigerator (and spaced out the shirts in Stan's closet in case somebody went in there).

"Abby, how about if we help you do some landscaping here?" her mother said.

But she and Stan liked this place the way it was.

A yard project would take time though and fend off the intimate conversation she could feel brewing. "Great. Sure."

So they drove to a nursery, which is never far down a Virginia street. When people get on your nerves, plant a garden. Even now on this wilting August day, folks milled about, blissfully loading plants into their wagons, pulling them quivering over the bumps in the parking lot to the trunks of their cars.

They bought azaleas, that southern staple which stays

green all year, sturdy through the snow. Inside those stiff little branches bloom awaits, come the next April. And April would likely come again.

Her father asked if she wanted a tree. It was too much. But sure, she said. That would take up the afternoon. Is it really possible to put a tree in the ground and have it grow? In Virginia that usually happens. They considered a redbud, the first to bloom, with its startling fuchsia clusters popping out along the trunk in early spring. Or a weeping cherry, trailing pink lace to the ground, where she might kneel and rake it. But a cherry tree would be too big for the yard of the condo.

Then they came to her favorite, the dogwood. The crooked little tree that brings forth flowers in the shade. The bent gray trunk seems fragile, yet it is of the strongest wood, so resilient against violent jarring that it was used to make gun handles. The bark is rough, but the wood wears down smooth.

They selected a white flowering dogwood over the pink variety and tied it on top of her Honda Civic. Carefully she drove home down Shenandoah Street.

"You're sure Stan won't mind us doing this? It's his place too."

"Mother, I'm sure."

It was too hot an afternoon to plant a tree. The best time is a wet fall day. But her father wanted to do it. And she let him.

The leaves of the dogwood wilted as it leaned against the wall of the condo, looking lonely away from its companions at the nursery. It is pleasant to imagine that something you plant is glad to find a home. But plucked out of its familiar surroundings, surely it could die.

Abby helped her father dig the hole for the tree, both of them dripping in the humid air, which everybody complains about in this part of the world, but she had come to crave. Humidity makes your skin soft. Sweat lubricates and cleanses. It felt good digging this hole. Better than waiting for someone else to do it.

However, her father's face was getting red. The veins of his forehead pulsed. He could drop from a heart attack, just so she could perpetuate the lie that she and Stan would be living in the shade of this tree. "Daddy, stop—"

It was too late. He kept on digging. A mighty thrust of the shovel, and he hit a rock. Rather, a chunk of concrete left from a previous tenant, something of the past retained, even in a condominium.

Together they lifted the little tree with its big root ball and fit it in the ground, patting the dirt tight. The dogwood still didn't stand entirely straight. Well, maybe it wasn't meant to. "Stop, Father. Rest and drink."

Abby hunted for a hose, which is not a fixture in a Virginia yard as it is in the west. Out there the sizzle of sprinklers is the very sound of summer.

As the tree absorbed its water, the three of them drank their frosted gin and tonics until long fingers of shadow reached across the concrete patio, and the murmur of rush-hour traffic echoed from distant roads. It must have been the gin that brought water to her eyes. Or maybe it was seeing her father's damp, flushed face, the way his hair was getting thin where he parted it. Abby looked over at her mother's enlarging knuckles around the glass she held, the hand that before long would be her own. She remembered her mother doing the ironing with that capable hand when Abby was barely the height of the ironing board. And she was sad that she would never be a parent, giving more than you got.

"Please bear with me a little longer." She could hear Stan's words.

But that wasn't why she didn't share her secret. The reason was cowardice. *Tell your parents now*, a voice from her former, straightforward self cried out, although it would make her mother weep for her, and her father look in a stricken way over at his tree.

She thought how hard it must have been for Stan to tell her when he left, getting out those awful words. But as bad as they were to hear, it might be worse to say them. How many versions did Stan rehearse, she wondered (being the careful man he was), before selecting the correct one? What other choices did he imagine besides, "I don't know if I want to continue in this relationship"?

Abby whispered against the rim of her glass. "I need to tell you something."

Her mother turned with mildly questioning eyes. She heard. But this was her happy daughter, so she was probably expecting good news. Of course she was.

The phone rang then—it really did—just like in the movies at the crucial time. She could have let it go, finishing what she had to say. But you don't want your mother to see you ignoring your phone. She'll think that you are antisocial. She will think that when she calls and nobody answers that you don't want to talk to her.

Abby went in and got the phone. She heard the faint crackle of a long-distance connection. Then came the voice she would recognize if it came from the end of the earth. "Abby, love. How's it going with your folks?"

When she and Stan had finished talking, she took the phone out to her parents. "He wants to say hello to you."

13 Night

It was a moonlit night in November. The blue-white streets of the neighborhood still bore the warm air that summer graciously leaves behind in the south. A fine evening to go out.

Stan had gone back to Geneva for more meetings on jute as the earlier ones had failed. Jute to make rope. Little hope was left for their marriage. Abby knew that. The books she read said that if the departing partner doesn't return in six months, he probably never will.

Yet as she looked up at the stars she thought, what was another month, another year, to that firmament? She required patience of her students in their writing, reminding them that it took three billion years to make a grasshopper.

Stan continued to say that their situation was "negotiable," thus leaving the pilot light aglow. It died out when she was tired. Then the tiny flame gasped alive after morning coffee. When she won at tennis, hope sang in her the whole way home.

And when Stan was out of town, she could think what she wanted. At least with him away, he couldn't show up and ask for a divorce. Being overseas for an extended stay this time might even bring him around. That's what he suggested. Even more foolishly, she almost believed.

Maybe it was the moon tonight that buoyed her, the same moon that had shone down on the backyard where she and Elizabeth used to sleep out under the stars. A shoulder of tonight's moon drooped. Still, it gave plenty of light along Shenandoah Street.

She started to run, wearing new Adidas with excellent arch support, yet they were light as marshmallows. A dark shape slipped out of the bushes, a cat, trotting across the street in front of her with a cat's confidence, going where he had to go. Good luck as she saw it.

The leaves were silver in the moonlight, staying on the trees well into winter here in this gentle climate, often beyond.

On this quiet Sunday night, she moved into the middle of the street, running silently past windows where colorful heads bounced on TV screens through the filmy curtains of dark bedrooms.

She happened down a street with spacious parking where Stan left his Cherokee when he was out of town. He parked it there for her to use in an emergency. Or anytime. He encouraged her to do that. After his trip Stan came directly here from the airport to get the Cherokee. Then he always dropped by to see her, bringing gifts.

She jogged toward the familiar tree, the vehicle. A man was approaching it. He was getting in. Stan? Could Stan be back? "Hello!"

The person was somebody else. "Sir? Sir?" she called,

racing to get there, in time to see a Pathfinder drive away.

In this neighborhood of Virginia, red-brick buildings, it was easy to be mistaken. Stan might have parked in a different place, although he had his patterns. Worthwhile habits she had relied on once. He taught her to go to bed early, wake up alive. To get rid of things you didn't use. He knew how to live she had always thought.

The Cherokee had to be here. She saw it a couple of days ago.

She ran down other streets, sweat collecting on her clothes until they were heavy, clammy. Her throat grew dry from gasping. She came upon a white Trooper, an Explorer, a Bronco. She had not known there were so many sport utility vehicles.

But the Cherokee wasn't here. Not anywhere on these streets. Her heart grew faint.

Slowly she walked back to the house. The air was chillier than before. Stan's flight could have arrived late, in the middle of the night when he wouldn't have come over and rudely awakened her. Maybe he was ill. Nothing personal. When you are sick, you don't want to see anyone.

She went out in the backyard. A black rope of cloud stretched across the moon, thickening. She sat and watched the patio grow dim. The azaleas her father had planted were black clumps, trying to dig in and live after being planted so late in the season. Probably they were dead. The bent shade of the dogwood tree sharpened on the concrete then it was gone.

If she had been a person to pray, this would be the time. She hadn't believed in a god since Santa Claus. Certainly not the Old Testament terrorist, with his threats and his punishments and his jealous rage. What did he know of sorrow in marriage? What did he care?

Even if she were to hurl her prayer into the sky, in case some kindly hand might catch it, or it might brush the ankle of the divine, he would know that it came from a disbeliever. One more desperate person having a bad day. Her message would blink away on the machine in the sky, unanswered like a trillion others. If she could offer a gift—the prayer of music—a song so lovely that even the huge hands of deity would stop in their molding, he might hear her then. If she had Shakespeare's words, surely they could penetrate that mountain of chest hair and find a way to the heart of God.

What she had to offer was love for one man. It was her best gift.

But what if it wasn't love at all? Maybe it was just a selfish desire to be comfortable. To hug someone daily. What she had thought was a great love would fade soon enough, turning to bitterness with divorce. She would look back and be amazed at her delusions.

If a god did take his little finger and nudge Stan back home, the debt might be too huge. She would have to pray, pray, pray every day. It would not be seemly, even for one of callous heart, to have a one-night stand with God.

But if she were to pray, going to her knees, thus, on this cool cement, she would say . . .

"Oh, Lord, you who made the world—this human heart that can tick for a hundred years. Skin wrapped around me that heals in a week. Surely you can bring a single husband home. He is only five minutes from here, living in a basement. A small fellow and very nice. Never violent.

"I have lost all courage. I lie and deceive. I cower, living for the words of another, that sin. I truly wish I loved the people of your fair world. But what do I care for them? All I can think about is him.

"Stan is suffering, I know. Help him, Lord. He doesn't want to do a bad thing. Help him as only you can. You who are a god, you who are male, maybe you can comprehend his mind.

"If you do this one thing, I'll be a different person. I can change. I'll give to the homeless, drive around looking for them. I'll send a contribution to public radio.

"Surely you want to be a nice god. Better than sitting in a funk on your high chair, thinking up punishments. What would be the good of having this marriage end? What good? Do you really want two more divorced people down here screwing things up?

"It's not that I can't live without him. Only that life will be less. If I knew a thousand men, I still would have chosen him.

"My fear is that I cannot undo what I have done. I cannot undo my marriage ever. You know. You have said it.

"How might I ever begin to put it asunder?

"Lord, help me in my night, I pray."

14 Day

My lady goes out in the dark. I slip out too, rubbing against her leg. She does not reach down and scratch my head.

I sniff the air and dash about. I eat grass. I throw up. A light floats in front of me. Swat. Another little light is bouncing. I reach. It's gone.

I roll on the ground, scratching my back. Feeling good.

The door swooshes shut behind me. I race over and paw the glass. I whine. I cry. *Let me in.*

Being outside is fun. Being locked out is mean.

I gallop away, stopping to scratch my paws on a small tree trunk. It moves when I push. I used to climb trees when I had claws, hanging on the whole way up. Now I slide.

These teeth though, they bite. These feet can hit.

I sniff around for a place to relieve myself, looking for loose dirt. Sticky mud here.

There's a hole in the wall, and I squeeze myself through, flopping to the other side.

Something smells over here. It's a food smell, but nothing I want. I step through weeds. This is not a nice place.

I tense, hearing a sound I hate.

Dog.

The snort is coming from outside. The rattly gate opens, and the slobbery smell is here. A big dark dog is pulling on a leash, growling in my direction. I don't move. The man yanks at the mutt, dragging him off into the house.

In the dark the rain falls on me. Miserable rain. It makes my fur heavy and smelly. I go back and squeeze through the fence, dropping wet and dirty on the other side, back in my yard.

A bird comes hopping along on stick legs. I quiver. This always happens to me with birds. I tense up. Pounce. I miss. The bird flaps away in the dark, where birds go. Me, I like the ground. Not living up in branches.

The night is long, and I am lonely. How could she leave me out here? I always sleep on her bed.

I stare at the door, hoping it will open. Just let me inside. I want my dish.

The sun is warm on me. The ground is bright. I am hungry. I stretch and wander around looking for food. Not nasty grass this time. Give me tuna fish. Or even the crunchy stuff.

Nothing. Oh well. I settle down, folding my paws under my chin, watching. The door slides open. Here she comes in her robe, calling, looking this way and that. I stay over by the wall, lying there with slitted eyes. I do not bound over and say hello. However, I do feel a purr coming on.

90

She hurries across the yard and out the gate, hollering. I don't follow her this time. I'm staying here.

She comes back and drops into a chair, putting her head down.

In a while I stroll over and lick her hand. Softly she touches me, ever so carefully. She picks me up and holds me close to her for a long time.

She pays attention to me now. She pets me all the time.

15   Iron Lung

It was a note on white paper this time, slipped under the door like a flyer for a car wash or an ad to have your gutters cleaned. In romantic tragedies of the past, the missive gets lost under the mat, completely altering the plot. It was her misfortune to find this one.

Abby,

The reason I didn't drop by when I got home from Geneva the other night was that I needed time to unwind before seeing you. I wasn't in a very good mood and would not have been pleasant company. I did get Waterford crystal, which I am sure you will like. I'll bring it when I come for our Saturday night outing.

I know I haven't been very forthcoming in our recent discussions. That is always easier when the topic is a happy one. Isn't it ironic that we have trouble talking when we both value communication so much.

I really hurt inside. My chest is being ripped out of my body. I've wakened in the night with the feeling that I'm in an iron lung. My mind floats. I don't know why this is happening, why the pressure has built up recently.

I guess what's happening is that I am realizing marriage simply isn't working out for me. I can't explain why. I always feared this. But I loved you so much and wanted us to be happy always. So I tried. I really tried. I just can't seem to adjust.

There is nothing you could have done differently that I can think of. You give me plenty of freedom. But maybe that isn't enough. I guess the freedom just has to be there.

I'm sorry, very sorry to put you through this. But I have never done anything more difficult nor have I ever felt so much pain. I had to have a release.

Another part of me says it will hit me what a wonderful wife I have, and I will joyfully come back to you with every intention of staying forever.

I cannot foresee when this might happen. However, I wouldn't want to shut the door on such a possibility.

You might let me know how you feel on this matter. Or if you prefer, we will just let things work themselves out. I still enjoy seeing you, Abby, and hope you feel the same.

Talk to you soon.

All my love, Stan

Later that day Abby stood in front of the mirror, polishing her speech. She added hand gestures to calm her trembling fingers. Eventually she struck just the right professional tone. Clarity at last. A man in an iron lung. Unplug the poor devil.

She dialed Stan's office and announced that Mr. Swan's wife was calling, envisioning the scene in a show where the man cowers at his desk, waving off his secretary. But Stan wouldn't do that. He had encouraged her to call.

Stan came on the line immediately. She said she wouldn't be seeing him anymore. He asked why. She said she didn't want to. His voice grew cool. "If this is what you want, Abby. I guess I just don't understand such an extreme measure."

When she hung up, she felt light, emptied. If you take action, supposedly you will experience power. She was free. Or like a balloon not knowing it is punctured yet, floating along before the air sucks out and the contracting rubber wobbles into a chasm.

Anyway, Abby called Marge immediately to brag about what she'd done, and they planned a major celebration.

Stan respected her wishes that he not call or come to the house. No more Saturday morning memos. She put fresh fruit in the bowl. Marge still thought that Abby should change the lock. She said that wasn't necessary. Stan wasn't a stalker. He was not a creep.

Blithely she turned on her computer. "You've Got Mail," and there was a message from Stan. He had found her on AOL.

Subject: Christmas Plans
Abby,
    Since you have asked that I don't call or visit—a decision you reached by whatever logic—at least we should be able to touch base by e-mail. I am not doing this to

distress you. If this bothers you, just delete the message now. I do have a simple question. In your recent communication with me by phone, did you intend to cancel the plans to spend Christmas with my parents as well? You needn't think of the occasion as a date for us if that is your objection. Knowing you, I don't think you would want to disappoint my mother even if your purpose is to punish me by your recent actions. As you know, she enjoys her holiday preparations and is looking forward to having us there. Please let me know. Of course the choice is yours.

Love, Stan

Damn. Christmas. She didn't want to go to Utah. What, tell her family all this and ruin their holiday? Only when Stan told his folks would she talk.

Meanwhile, no, she wouldn't spoil things for the Swans. She would be extra nice to Stan's parents—and ignore him.

She sent a crisp reply saying that indeed she would come as promised. No need to confirm this message. Or e-mail her again.

Minutes later Stan flashed back a reply.

Abby,

I'm surprised that you, of all people, being an English teacher, can't see the importance of keeping the lines of communication open. For me this would be easier in person, rather than the impersonality of electronic mail. But I am trying to respect your wishes, although I really don't see the necessity here.

Abby, I miss you terribly. I'm sure this doesn't make sense to you, considering my behavior. I am not proud of my actions. But I have tried to be honest with you.

I have always seen you as a reasonable person. So I don't understand this need you feel to cut off negotiations, so to speak. Sorry about the jargon, but it does seem applicable. I never intended to break off completely with you. We've had many good times in spite of the circumstances. Wouldn't you agree?

Abby, I still love you. At least couldn't we meet as friends? I simply can't accept the thought of never seeing you again except in the presence of my parents.

If you prefer, we could meet some place other than the house. I would even schedule an indoor tennis court. I am a lonely person. I need you. I guess my preference for our get-together would be a casual dinner. What about your favorite ribs? Afterward we wouldn't need to be intimate, although I must admit that the thought of never making love to you again is something my mind can't handle yet. However, I will respect your wishes on the matter.

My life is empty without you.

At least consider our friendship. I guess I just don't get it, this need you have for total abstinence.

Love always, Stan

Abby filed the message, put her computer to sleep, and serenely left her work station.

Then she woke up in the night, burning to reply. She would have her say. Now, finally. In the gray light of the

computer screen, at this dim uncompromising hour, she
took to the keys to tell the truth at last.

Stan,

How right you are that people should be able to meet as
friends. Ah, but what is a friend? I can assure you that
students, who know much more than you or I about these
matters, consider this *f* word to be foul when it is used by a
person who is dumping someone.

Yes. Go to the mirror and say it, "I dumped my wife."

Good.

And where better to meet a friend than on the tennis
court? Right again. You would graciously hit the ball back to
me, I'm sure. Afterward, tasty barbecued ribs. We know the
place, don't we, where the meat is infinitely tender, sliding
off with no resistance. I would sit across from you, scraping
my bones white and wondering what your next move would
be. Maybe you wouldn't know yourself. Or it might not
really matter if you have known the final outcome all along.

Yet friends, you say? Silly man. You are far too expert a
lover for that. I don't think so. Surely I have told you how
good you are.

After such a lovely evening, it wouldn't be easy to
refuse one more night with you. Yet by remembering the
sound of your footsteps leaving, I probably could manage it.

But no.

When people ask, and they will, "What was the hardest
thing about having your husband leave?" do you know what I

will say? Maybe you don't want to know, Stan. Well, I'll tell you anyway. I'll even number the items to show how rational I am.

1. Some say *humiliation* is the worst thing about getting dumped. It's a burning sensation that makes you want to scatter like a cockroach. Not that I expect you to understand. How could you? Humiliation festers and feeds on thoughts, flaring up on unexpected occasions. I will say, you have expanded my repertoire of emotions. This one is new. And I expect to feel it the rest of my life—forty more years of this shit, you little worm. Put that in your resume.

Ah, but even humiliation is not the worst part.

2. One man whose wife surprised him by leaving said that the *feeling of stupidity* was what tortured him. He could no longer trust his own mind. You certainly blindsided me, Stan. I didn't know you were suffering. I regret that. How very much I do.

I'm also sorry that you didn't tell me.

Well, perhaps one can forgive such stupidity. It's comic really. Marriage for dummies.

3. Some say that *failing at marriage* is the rub. And we failed, Stan, you and I. Ha, both of us. Sociologists (to sell their books) and casual practitioners of the art (to diminish their acts) speak of divorce as a major opportunity, one of the "creative passages" of life. These people are morons.

Letting love die is a terrible thing. That's what sin is. The failure of love.

Most people today don't believe in a great love. *Romeo and Juliet* is just a silly story about infatuated teenagers. The word *romance* refers to a trashy novel read by a housewife in a trailer who stuffs her paperback under the bed when her real-life husband comes home.

I do not agree. Even yet.

But failure, poof, is nothing. I plan to hold mine as a badge of honor, the stripe that puts me in touch with the human race. By the time I get through with this life, my scar will glow in the dark.

Everyone needs to go down the toilet once. It's part of the American dream of rehabilitation. You can't get on a talk show without some really ugly failure.

4. People say when you've been dumped (that's right, Stan, say it again, "I dumped a perfectly good and wonderful wife"), "What about the *anger?*" Guess what? Anger isn't the worst part at all. It's the best! When I can curse you for ending our marriage all by yourself, you selfish little man, I dance in the street.

Then you take away my anger, don't you, coming with your tenderness, your touch, words of hope. False though these things may have been, what joy you brought. I cannot erase it from my memory. Nor would I.

When you returned—stirring us to new life—I swooned with the possibility. Still do.

No, indeed. Anger is not the worst.

5. Well, the list could go on. Who knows the side effects, what neurotic ticks will be mine in time.

Anyway, here's the final item, the worst thing of all about having you leave. Do you know what is? Can you possibly imagine?

Missing you is the worst. Knowing that I will not see you in the morning, or again at night. I will miss you every day of the world.

So, I fear I still am, and may always be,
Your Abby

When she finished her message, a peculiar lightness came upon her, borne of the truth. Day was coming through the window, day again.

She slid the cursor to the Send Now icon. The faint whirring of the computer indicated that she was still online. In an instant her message would fly to Stan, the miracle of e-mail. He would read it and be gratified, maybe even grateful. He would be assured that their relationship was secure. He might even think that they were friends.

But he wouldn't understand, would he. He would not understand if she typed her words upon a thousand screens, wrote them on a stack of yellow memo pads, if she penned them on parchment with her blood.

The sun was coming up.

She slid the cursor down the screen, darkening it, selecting all. Then with the featherweight touch it takes, she clicked Delete.

16 *Silent Night*

What do you give your in-laws for Christmas when you may never see them again? A slight gift, wrapped well, perhaps? Or she could overdo it. Better. She would give such ostentatious items that Fred and Edna would forever proclaim what a wonderful daughter-in-law they'd had.

Edna was easy. She couldn't get enough Waterford crystal to display to the ladies in her bridge club. Champagne flutes (although she barely sipped alcohol herself), brandy snifters, little shot glasses glittered from her dining-room shelves. Jam jars, candy dishes, a salt bowl the size of a thimble adorned her tabletops, along with several swans. Someone had also given Edna an owl that looked like a hand grenade.

Fred wasn't so easy, not if you wanted to give something decent. His taste ran to the disgusting, objects to be found in the back of the dollar store. A plastic cow pie had gone over well. And last year's whoopee cushion was his favorite gift.

But what for Stan? A clock ticking in its box? Abby considered having a boutique photo album made of herself in exotic poses. When Stan turned those pages he would groan

101

with regret. Fred would hoot seeing the sexy pictures, applauding his son's taste in a wife. Edna would cheer. However, Stan might take the gift to be a genuine memento of their good times, not the slap it was meant to be.

Thus Abby stalked the mall at Christmastime with evil in her heart. She growled at Christmas music, scorned children waiting to sit on Santa. She envied couples, and not just happy-looking ones. Slouching teenagers in pairs with a ring pierced through a nostril or lip. She envied the old couple sitting on a bench. How did they do it?

She also imagined their dark secrets. Which one at this very moment was planning to leave? The woman listening all too intently to her husband as she licked an ice cream cone might be figuring out her strategy. The gentleman a step ahead of his female companion could be counting the days until spring when he would go.

From a manger in the mall, an oversized baby Jesus looked out with blue eyes, his placid mother showing no sign of strain after delivering her fifteen-pound miracle. Nor did her youthful face reflect the terrified wonder she must have felt for the child's father, who came through the window and said his name was God.

Joseph stood off to the side. What was his life to be? Stepfather to the savior of the world?

Abby trudged on in her Scrooge mode. Maybe this was her true identity. She could rise above her happy childhood and be a bitch! It is a relief when you have lost something. You don't have to be so grateful all the time.

Pleased with her new insight, she stopped and bought a

Mrs. Field's cookie, biting deep into the chocolate chunks, gooey and warm. When your husband goes, you can eat all the cookies you want.

She passed a florist and was struck with an inspiration for Stan. There is a store in the area that will send dead flowers or rotten fruit accompanied by an original poem. Sacked by your boss? Surprise him with decomposing mums at his next staff meeting. Imagine Stan opening his hand-delivered gift amidst his colleagues in the government to find shriveled grapes, strawberries decorated with fungus, peaches with holes in them.

Abby jogged up the escalator at Bloomingdale's singing "Jingle Bells."

Now for Edna, something wonderful. The store had a whole shelf of Waterford animals. Not the dog. Maybe the porcupine. Edna would think it was cute, and Stan would grasp the significance of the needles. Then she saw it. Perfect. A unicorn, poised on its haunches, expensive. "I'll take that." Just the thing, this mythical beast enamored of virgins, whose horn was presumed to cure all ills. Nice horse, with a dagger in his head.

She couldn't find anything gross for Fred in Bloomingdale's. But in the lower level of the mall, past the fake leather jackets, a green and orange plaid blazer called out. Stan would hate it. And Fred would show it off at work.

Delighted with her purchase, Abby headed out of the mall. Enough of this Christmas giving. But she made the mistake of going through Nordstrom on her way out, and there before her was a jacket of a smoky blue, the very color to highlight Stan's eyes. The easy fit of the shoulders, the touchability of the fabric, made her want to stroke the manikin on the spot. Stan had plenty of business clothes but nothing casual that was this nice. Even if he didn't wear it with her, surely he would think of her every time he put it on, looking back with fondness after all. And he wouldn't give this jacket away, not anything this expensive.

The weather had been gentle here in Virginia. So far, no snow. Grass that stiffened at night, holding bicycle tracks, paw prints, softened with the light, as frost etched on car windows slid off in the sun.

Christmas Eve brought mist, adding halos to the street lights, fur around the colored bulbs in the trees all along Shenandoah Street.

Stan came bearing a poinsettia. It eased their greeting, giving them something to talk about, where to put it high enough that the cat couldn't get at it. Dwayne did not stir from his windowsill when Stan came in, remaining stretched out regally with his paws crossed.

So this is how it ends, Abby thought. Politeness, a potted flower, and your cat giving you that look.

She brought a chair so Stan could climb up and put the poinsettia on top of the bookcase. She stood there holding the chair and thinking this wasn't so bad. She had said no to him and gained control. Gradually they would become more distant until she could be quite objective about this man.

Then a thread undid her. A single stitch showing in Stan's trouser leg where she had hemmed it, back when he asked her to do such things. She wondered if it was hard for him being short. Maybe that's the reason he was unhappy, because he felt short. She wanted to fling herself around his legs and invite him to come back to their good life. Ask him once more, "Why are we doing this?"

They went out to get in the Cherokee; Stan had left it running. She climbed up on her high seat where she had always enjoyed being, going to the movies or even to the drugstore. Stan had turned on the classical music station for her. It was playing the *Messiah*, "Every valley shall be exalted," as they drove away.

Traffic was sparse around the beltway on this Christmas Eve, just those few, last souls speeding to their Christmas celebrations, let us hope. And the occasional truck driver alone delivering his load.

Over in Maryland the neighborhoods were brightly lit, each house trying to beat out the next with a more spectacular display. Fred usually won on his street. Last year's strobe light dominated with its bands of red, white, and blue sweeping across the crèche in his yard, where among the creatures gathered to honor the Christ child was a panda from the National Zoo. A fourth wise man had also arrived, bringing a box of Pampers as his gift.

Tonight the action was on Fred's roof. Santa stood and sat in rhythmical motion. Notice his throne. Oval, white, porcelain. Santa grinned and waved, taking his pit stop.

"Shit," Stan said, who rarely cursed, not wanting to be like his vulgar father. Then she and Stan laughed, and still were laughing, with relief perhaps, as they went up the walk to where the lights of the Christmas tree danced in the window. Inside, the candles on the table were lit, gleaming off Edna's best crystal set out for the occasion.

Fred greeted them with a Bloody Mary that nearly jumped out of the glass with its big celery stalk. He leaned and kissed Abby on the cheek.

She went to find Edna, who was tending a steamed pudding she cooked in a coffee can protected with a cloth cap. Bits of the batter escaped anyway and floated in the boiling water, looking like seaweed. "I hope you like pudding, Abby. I shouldn't make it every year."

"You know I do." Abby put her arm around her mother-in-law's small shoulders and wished her a merry Christmas. Edna smiled, and her capped teeth were white. "Can I help?"

"No, you go relax. You're a teacher."

Abby wandered into the living room with its mustard walls and floral couch that had once seemed tacky. Now they were a fond part of her life. The silk ficus tree she'd watered along with the living plants when Stan's parents were on vacation. The family still kidded her about that.

She knelt on the ocher carpet by the tree, arranging her packages with their expensive wrapping and cynical contents, and she was ashamed. Maybe the family wouldn't see how inappropriate her gifts were or read the unkind messages in them. After all it was Christmastime.

The sound of Fred playing his new organ came up from the basement. The organ was an early gift from Edna, something he had always wanted. Fred knew nothing about the keyboard, but by following the numbers in the manual, he managed "Up on the Housetop" so you could tell what it was.

Abby went downstairs to sing along, standing behind her father-in-law. His thick hair, with the same soft wave as Stan's, had turned an early white. Stan was getting a few gray hairs himself. Maybe he would go white at a young age, and she wouldn't recognize him on the street.

Stan's arm came around her waist. And he who usually did not sing, sang now. The three of them lifted their voices, swelling with "Joy to the World" for one more Christmas Eve.

They had red wine with dinner for its seasonal color, and Fred said a prayer over the food, as he did twice a year. "Thank you for the fabulous meal prepared, and for the family here. Have a great day, yourself, Lord. Amen." Then he hacked off a turkey leg and passed Abby the dark meat, remembering that it was her favorite. She chewed and watched the white slices fall away from the chest of the cooked bird, until it was a bird no more.

"Did Stan tell you about our cruise?" Edna said. "Here, have a hot roll."

Abby put butter on hers and watched it disappear. Stan gripped her knee. "Guess I forgot."

"We're going to the Caribbean—St. Thomas, the Dominican Republic. If the weather isn't good, they give you a refund. You two should go back there. Celebrate your anniversary."

A pea rolled across Stan's plate, and he stabbed it. "Sounds good."

"You were smart getting married on New Year's, Abby. That way Stan can never forget." Edna looked at her son. "So, where are you taking her this year?"

Without stopping for a swallow of wine, Stan turned and said, "Want to go to our regular place, Abby?" It was a restaurant in Great Falls, the Serbian Crown, where a violinist comes to your table and plays romantic tunes.

Well, she'd had it with this crap. *Your son has something to tell you.* Abby stared at these people, the eagerness in Edna's face, all based on a lie. The contented look Fred had, never considering that there is suffering in the world.

If this were a stage drama, here's where the character would shout the truth. But the moment passed. Abby lifted her wine glass. She did sip carefully, however. Too much of this stuff, and she would spill.

The Swans opened their gifts on Christmas Eve (unlike Abby's family, who could wait). Stan looked wonderful in his blue jacket, and Edna was pleased with her unicorn. "I don't have one of those." Fred put on his green and orange blazer with a red shirt. Their gift to her and Stan was a Cuisinart. "My," Abby said, peering down into a pit of knives.

Then Stan grandly brought out his present for her (his guilt gift), which she already planned to take to the Salvation Army. Stan was good at giving gifts. The backup tennis racket that had become interchangeable with her other one. Stylish clothes that fit.

This year's box was square and heavy, no doubt some mechanical appliance she could do without. OK, get this over with. She ripped off the paper as everyone watched. Stan was smiling, that wonderful smile. She pulled the stiff cardboard lid out of its slot, ready to disdain the contents. Then a gasp came out of her. Inside was something she wanted more than she knew. Transportable, easy to use, divinely lightweight—a laptop computer.

They always stayed here overnight on Christmas Eve, so up they went to Stan's boyhood bedroom with its picture of him in a mushroom cut and his arm around his dog Jackie. They lay quietly in the dark with just enough light from the window to make out shapes. She could have seen Stan if she had turned to look, as once she would have done, marveling at his excellent profile.

Abby closed her eyes, although sleep would not come soon. Not with him here. Yet he didn't disturb her. Stan knew when to touch and when to wait. Never insisting. Never hurrying. Their first kiss had come easily, after a time. They were in a park. The sky was pink. His lips were even softer than they looked.

They had never turned back after that, going with the wave that carried them.

Stan took her hand as they lay there. That was all. See how civil they had become. Their love had simply followed a natural drift toward death. The only shock was how soon the end had come. But her detachment and resolve now let her see reality. She would grow calmer with time until she could speak to Stan without a ripple in her voice. They might even become friends.

Sleep was easing in, bringing its gracious release of the will. She had done what she could do. There was no more hope.

Then from somewhere came the strains of "Silent Night." It might have been carolers on the street, or maybe a car radio. The song could even be coming from Fred and Edna's room, a nice thought, wasn't it, music beside their bed after all these years.

"All is calm, all is bright." She did still believe in miracles. How is it possible not to? Lungs working at this moment, despite the small deaths of the soul, breath even yet.

And that other miracle, a man born two thousand years ago, bringing new life, a new way of being. Forgiveness not once but a thousand, thousand times.

Believe in one miracle, and how can you deny another?

She turned to Stan, and he was there.

17 A Cat's Christmas

It was the night before Christmas and not a sound in the house. A cat looked out the window, home alone while the family dined on turkey in Maryland. He didn't seem to mind. He knew these rooms. He knew their smell. There are worse things than being by yourself.

Christmas is a holiday, we might note, which honors a host of animals—the ass, named for the word *heap* after the things it carries, for bringing Mary to the stable, the camels arriving to kneel before the newborn child, and the lambs that came.

Biblical creation abounds with creatures, ant to whale— bat and behemoth, caterpillar, chameleon, cock, and crane, dogs aplenty, dove and dromedary, eagle, ferret, fox, and frog, the grasshopper, hart, hornet, and horse, leopards and lions and locusts and mice and moles and mules, ostrich and owl, partridge, pigeon, and quail, the raven and the roe, scorpion, serpent, snail, and swan. Yet nowhere in the bible is there mention of a single cat.

No one seems to know why. Perhaps it's because the Egyptians were cat worshipers. Cat torturers were Christian.

They stuck black cats on sticks to be used as torches. An effigy of Henry VIII was stuffed with living cats so that as the figure burned their dying screams could be heard. The cat was assigned to the devil, this accomplice of witches, feared for its ability to change shape and escape enclosures miraculously.

Or maybe the cat wouldn't kneel before a god and lick his feet, so that's why it was left out of the story. The swallow has its promise, but the cat must go alone.

Dwayne had been invited to the Swans' for Christmas one year. The evening did not go well. He wailed in the car all along the beltway, nipping at the ribbon tied around his neck. In the foreign-smelling house, where no bowl was set out for him, he got on the counter and gnawed into a bag of donuts. In the night he attacked the Christmas tree, swatting the decorations until the tree came shuddering down, scattering shiny balls and tangled tinsel across the room.

Now on this Christmas Eve at home, Dwayne purred from time to time, looking out at the lights in the windows and in the trees. He dropped to the floor with that pleasing thud a cat makes and headed to the kitchen for his dinner. Sliced beef in gravy. Salmon supreme. And tonight something special in a dark bowl, cream.

When he'd had enough, which was quite a bit, he licked his paws and cleaned his bib. He padded on down the stairs to his spot on the bed. In a swoop he was up. The blanket was warm, turned on the way he liked it.

God bless us every one.

18 New Year

Abby's mother looked out at the new snow, coming last night on New Year's Eve. Frank had turned on the lights out back, and they watched the yard fill up with white. It used to be that the kids in the neighborhood would bang pots and pans when midnight came. These days they set off fireworks, squealing up from next door, diving into nearby shrubs. Seeming dangerous. Yet no one complained.

Today was quiet.

Helene liked this time after the holidays, when the decorations were put away, the dying tree taken out. The little angel was packed away for another year, although her dress was far from white, her platinum bouffant long out of style. Frank was fond of that angel. She had been on every tree since their daughters were young.

A gladness rose in Helene for her life. At this moment she knew that she was happy. She would rather be here in her home than any place on earth. She liked the smell of the house, today with a hint of lemon furniture polish.

She'd had the family she wanted. Two fine girls. Two growing grandsons. All in good health. Maybe Roy would come over this afternoon and build a snowman.

Something moved in the back of the yard. A bird, a breeze could disturb the snow that balanced inches high on the slimmest branches. She saw no bird.

A dark branch sprang up out of the white. A deer could be back there. They come down from the foothills, destroying people's yards. They were a real menace on the roads.

Yet the sight of a deer, suddenly—

A doe stepped over the hedge into the yard. Head up, motionless now, listening to something. Then Helene could hear it too, the faint rattle of Frank's snow blower going down the block. He cleaned the walks of women living alone on their street, several widows by now.

The doe turned and soared over the bushes, floating as deer do, lovely even from behind. A graceful exit indeed.

The throbbing of the snow blower faded, and the yard was as before except for the prints of the deer.

As Helene turned away from her upstairs window, she noticed Frank's hat lying on the bed. She must take it out to him. Men die of heart attacks in this cold.

She was on her way out the door when the phone rang. She could have kept on going. She had learned to let the answering machine take calls. Her daughters had finally taught her to do that. Yet it might be one of her girls, so she went back.

It was Abby out in Virginia. Helene settled into a chair, feet up, ready for conversation. She described the snowstorm to her daughter, who preferred the milder climate of Virginia where she had lived for several years. Abby reported that there was no snow in her area, that the weather was calm.

Helene told her how much her father enjoyed his new snow blower and that he was outside cleaning the walks.

When Helene thought about this conversation later, as she would do for the rest of her life, she realized that she had forgotten it was Stan and Abby's anniversary. This was the first year she hadn't sent them a card.

What she did remember afterward was the stark look of the snow, unforgiving and bare, glaring in the sun.

"Stan has left me, Mom."

Helene, the drama teacher, coaching others to prepare speeches for life as well as the stage, had no speech now.

When you become a parent you imagine a call from the hospital, even a policeman coming to the door to announce that there's been an accident. Never this.

"Oh, Abby. My dear girl." What were Stan's reasons for leaving? When did he go?

Abby would not say. "He said it had nothing to do with me" was all her daughter's voice answered from two thousand miles away.

"I'll get on a plane," Helene said.

Abby wouldn't let her, not this independent child who hadn't allowed her mother to tie her shoes.

"Surely the two of you can work it out." Helene heard herself recommending marriage counseling, which she had always thought was a crock. But something had to be done. Something!

How could Abby not have known there was a problem? What was the matter with her? Maybe she was the one driving Stan away. A mother doesn't know these things.

Stan wouldn't just leave. He was a faithful federal employee.

There was a silence on the line, which Helene wanted to fill with words, the way you want to fill your child full of food when she falls off her bike, not knowing what else to do. "Stan will change his mind. I've seen how content you two look together. Surely he will be back."

Abby said it was too late.

What was wrong with these young people, giving up so easily? They were smart, exceptionally bright. Abby and Stan were a good match, a fine match. He was a negotiator, for heaven's sake, handling trade agreements around the world. "I'll have your father call and talk to him."

Abby did not answer. And Helene knew that her daughter was crying, although she wouldn't let her tears be heard.

Helene stepped out the front door into the blinding white. How could she have thought that she liked winter? It was sick to like the cold. It closes people in. Not that they talk to each other, do they, just about the damn weather.

Stan obviously hadn't talked to Abby.

Helene had little reason to hate in this life, but a fury rose in her against anything hurting her daughter.

Yet it must be Abby's fault too. She had always been cool with men. Never cared a hoot about anybody before Stan. (Was she possibly frigid?) Why she chose him, the family didn't know. Yet nobody doubted how much Abby cared for Stan or that she had changed for the better since she had been with him.

Helene noticed her bare hand stuck to the porch railing.

116

She removed it and pulled gloves on her numb fingers, setting out in the sharp air, down the aisle in the snow that Frank had made. The sun was bright, but there was no warmth to it. No snow was melting. Even the powder on the walk stayed as it was. No sound of dripping anywhere today. The air was stiff.

Is a good marriage just luck? She had always been rather proud of her own. Maybe she had nothing to do with it. Frank would have stayed with any wife he had, wouldn't he. It was in his nature to do that.

As she approached the rattling snow blower, the squeak of her boots on the snow disappeared into it. The words swirling inside her were lost in the sound.

Frank saw her and wheeled around. He waved.

Helene raised a mittened hand.

He turned the motor off. "What's up?" His lips moved slowly in the cold, but he managed a smile. His nose was red.

Her mouth felt too frozen to move. She gave him his hat. "Men die in the cold," she managed to say.

He laughed good-naturedly and put the cap on. He didn't fasten the ear flaps, and she wanted to reach over and snap them shut so he wouldn't have to hear. "Want a ride?" he asked, patting the seat.

"Frank?" He looked at her with those brown eyes she would trust with the world, and she had trusted with her life. "Thank you," her chilled lips said. Then the icy air sucked in and closed her throat.

"What's that for?" He appeared to blush, although it was probably just the cold.

"For never making me afraid."

He laughed again. That's the way he reacted even to serious things, a habit which often irritated her. "You are many things, Helene. But I can't imagine you afraid."

Well, she was afraid now.

"Glad I did something right," he added.

"You are a most wonderful man." Surely she had told him that. She must say it more often. Then the cold burned her eyes, making her blink, and she wrapped the scarf around her mouth.

Frank pushed the snow blower so they could walk together. Why couldn't Abby have chosen a good man like him? They do exist.

Well, she and Stan would just have to work on their problem. Do something. Whatever was necessary.

Why, here in this park across the street (vast and white and barren today), the city had wanted to put a picnic canopy—out in the middle, spoiling the space for sports events, any activity. Utter stupidity. Picnic tables should be put at the end of the park, out of the way. Helene had carried a petition, which twenty-nine neighbors signed. That didn't stop the ridiculous plan. So when the lumber arrived, she marched over and sat on it. Every day she stationed herself there until the city relinquished and put the picnic area where it belonged. So there.

As she and Frank approached the house, Helene announced that she was going to use the snow blower. "You go get warm. I'll be in soon."

She watched Frank enter the house, wearing trousers that

were too long. He was whistling as he pushed open the door, that delightful whistle he had, genuinely joyful she had always thought.

Let him whistle a little longer. She got up on the freezing seat of the machine, ripping at the cord until the motor chugged alive. She aimed for the blinding white of the untouched walk, taking off in a spray of snow, waves of it flying as she made a path for unsuspecting neighbors. On she forged, clearing driveways, that she might give someone a pleasant surprise before she had to go home and deliver her news.

19 Ice

Snow fell on Virginia at last, closing roads, schools, the government. Even the health club went dark as tree limbs brought down power lines. A glaze of ice then covered everything, making it treacherous to step on sidewalks, streets, even piles of snow. People inching out to take their trash fell and broke their bones. You knew the ice was there. Surely you could make it to your car. Then, comically, as you grabbed the handle, you'd swoop under the car door.

The ice stayed. Interminably it lay in wait on roads, greased every path, and cunningly coated the snow, which looked like ordinary snow, sooty at the edges and crystallized with age. Yet a boot heel would not dig in, and down you'd go again. People bought cleats to get around. Do that or crawl.

Abby brooded in her confinement, entrenched in the rooms where she and Stan had lived. She missed his parents. She hadn't talked to them since she visited Edna shortly after Stan made his announcement on New Year's Day.

It had been a steely gray afternoon when she drove to Maryland to see Edna, snow predicted. Watch out, as cars

120

spin out of control in the slightest storm. Get caught in a blizzard, and you might not make it home.

That day Abby didn't care. But the cold sky held as she drove around the beltway, past tangled, dead-looking foliage onto the Woodrow Wilson Bridge. Only the ice in the Potomac was alive, slabs of it sliding along like crocodiles.

"I have pineapple pie," Edna said at the door. "I hope it isn't stale. I didn't know you would be coming."

Abby waited on the flowered couch while Edna got the pie, taking longer than she needed to. The Christmas tree was still up, perky as ever with its artificial limbs stuck in their appointed holes, where they would fit again next year and in the years to come. However, the little lights strung in the branches were turned off. Plastic icicles hung like daggers. A candy cane was crushed in its cellophane.

Edna brought out the pie, cut in lady-like pieces, and placed it with the pointed end toward her guest, the proper way. She steadied her hand as she poured the coffee. "Would you like cream?"

Edna surely remembered that Abby took it black. It was just something to say.

"It's supposed to snow." Edna took quick little sips of her coffee as if to keep from getting burned, although no steam came from the cup.

"Yes." But the worst storms in Washington catch you by surprise. You wake up to an unusual quiet. The window wells are dark.

Edna put her cup back on the saucer, in a slight puddle there. "It's my fault, Abby."

"No, Edna."

"He said it was nothing you did. Those were his exact words. I'm not making this up." She went on breathlessly. "Stan was always a good son. He took perfect care of his pets. He slept on the floor by his dog the whole summer before she died."

"I remember that story."

"I won't say anything bad about you, Abby. When someone complains about her daughter-in-law spending the son's money, you know what I say? 'Our Abby is a teacher.'" Edna's face held firm. Then her lips gave way, quivering. "My friends at the bridge club will be so surprised at this. More than if Fred left me. The reason he wouldn't is he's too dependent is what I think. Would you like ice cream on your pie? There's vanilla. And mint chocolate chip."

Abby shook her head, taking one more taste of the delicious pie.

When there were no more bites to take from their plates, and they had cleaned their forks with their lips, they finally looked at each other. "What happened, Edna? You must know something."

Edna held her napkin to her lips, pressing it tight. She took a moment. "You were the only one he ever wanted to marry, Abby. And Stan had plenty of girls. It seemed he got bored with them. The one before you was a nurse. We knew he'd never marry her. We thought Stan would never get married."

"So, how did it end?"

"What?"

"With the nurse."

Edna smoothed her napkin on her lap. "Oh, Stan never talked to us about those things. And he's barely talked to us about, you know, this." She blinked. "But he does come over and fix things. He put in a new fence in the backyard, although I liked the old one better, gray wood covered with moss. Let's see, he built that fence around Halloween time. Uh-huh. Fred was hanging a spider web in the tree, making a nuisance of himself. Meanwhile, Stan was shellacking his wall so pretty. You'd never know he was having trouble at home. He couldn't have been thinking of leaving then. When did he?" Edna asked with fearful eyes.

Abby paused. "Awhile back."

"I could show you the new fence. Fred never was the handyman type. It was Stan who fixed everything. I held him too high. That's what happened. I was a bad mother." A tear fell on Edna's pink silk blouse. "I thought Stan was the nicest man I ever knew. Not just because he was my son."

"And he was."

"Well, he's not *that* nice." Edna shook with a silent sob.

Abby reached for her mother-in-law's hand. "This is hard for you too. Maybe being a parent is the worst."

Edna dabbed her eyes. "Oh no. What could be worse than having your husband walk out on you?"

Well, let's see. Maybe leaving him.

"Fred should be here soon." Edna looked out the window to the street where her husband would arrive. "Won't you stay for dinner?"

"I better go."

Edna stood. She went out on the porch for their good-bye, rubbing her arms in the chill. They gave a quick hug, then it was over. "You'll be happier with somebody else, Abby. Stan isn't any fun, you know."

Since that day Abby had not spoken with Stan's parents.

Then one night during this February freeze, when the power was out all across the area, the phone rang. She fumbled for it in the flickering light. It was Fred. "How's it going?" he said in his usual jovial voice.

Abby set the candle down, spilling the wax. There was no heat. No electric blanket. No TV. Soon Stan would ask for a divorce. *How was she doing?*

"Not well."

"So, what do you think of this ice," Fred went on.

"They even canceled my bridge game," Edna piped up on the extension. "We need to have you over, Abby. But you wouldn't want to drive on these streets."

"She's making crab cakes for supper tonight," Fred reported. "What a woman, going out in this weather and finding crab in the store. Well, take care. We're glad everything is fine."

Abby was relieved that she didn't hear from Stan. As the days went by, she felt a certain solace. If he wanted a divorce, he would ask for one. This silence meant he wasn't sure. Some couples are separated for years, simply unsuited for marriage perhaps. That's how Stan described himself. A clean break is better for some. But others can't go that far, bonded still.

Stan said one time—true, back when it would have seemed impossible for them to fail, but he said it so touchingly—"If I ever did get divorced, Abby, I would marry you again."

The ice melted. A thaw brought summer heat into mid-winter light, startling the shrubs, calling back the birds, sending the heart on vacation. A person could walk down the street upright again. Abby came in the house with a beat to her feet. She stretched out with her laptop, enjoying its warmth on her legs, and checked her e-mail.

Abby,

I saw a lawyer. I'm still depressed and shaky, but I guess I should outline the main details. The Agreement would read something like this. Please remember that even when written into the Agreement, all items are negotiable.

1. The effective date of separation would be January 1. This means if I go to court, six months later (July 1), we would no longer be married. There is nothing magic about these dates, so they can be changed.

2. All property we each owned prior to the marriage would stay with that person.

3. Everything purchased after getting married can be identified and belongs to the person who bought it. For example, the bed in the guest room is yours, and the dining-room furniture is mine. All gifts remain the possessions of the recipients, such as the jacket you gave me for Christmas and the laptop computer and other items I have given you.

4. I will make out a check for your share of equity in the condo from the payments we shared. Naturally, I will continue to pay my part of the mortgage until you find another place.

Does all this seem fair? I emphasize that everything here is flexible. Nothing has to occur on the exact date. If you have any questions, let me know. Otherwise, I will assume that you think this is acceptable.

I'm sorry.

Love always, Stan

20 *Wheels*

My lady goes out. I hear wheels screaming in the street. I have known the terrifying wheels of the highway.

The boys where I once lived took me for a ride (I hate riding in cars). I howled in the back, crouching on the floor. Music was pounding from the walls. I leaped up behind the driver's head and gnawed his hair. He swung around and knocked me off, laughing cruelly as I flopped to the floor.

I crept to a corner, trembling. There was no place to hide.

An arm came over the seat. I hissed at it. I was grabbed and hauled up by one leg. It hurt. Fingers dug into me. I squirmed, hollering, writhing to be free. Then I went limp, as a cat will do at such a time.

My captor sat me on his lap and petted my head. I did not purr. However, I was not so eager to bite him as I had been. We were slowing down. Maybe we were home. I could go to my dish. My box.

The side door swished open. Air sucked in. We were still moving. Hands clamped around me, squeezing off my breath. They held me up, out into the wind. They let go. I was dropped, falling, slamming to the ground.

I scrambled up, along a road where great wheels came roaring at me. I lurched out of the way, slid into a ditch where I muddied myself, shook off the disgusting water, and vaulted to the other side. I trotted through a field, head up, as if I had someplace to go. I stopped to clean myself, licking off wet dirt, blood on my paw.

Thus began my life on the streets. Screaming midnight fights with other cats. The wet. Cold. Hunger.

But nothing was as bad as being dropped from a moving car, being let go by hands I knew.

21 *Moving On*

How do you go back to being single? Wear a training bra again?

It was agreed that Abby would move out of the condo. This wasn't necessarily Stan's idea, although he mentioned that he didn't like living in a basement. She could have stayed in their place. But he would be there in every room.

So, one foul day in March, she forced herself to go look for an apartment. She was in a bad mood, which got uglier when she discovered that most rentals do not allow pets. As if Dwayne would pee on their precious rug—no more than the landlord would if he got locked in a closet. And this cat could hardly hurt their walls with his soft paws.

In one dreadful building that did allow animals, a dog was yapping through the wall. A high-rise out in Reston advertised "Pets welcome." Then they wanted a two-hundred-dollar deposit for carpet damage. Plus, your pet couldn't weigh more than fifteen pounds. From their highest window, Dwayne couldn't pass for that.

Abby drove down dead-end streets in the rain, along roads where signs mocked with their cruel sayings—Detour, Wrong Way, and the most vicious of all, This Lane Ends.

She cursed drivers who cut in and those who went too slow, exhausting even herself with her vile remarks. Then she grew sad that she wasn't a nice person anymore. So, she would find someone needy and give, give, give. But where are the homeless when you need them? Not here in Fairfax County. She might have to drive into the District.

However, as she approached Seven Corners, where Route 50 meets Leesburg Pike going to Bailey's Crossroads (former home of Barnum and Bailey elephants), there in the median stood a homeless man. Don't go away. She had her money ready. But the light wouldn't change so she could hand it to him. She slowed down anyway, causing honking behind her. A BMW swished around, the driver's hand up. Yet with her emergency blinkers going, Abby held her ground.

The light finally turned red, and she eased to the side. Drivers in the next lane did not turn their heads to look at the man. She knew the routine for ignoring the homeless. You appear to be intent on your driving (meanwhile, screaming inside for the light to change). Or you busy yourself. Put on lipstick. Read a map. Tennis players have been known to change clothes in the driver's seat on the way to a match.

The man wore a cardboard sign saying that he'd been evicted. That diabolical act. Abby put away the dollar bill and got out a five.

He didn't hurry over to get it. Rather, he glided with a practiced dignity, a tall, thin man with a red beard and pale blue eyes. "God bless you," he said.

He said that to everyone of course. Yet the words lifted her. For miles after that, other drivers no longer appeared to be cursing in their cars; they were whispering their disappointments. The fellow on his cell phone in front of her might be asking for another chance. Not everyone is selling real estate.

One woman cried as she drove along. The car is a good place for that, with its illusion of privacy, a blessed cubicle away from the family member or whoever caused the tears. And if your commute is long enough, you might be dried out by the time you get home. Several of Abby's drives had lasted that long.

Just when the search for an apartment seemed hopeless, one balmy afternoon she happened upon a modest garden complex out in Falls Church. The old brown brick was not pretty. But the trees were big, and the pine needles on the ground smelled good. Away from the singles high-rises closer to town, where couples leap out of sports cars and ride elevators to the sky, the pace here was comfortable. Hispanic children skipped down the walk. An old woman sat on the steps looking at the sky. Next door was a library.

Abby got out and walked to the end of the street, a wooded area. She heard it before she saw. The pop of a tennis ball. The court was back in the trees, with enough shade so that you could play on the hottest day. Two Asian boys were hitting with topspin, making the ball leap up impossibly from the baseline, or sometimes it sailed way out. When they made an error, how quickly they laughed. A habitual laugh to save face perhaps, but it was a wonderful thing to see.

The court was cracked, and grass poked through. One end of the court was slanted and held a puddle at the baseline. The boys played around the wet spot, having a grand time. The net was new.

Her heart did a little flip.

She would live here. Smuggle Dwayne into the apartment. People do that all the time with cats. Put a shroud over the cage and arrive at night. The sound of meowing? It could be something on TV. She would have to shut the blinds where Dwayne sat in the window. Ah, but these tricks were nothing. She had learned deceit.

Abby nodded politely as the receptionist in the rental office recited the conditions of the lease and the deposit as she munched Dorito chips. "Want one?" Nice girl.

"The maintenance people don't barge in—"

"Not usually." The girl brushed cheese dust off her fingers. "Only lap pets allowed."

"A cat?" Abby asked, stupidly. Obviously not a goldfish or a Doberman pinscher.

"A cat is fine."

Fine? This was splendid news, the best in a long time.

April returned, bringing its blossoms and its promises and the horror of the year before. Just move your things out and go. You can do it.

Packing books should have be easy enough. However, her fiction and Stan's economics had commingled on the shelves. Every book she took left a gap like the place where a tooth has been knocked out. John Maynard Keynes slumped to his side as his neighbor Langston Hughes left the area.

What does happen to a dream deferred? Does it dry you up? Turn you icky sweet? Or make you crazy.

Abby paused holding *The Adventures of Huckleberry Finn*, not so enamored as she once was of that lonely boy, the kid everybody wants to be. Where was he now? A solitary in the midwest, driving a truck through the night? She took a copy of *Shakespeare's Sonnets* off the shelf, thinking it was hers. But the inscription read, "To Stan— Even though our time together was all too short, I will always treasure it. Suzanne."

Suzanne, was it. That wasn't Stan's nurse. Her name was Alice. Stan and Suzanne. The names did go well together. When she wrote her dream name on a paper napkin, Suzanne Swan, how could it not be right?

So, then, would Stan have divorced Suzanne? Maybe she would have found a way to make the marriage succeed. Or she could be packing her things today. Suzanne, wherever you are, be glad.

The phone rang once more. First, the movers had called to confirm that tomorrow was the day. Next, it was Marge setting up a housewarming in the new apartment. Then Abby's mother called, knowing this was a bad time, wishing her well. They were kind.

It was Stan on the phone, asking in an upbeat voice if she wanted him to come and help her move.

Down, down she went again into the dark.

The day of the move was too lovely to leave a home. The azaleas were in full bloom—bouquets of red, coral, lavender bursting out in every yard. The road was pink, strewn with cherry blossoms. The flowering dogwood had turned from pale green to white.

Load the boxes. Just do it.

Abby marked the items to go. Her desk from graduate school, calling back those honorable spartan days. She paused before the white leather couch Stan had known she liked and bought while she was out of town. The note said, "For my lovely wife." She probably still had that note. She never threw away anything Stan wrote to her.

He would feel bad if she left the couch. But not bad enough.

Of course she would take her pretty couch. Cat hair wipes off leather so easily.

A white vehicle passed the window. Damn. She had told Stan not to come. But it wasn't the Cherokee. A van with Maid in America on the side, delivering a perky team to clean the neighbor's house. Even when it came to housework, she and Stan got along. He enjoyed vacuuming, making neat lanes in the carpet. See, a path still showed at the edge where nobody had stepped since the day he left.

Abby was down cleaning under the kitchen sink when the knock came, sounding quick and intimate. She jumped. Get a grip. Actually, it was the official knock of the man from the Ace Moving Company.

Manuel was his name, stitched in red on his shirt pocket, a slight fellow you wouldn't expect to find in the lifting business. Yet in no time he gracefully hoisted her things onto his gurney and rolled them out into the hall.

"No, not that." Abby stopped him at the dining-room table.

"Sorry. I thought the missus always took everything when she left."

"Oh, I'm not leaving him."

Manuel stopped what he was moving, leaning thoughtfully on the handrail of the gurney. "Well, then, he'll change his mind and be wanting you back, won't he. We moved a grand piano for this one lady, then it wasn't two weeks time before we were hauling that big old piano back into her same house. You'll be calling me. What'll you bet?"

Manuel grinned and handed her his card.

Abby stuck it in the pocket of her jeans, shaking her head with a smile. But Manuel knew things. He could even be right.

"All these comings and goings is good for the business, I must say. Now me and the wife, we've lived in our same house twenty years. Never moved once. You couldn't pry her out of there."

Just sweep the place and go. She put fresh towels in the bathroom. All right, to make Stan feel guilty. The closets were cleaned out, all but a garment bag in the guest room. When Abby touched it, she knew the contents. What else would fill the bag so completely?

It was her wedding dress.

135

What to do with that, sell it? The Salvation Army might take it. But the thought of a bride needing to buy her wedding dress at the Salvation Army was too sad. Or having this dress hang with a shabby price tag on the rack and nobody buying.

Abby tugged at the stiff zipper of the bag, and it dislodged, letting the dress spring out as if alive. There was the torn hem where she had stepped on it going to their mountain cabin, in the moonlight, in the snow. The bodice of the dress sparkled.

All right. Here's what she would do. Leave the wedding dress for Stan. Let him deal with it.

She took the gown out of the bag and fluffed up the skirt so that it filled the closet. When Stan rushed in here, thinking he was free, hello.

Vengeance complete, she went into a cleaning frenzy, sweeping up dust balls, cat hair, all of it. She scoured woodwork she had never touched. Housework had not been one of her specialties. Maybe that's why Stan left.

Now just leave the mailbox key and go. Where was that little key? You can't get a duplicate made. It was in an envelope around here somewhere.

Please let her find the key. Was that asking so much? One small key. She so wanted to exit with dignity.

Instead, Abby found herself clawing through bags of trash, tunneling into junk mail for that certain envelope, sifting coffee grounds. All she needed now was for Stan to come in and find her in the garbage.

She pulled out a plate Edna had given them, cracked for

years, which Abby had finally been able to throw away. She sat with it in her hands, blurry. A sweater from Stan she'd triumphantly flung in the trash bag before dumping in the kitty litter reached out a sleeve, forest green.

Where was that mailbox key?

She knelt in the trash and wept. "Oh, Lord, please help me find the key," though there wasn't any reason why he should. She had insulted him. She didn't even believe in him. Yet as her tears dropped into the orange rinds, she called upon his tender mercies now.

OK, Abby, up off your knees. So she had lost a silly key. Stan could cope. He would just think that she took it so she could come back and get the mail, and she would have to explain. She had so fervently hoped that after today they wouldn't have to speak again.

She heard a rustling sound. It was Dwayne in the other room, playing with something. She stood at the door and watched as this magnificent cat batted his toy about, a small white envelope with the word *key* on it. Maybe there is a god.

One final gesture, and she'd be done. Something never to be mentioned. Elizabeth would be disgusted. Her mother sad. Marge would scream at her.

In their bedroom downstairs, Abby opened the bureau drawer and reached to the back for the tissue paper she had stuffed there. From the tissue she took a red silk rose. The vase was ready. There.

Now she could go.

For one last moment she stood and looked, where even

at this moment the sun found a way into this basement room, spreading a gold band across the floor. Perhaps in some unguarded moment, Stan too would stand here and remember how they had loved each other once.

She put Dwayne in his cage, howling as she carried him out to the car. Wildly he pawed through his bars, swatting the air with his clawless paws.

He cried along with her for the whole way, as they drove down Shenandoah Street and out onto the beltway.

22 *The Hedge*

As Edna drove home from her bridge game, she didn't want to see her husband. They had argued before she left. It was about yard work. He didn't care if their place looked nice. He liked to cut things down. Or pile on the mulch of the stinkiest kind. The only plants Fred ever bought were on sale, half dead. He would never think to ask the color of the bloom.

The azaleas were fading now. Little pink ones disappear. Red ones shrivel. The bigger white bloom hangs like wet tissue and turns brown.

Edna looked down her street. What? That couldn't be her yard. It was naked. The azaleas going up her front walk were gone. Fred had chopped them down. Murderer! He had threatened to "prune" that hedge. Not get rid of it. Now it was just sticks. And he'd pulled some of the plants out by the root and thrown them in the street.

Fred was down in the dirt, supposedly filling his holes. Neighbors were standing there watching this hateful person acting as if the yard was all his.

Well, Edna refused to go into such an ugly place. Their front door was exposed, looking cheap. Tin.

Fred grinned up at her. "Guess I got carried away."

"You know I loved those azaleas." Edna was glad her voice sounded mean, not quivery. She had cried enough lately. "That stuff was way overgrown. You could barely get up the walk."

"I liked it that way," she snapped. "But you'll do what you want, won't you, no matter what I think." He tossed a twig out to the curb. "Well?"

Fred sat up on his haunches, proud of himself. "This will give us a vista."

Vista. He used words like that to show off. "Of what?" The best "vista" she could imagine was her flowers out the window—pink ones and purple and white intertwined with green. That was all you saw. Now the view was trash cans on the street.

"They'll grow back," Fred said.

"What about those?" Edna gestured to the azaleas in the gutter, still green. "Look at how healthy they are. I hope you're satisfied."

"You can plant some more." Fred played in the dirt.

New ones die. He knew that. It takes years for shrubs to grow up over a window, which is exactly the way some people like them. She did. With that hedge for protection, she could go out in her bathrobe for the newspaper without have her nosy neighbor Alberta watching her. The once in her life Edna ordered a pizza delivered, there stood Alberta when the Domino's man arrived. "Having our dinner delivered, are we? You know, Edna, pizza is junk food."

140

Now their yards ran together in one bare piece. You could see Fred's pink flamingos all the way down the block. People make fun of them. Why didn't he get a real bird?

Here came Alberta wearing big clunky running shoes, as if that made her athletic. She came over to Edna sitting in the car. "Guess he's done it this time."

Edna leaned out the car window. "Oh, that hedge was way overgrown. Have I shown you these earrings Fred gave me?" She turned her head so that her zircon studs could catch the light. "And not for Christmas."

Alberta moved closer, squinting. "They're not real."

Edna pulled back. "Don't be silly. Now I have to be some place." She started the car and took off down the street, although she had no idea where she was going. As she swung around the corner, she nicked a trash receptacle. It couldn't have hurt the car, but the dumpster tilted and clattered into the street, rolling noisily. Meanwhile, Edna drove on like a hit and run.

She would just keep on going, that's what. She never wanted to see Fred again, with his clippers and his vocabulary words. Vista, my eye.

She would go on down to Florida. A friend of hers had moved there, and they could play bridge every day.

Besides, with Stan and Abby breaking up, family life here wasn't fun any more. Edna missed her daughter-in-law. Well, don't think about that. Stan rarely came to dinner by himself. He'd always been the one who listened to her stories from the bridge club. Not Fred. He watched TV. But as Edna thought about it now, maybe Stan was only being polite and wasn't entertained in the least by what she said.

A mother naturally wants to praise her son no matter what. They do it on the talk shows. Mothers of Convicted Murderers say that their son was such a good boy. He couldn't have done that terrible thing. Neighbors say it too. "Oh no. Not that nice boy next door. He would never do that."

The people here all liked Stan. He was never rude. He shoveled more than his part of the walk. Ellie Naylor down the street, whose son Nelson got into drugs and every kind of trouble, said she wished she had a boy like Stan. When she heard he'd left his wife, Ellie just knew it couldn't be Stan's fault. "His wife probably had it coming. I know you liked that girl, Edna, but you never know what goes on behind closed doors."

Only know-it-all Alberta wasn't surprised when she heard what Stan did. "He was obviously a loner." She could have said that because of her own husband running off, which people figured he did because of Alberta's orneriness. But it's possible she was once a likeable person and went sour because of what happened to her.

Having the hedge between them chopped down would be a shock for Alberta too, not that she would admit it. Those azaleas from her window surely looked as pretty as what Edna saw. She should probably try to be neighborly to Alberta one more time. However, that isn't easy when the person doesn't even like a piece of pie.

Well, down in Florida none of this would matter. She would take Route 95 south. It must go all the way.

Then as the light ahead of her turned yellow, Edna hit the brakes, realizing it really was her fault what Stan did. Here she was, running away too. Fred might be mean to live with, but he had never left her. Not even for a day.

She pulled into the 7-Eleven, one of her favorite stores. They have gourmet coffee. And she could read the *National Enquirer* in peace (which Fred made fun of when she brought it home). Well, the *Enquirer* is more than just pictures of celebrities having a bad hair day or a baby born without skin. You find stories of amazing accomplishments, such as the man who ate an entire shopping cart.

Edna sipped vanilla nut coffee and ate a Dove ice cream bar. She liked watching the people go in the store for their favorite treats. A black fellow wearing earphones came along snapping his fingers, making his skinny braids bounce. Maybe it was racial prejudice, but gangs of black boys made her nervous. Yet their mothers loved them the same as any mother. A person isn't necessarily a criminal because he has big pockets going into a store. Somebody seeing Stan in his gray suit working for the government would probably think he went home to his wife, never guessing that he walked out on her as if it were nothing. That is the way Stan acted. You would hardly know he had been married. He never even mentioned Abby's name.

On her way home Edna stopped at the Safeway. Yes, she would fix Fred's supper. But not anything that was his favorite. Tonight they were having salad. And when he stuck his fork in the tomato thinking he was getting a jumbo shrimp, or at least a piece of chicken, not this time. Celery.

Personally, she wasn't all that hungry after eating that delicious Dove bar.

As Edna drove back down her street, she tried not to look at her ruined yard, although you can't exactly drive with your eyes shut. Furiously, she pulled into the driveway behind Fred's Land Rover, wanting to smack it. She kept going, right up to it, stopping, pow, just in time—also hitting her face on the steering wheel. That hurt.

Whenever Fred heard the shopping bags in the kitchen, he made a big show of coming to help her carry them (after refusing to go to the store with her). Here he came just like any other day.

He gave her an odd look. "What happened to you?"

Edna felt her nose dripping. She didn't even know that she was crying. When she took the Kleenex away, it was red. "Just a bloody nose." In the bathroom she saw the red blotch above her lip from banging the steering wheel. That spot would turn purple and make her look like Hitler.

Fred didn't ask another question about her bloody nose, not anything. That was him, not even caring that his own son was about to get divorced. "Guess he had to do it" was all Fred said when he found out. He wouldn't discuss how such a thing could have happened. Of all people, Fred should know something, being the father and another man.

Or maybe he did know what their boy was feeling, and that's why Fred wouldn't talk about it. He might be proud of Stan for doing what Fred himself wanted to do but never had the nerve. So he stayed with his wife and cut down her azalea hedge instead.

Edna went to the mantle in the living room and snatched the bowling trophy won by Fred's office, making a space for what belonged on that spot. He'd made her take down the family picture with the four of them, claiming that her friends from the bridge club would think she was living in the past.

What's wrong with the past? A lot of good things happened there.

She went to her bureau. Under her lingerie was the picture, smiling up through her panties. Fred was wearing his barbecue apron, with that big grin he got after jumping in the picture when the camera was set. The blinking red light made all of them laugh. Stan and Abby looked so happy, wearing the same white T-shirts and blue jeans. How could so much have changed?

Edna put the picture back on the mantle. There. If she couldn't look out at her azaleas, at least she could see this picture and remember happy days. Besides, nobody had told her about any divorce happening. Stan had never even mentioned wanting one. He might still come to realize that they loved each other. It can happen at any time. The *Enquirer* had a story about a couple who got back together after twenty years.

Edna was chopping celery in the kitchen when Fred came in and grabbed her around the waist. "Looking good." When he said that about something green, you knew he was trying to make up.

Edna hummed a little hum as he went on into the living room. She heard Fred grunt as he noticed the family photo

145

in its proper place. But he couldn't complain about that now, could he. After cutting down her azaleas, he would have to be nice to her for a long time.

23 *Have a Good Day*

How can a mailman whistle, stroll in his Bermuda shorts, with what he carries? Under the magazines lies the slim envelope that can change a life. The notice of nonpayment is dropped off without a thought, saying your lights will go out. A rejection slip is just a piece of paper to a postman. The Dear John letter, no doubt still a handy closure for some, may be delivered along with pizza ads.

Yet the mail brings its paychecks too, glad green through cellophane. The occasional handwriting from a friend. With unbridled anticipation, people look to some happy surprise.

The sound of the mail arriving catches the breath, the thrust it makes coming through the door, the soft thud as it lands on the floor. In apartment buildings the click of the mail carrier's key, the wall rattling open, alerts the residents in their rooms to come out. On a country road the little flag pushed up on the box brings the person hurrying down the lane. The mail! It's here!

Mail affirms the inhabitant's existence, even when the item is addressed to Resident. A homeless person does not get mail. After a move to a new place, whatever shifting of the earth brought about the change, regular mail delivery announces that something has returned to normal. Advertisements in the mailbox await patiently, asking for but a moment of your time, the lick of a stamp in reply. Sweepstakes Winner—there's your name in gold—and for a moment you believe. Anything is better than an empty box. Well, almost anything.

In the apartment where Abby lived now, the mailboxes in the foyer had holes so you could see if you had mail, sometimes even what it was. She would shake out the glossy ads in case something personal was inside. Then with relief when nothing ominous slipped forth, she would bound back upstairs, keeping the flyer for Chinese food since she and Dwayne had become particularly fond of Kung Pao chicken.

Dwayne had hated moving here. At first he crept under the sheets at night, trembling at her feet as she lay awake in the dark. He hid behind the couch for a week. Then one day he strolled out as if nothing were amiss, the way cats do.

One morning in June on her way out to the tennis court, Abby spied the familiar blue of her mother's letter in the mailbox and stopped to get it. Her mom wrote without fail, although they hadn't always been close. Abby had shut her out in high school and kept the habit going. Moving east and living the single life didn't help. But when she got married things improved. Someday with children she was destined to share much more. Now what?

Yet here was her mother's faithful letter, ever encouraging, always kind, and Abby was grateful for it. This time when she wrote back, she would share something about her life, not just fill the page with words.

She was standing over the trash can in the hall dumping catalogs when an envelope dropped on the floor. Long, cream-colored, of good bond paper. Her name was typed on it, not stuck on with a label.

She knew before she saw the return address what it was. Attorneys at Law—Weiner, Avery, Crouch & Klein. How many lawyers does it take for one divorce? She had hoped by some miracle that this notice would never come.

Now here it was in her hand. The end.

All right, then. Face it. Move on.

Damn. The letter said she had to appear at the attorneys' offices in the District of Columbia on the first day of July, "to sign the papers for the final disposition of the marriage."

Well, she wouldn't go. She could pretend that this piece of paper never came. Things get lost. Many things do!

The dreaded day came, as dreaded days will. The air was heavy. The sky was white.

What does a person wear to a divorce? She had become fond of black and considered herself entitled to wear it year-round. However, Marge had bullied her into looking upbeat on this occasion.

So on the day of her divorce, Abby tucked a navy silk blouse into white linen pants, donned a white blazer (to cover possible heavings of the chest), and combed her long blond hair. Hell, just get this over with. Maybe it wouldn't be so bad. She put on oversized sunglasses and stepped out into the glare of summer, dressed for success.

Nature knew better. The cicadas had come out, screeching in the noonday sun like the soundtrack of a horror movie. A cicada leaped on her leg then fell to the pavement, there among other scattered carcasses of these ill-fated creatures who come out to mate and die. On the way to the car, she heard them crunching beneath her feet.

She took the long way downtown, crossing the Memorial Bridge as if to the drumbeats of entourages taking their last ride here, over to our exquisite capital city, underloved and without a song.

She parked blocks away from the offices of Wiener, Avery, Crouch, & Klein—WACK, clever—and walked back along 14th Street. A young girl stood in a doorway wearing a leopard miniskirt and chewing gum, caring no more for her clients than they did for her. Smart gal.

Stalls for the Fourth of July lined the street, laden with T-shirts and flags and plates decorated with the United States capitol etched in gold. A boy stopped to squeeze mustard on a hot dog. A yellow worm. She gulped and turned away.

The number on the building was carved deep in the dark stone. You couldn't miss it. She could run the other way. Be her familiar, undivorced self even yet. Oh, God, she didn't want to do this.

Yet the stranger in the glass next to her, a tall person with pretty blond hair and stylish sunglasses, marched on as if she knew what she was doing.

As she pushed through the revolving door, all went dark. Even when she took off her glasses, the place was dim. She focused and found herself in front of a jewelry store window, where diamonds were on sale for thirty percent off. These lawyers really are bastards, aren't they.

Stan had never liked diamonds. She should have seen that as a sign. In fact, different gems should be used for the various types of marriages. A wee pearl would be just the thing for those who marry lightly. A rhinestone should be required when the intent is false from the start.

She looked down at her hand, where just this morning she had taken off her wedding band. It left a pale place on her finger. She saw it and felt sad. Maybe by tomorrow she would be ready to rush out and hurl her ring in the river the way feisty people do when a marriage is over.

Not today, not if that river rose up to her lips.

She took the stairs to the sixth floor. Just keep moving. Blind people like stairs, so it is said, because the measured steps let them know where they are. One, two, three, four, five . . . .

On the sixth floor she passed a dentist's office. Give her the needle. Or how about some laughing gas to get her down this hallway. "Dead woman walking," she whispered, on the lookout for Stan.

The receptionist in the offices of Wiener, Avery, Crouch & Klein checked her appointment book with a square white fingernail. "Mrs. Swan? You can wait around the screen."

A screen? Why, that's the oldest comic stage prop of

all. And what would her exit line be? Her mother the drama teacher believed you can prepare speeches for the occasions of your life. Yet what words for this? Abby refused to say "fine" when Stan asked how she was. Nor would she inquire of him, only to hear him say that he was wonderful.

Around the screen was a couch and a chair. Ah, the trick choice. If she picked the couch, Stan could choose to sit next to her or noticeably move over by himself.

She took the chair.

Five minutes to go. Stan was always on time. Or if he were late today, better for the divorce than the wedding.

On their wedding day he had been early. Waiting in front of the mountain lodge, in a black tuxedo against the snow, as she drove up in the Jeep with her dad. Stan hurried to help her out in her wedding dress, more eagerly than was necessary to be a gentleman. With his arm on one side and her father's on the other, there was no chance of falling. The three of them strode splendidly through the drifts toward the long room in the lodge with its glowing fireplace.

"Hello." Stan stepped around the screen, looking fine in a white shirt, dark suit, and the paisley tie she'd given him, which he always said was his favorite. "You look beautiful."

As he sank down on the couch, not a tall man, anyway, it would have been so natural for her to move over and sit by him. "How's your tennis?" he asked.

"Bad," she answered, not ready for that question.

"I know the feeling," he said, but she did not believe him. Stan's topspin cleared the net every time. His superb backhand never failed.

A man stepped around the screen. He had a nick on his neck from shaving. Either that or a client had gone after him. So, was this the Wiener? Perhaps the Klein? "I'm Ed Crouch," he announced, reaching to shake her hand. "Nice to meet you, Mrs. Swan." That lovely name, one more time. "I understand you're a tennis player as well."

"Yup."

Crouch zipped his briefcase open and pulled the papers out. Stan stepped up with no hesitation to add his signature, which after his many promotions had become completely illegible.

"You understand when you sign here, Mrs. Swan, that you relinquish all financial claims to the marriage." Stan passed the pen to her. It was one of those cheap black ballpoints with a fuzzy tip.

Their names were arranged on the paper as on a family tree, except that here under Stan's name in the top bracket was the word *complainant*.

But he never complained. Maybe he would now. Then she might understand.

Below her typed name, Abby Hopkins Swan, was the word *defendant*, although for the life of her she did not know how to defend against this.

She wrote her married name one more time. It was a name that looked good with every font on the computer. Yet she could find no reason to use it after today.

Abby Hopkins she had been. To Miss Hopkins she would return.

So, that was it?

Ah, but Ed Crouch, with blood stuck to his neck, pressed on. "You need to get this notarized. Both your signatures. They'll do it for you in the bank across the street."

Well, shit.

Stan's face stiffened with disappointment, a look that brought her down, down, again.

He picked up briskly. "Thanks. Let's go." He held the door open for her, standing back as if she were leading the way in all of this. The receptionist lifted her square white nails. "Have a nice day."

Inside her pocket, Abby made a fist.

They took the elevator down, one of those slow ones that doesn't let you know where you are. Although she implored the plastic numbers on the wall to light up, nobody else got on. Even Stan had nothing to say as they rode down. They simply stood and faced the heavy door with its crack down the middle, the way strangers do waiting for an elevator to open.

Then they were out on the streets of Washington, where music boomed from a van, and a siren wailed nearby. Stan took her hand, and they dashed across in the middle of the block, barely making it around a taxi. She thought that if they got hit then she wouldn't have to go through with this. She would never have to be divorced. As they lay bleeding in the emergency room, maybe then Stan would tell her where they had gone wrong.

They went into the freezing air-conditioning of the Citibank, where lines of lunch-hour people were waiting. Abby held their place while Stan went to check the CD rates listed on a poster across the room, although he surely knew them by heart, being the economist he was.

Finally, the notary put his imprint on their paper, squeezing down on their signatures until they were braille.

"Well, I'm off to Geneva this week," Stan said outside as they stopped at the corner for the light. "Would you like your usual chocolate?"

"Sure," Abby said without thinking. Rather, she was thinking of the delicious Lindt flavors he brought. Orange. Raspberry. Then, "No. Of course not."

Stan asked where she was parked, and she motioned in the opposite direction from his office.

And so, at the corner of 15th Street and Constitution Avenue, in the District of Columbia, on this first day of July in the year 1997, they parted as separate people.

"See you," Stan called cheerfully as he walked the other way.

She did not turn.

She drove back down Constitution Avenue, past Albert Einstein sitting on a rock across from the Vietnam Memorial, known simply as the Wall. It isn't visible from the street. Instead, you look up to the Lincoln Memorial. Elegant, lighted, symmetrical.

The Wall takes you down, sloping, black. You feel it before you see it there. Skipping children slow in its presence.

Teenagers stop and whisper. People coming for their first time, or returning to visit the Wall again, all grow silent.

She parked and went across the street, joining the slowly moving line on the walk beside the Wall, where the black marble goes into the ground, and your throat grows tight in the presence of the fifty-eight thousand names carved there.

You turn and your face is reflected among the names, in Technicolor on a sunny day, or gray and white in rain.

The Lincoln Memorial sits up splendidly, holding our great sad president on his high chair, tragic in victory.

The Wall digs into the dark earth, for the war nobody understood, nobody won, no heroes here.

The Lincoln Memorial is death.

The Wall is divorce.

A wheelchair rolled along the path, its driver grown thick in the chest, both legs gone. It was a speedy new chair that slowed down the last minute, bumping off onto the grass. There the man sat facing the Wall. He just sat and stared at it, wearing a bandanna.

A young woman, whose father might have gone to Vietnam, reached to make a rubbing on the Wall. He would always be the clean young man in the picture to her, still married to her mother, no doubt, if not for the war.

A little girl ran over and placed a yellow rose at the base of the Wall, next to a bottle of Johnny Walker, left for the thirsty dead. Some bring a letter for the deceased person who likes to read.

When the woman had finished her rubbing, she turned,

saw Abby there, and shared a look of grief. Abby nodded gratefully. Here, then, was a place where she might come, for there is no memorial to the divorced, is there. It would stretch to the sea by now, and perhaps few would come and visit it.

As she turned to go, whose face was that moving among the dead of the Wall, ghostlike in white? What would that person become?

Then she walked away, out into the vast world where it was now her job to learn to forget.

Part Two: After

24 Recycling

"He can't get married," Elizabeth told her mother, who sat reading the paper while her grandson was about to ruin his life. "Tucker's never been on a date. They would meet in the mall. Then he moved in with her. Now this." Elizabeth kneaded the bread dough in front of her. At least she baked good bread. But her other boy, Roy, had decided that he liked Wonder Bread. *Wonder Bread.*

Helene looked up with that serene expression she had. Other people's mothers were depressed. This one was happy. She smiled at something in the paper. She read it all. Sports, editorials, comics.

"Tuck is only twenty," Elizabeth reminded her.

"You were nineteen when you got married."

"You want my son to turn out like me? No ambition. One semester of college and all he cared about was the recycling on the campus. Paper, plastic, aluminum. That girl is the one with the plans, thinking she's going to be a veterinarian. The pets in that place! Tuck never even wanted a dog. Now she's got him changing kitty litter."

"Use her name, dear. Natalie."

"Why couldn't they just stay living together?"

Her mother laughed. How easily she laughed. "You had a fit when Tucker moved in with Natalie."

All right, so Elizabeth had overreacted. "And she's a vegetarian." Her son never having meat again. It was too sad.

The thought of being anyone's mother-in-law made Elizabeth feel sick. Even if Tuck didn't marry this wretched girl, it would be somebody else, wouldn't it.

"How about spinach lasagna for the engagement party?"

Elizabeth shuddered. "I will not serve a green entree."

"Just a suggestion," her mother answered. "Dear, I do hope you can enjoy this wedding."

"Right, with the bride's divorced parents glaring at each other. And what about Abby? This wedding won't be easy for her."

"She'll get along fine. We all care about Tucker. Now let's go plant those impatiens I brought. Your yard needs some color for the occasion."

So Elizabeth went out and knelt in the dirt, stabbing at the ground. "I don't want Tuck getting divorced. You know how it twists a person."

The spade next to her kept digging. "I think she's recovered quite well."

"Abby?" Elizabeth reared up on her knees. "She's a mess."

In went a pink flower. "That's not true. Abby has her teaching. She has a good life." A purple flower went next, then a coral one, according to the plan. This was a woman in control, except when it came to her daughters' lives.

"Abby is doing fine," her mother repeated, like a mantra she had come to believe.

"Just because she won't talk about her divorce doesn't mean she's over it. We still aren't allowed to mention the word—and it's been three years."

"It is her way." Her mother smoothed the ground in front of her. "It's what she does to move on."

"To what?"

"A good life by herself. Not everyone has to be married these days. She has her teaching. Her tennis."

"Right." Elizabeth got up and turned on the hose, squirting the gravel on the patio, sending it skittering to the edges. "Tennis is the most boring thing I've ever seen. Have you watched it on TV? The ball goes back and forth."

Roy dashed around the corner, into the spray. "Mom, stop it."

"Well, get out of the way."

"Hi, Grandma." Then Roy was gone.

He had always been a secretive kid, this surprise child she'd had. Maybe because he wasn't planned, Elizabeth often forgot that Roy was there.

She stood gazing at her altered yard. "I just hope Abby can handle this wedding."

"She'll be fine. It's you I'm worried about."

"Not Tucker?" Elizabeth watered a dead place in the lawn. She should have forced her boys to do yard work. "How could his marriage last when people like Stan and Abby break up? And this girl's family is hardly a model."

"It's a worry. But think of Stan's parents. They seemed

163

to be stable people. He was devoted to his job. You just can't predict."

"He never loved my sister."

A white flower went quivering into the ground. "Surely he did."

"Whatever."

"Do you suppose," her mother said in a calm voice, although she was picking dirt off the spade where it was clean, "that Stan could have been gay?"

Elizabeth hooted. "No way. Abby told me that much. He was quite the lover. Even when they were separated."

"She talked to you about that?"

"Yup. Stan was a hot guy."

"So, do you think there were other women?"

"Not according to Abby."

"You know, I always liked Stan. He was pleasant to be around. Not pretentious."

"He was a rat."

"Don't say that. But I suppose it's just as well they didn't have children."

Elizabeth tightened the nozzle that was leaking water down her arm and aimed it at a tree, anything. "I'll never forgive him for not letting her have a child. Stan told her he wanted kids. Abby let him walk all over her. I didn't think she was such a wimp."

"Don't be so hard on your sister. Whatever Stan's flaws, she was crazy about him."

Elizabeth finished and tossed the hose on the ground. It was true. Abby cared more for Stan than for anyone. "But why him? This little guy who worked for the federal government. She knew other better men."

"She said he was smart. Very intelligent."

"Stan was dumb. Leaving her like that. I know Abby can be bitchy. But after the way she felt about him? I never knew anyone so totally gone over another person except in some romance novel. Not just at first either. Abby always felt that way."

"You care about Jack. You just don't go on about it."

"I've never been nuts about him. Not wiped out. Maybe Abby got it from all those books she reads."

"Not her American literature," her mother said, with pride in her voice for her younger daughter's advanced degree. "She says Americans don't write love stories. They write about freedom. Huckleberry Finn."

"Always the intellectual. Every time I call Abby, she cuts me off to go do her school work. She hasn't gone with anybody since the divorce, not really. When she comes out for the wedding, I'm going to fix her up."

"Ask her first."

"Abby? She'll say no. I'll just do it. At least with everybody getting divorced these days, more men are available. She needs to get out. Abby used to be fun."

"This has been tough."

It was tough on all of them. A divorce is not a ripple in a family. It's a quake. Trouble supposedly brings you closer. But not when the person won't talk.

Anyway, Abby was staying longer this summer and helping with the wedding.

So much to do. Look at this grass. "Roy?" Elizabeth shouted. He was old enough to mow the lawn. High time he learned to be more responsible than his older brother.

"Roy?" Naturally, when there were chores to do, he disappeared.

25 *Roy*

I grab my bear and run out, away from the bad thing I've done. Bob's arm is loose. I swing him like a lasso. I've had him for my whole life. I'm nine years old.

I run to the park and throw Bob at a tree. He lands on his head. Once he got stuck in the branches, and I had to throw rocks to get him down. He only has one eye.

My brother Tucker used to hide Bob from me. He put him in the freezer, and he got stiff. Tucker is getting married to his girlfriend named Natalie. She's nice. She talks to me. Tucker walks her dog for her, but he never used to like pets. Not even our dog Sophie. She was mine.

Sophie was big and black and ran away. My dad drove us everywhere looking for her. I didn't want to look by the road. We never did find Sophie, but we put her picture on all the trees. Nobody called the number. My dad says she might have found another home.

I chase around with the sprinkler in the park. It comes after me, landing cold drops on my back. It feels good. Bob doesn't like water. It gives him spots.

We race away to our tree hiding place. The branches go to the ground. It's like a tent inside. I kneel on the pine needles, breathing hard. Nobody else knows about this place. Just us.

I try to forget the bad thing I've done. When you try not to think about something though, you do it all the more. I did it because of what my mom said about Uncle Stan. "Forget him. He's gone." I saw his picture in the family album and did a bad thing. I didn't mean to do it. Then I couldn't stop.

My Uncle Stan divorced my Aunt Abby, and my mother calls him swear words. She gets real bossy on the subject. "When Aunt Abby comes, I do *not* want you mentioning his name." People are always telling kids not to say stuff. Us with our big mouths.

Uncle Stan was smiling in the picture. I drew a beard on him with a black crayon. It was fun. I gave him spiky hair. He really looked different. I did it in all the pictures. I was going to get blamed anyway, as I'm the only kid. Tucker is a lot older than me. He gets away with everything.

The only one littler than me is my bear Bob. I'm bad to him. I beat him up and stuff. He would run away if he could.

The black spiky hair on Uncle Stan looked gross. So I cut his head off with the scissors. Whack, whack, whack. It was a pile of heads. His pictures really looked dumb then. There was my Aunt Abby holding hands with a headless guy. She was smiling at a hole.

I started crying like a kid (which I am). More like a baby. It's embarrassing. I hid the album in the piano bench.

I took piano lessons one time, but I stunk.

I squeeze my eyes shut, trying to forget what I did. But I

can see Uncle Stan's heads that I threw in the garbage. I take Bob and choke him around the neck. He must be pretty mad at me, this crazy kid trying to strangle a teddy bear.

Uncle Stan lives out in Virginia, over by Washington, D.C. We visited there one time. He and Aunt Abby took us to the fireworks down by the United States capitol. They were awesome. Uncle Stan put me up on his shoulders so I could see. I still wasn't that high, as he's a pretty short guy.

I don't know why he left Aunt Abby. Nobody tells a kid stuff like that. She's not that bad of a person. Actually, she's pretty much fun, although she hardly ever visits us.

Now my mom's afraid Tucker will get divorced when he gets married to Natalie. I never knew a grown-up could have so many pets! Sprawled on the furniture. Scratching in cages. Next she wants to get a snake, but I'm not supposed to tell.

What I'm scared of is my parents getting divorced. It happens to lots of kids at my school. They say it's not so bad. I think they just don't want to talk about it. My mom and dad probably will get divorced. They fight. Well, mostly it's my mom who fights. My dad just laughs it off, which only makes her madder. He takes me to the paint store. He's a house painter. You can smell paint on him when he comes home. His shoes have spots. He wears a mask and uses a neat spray gun.

My dad isn't into sports. Me neither. I'm totally un-coordinated.

I crawl out from under the tree. It's bright outside. Guess I'll go find my friend Thurman and see if he can play.

169

My mom's car is gone, and I get my bike and ride off, almost forgetting the bad thing I've done.

Here comes Thurman on his bike to get me. I feel happy! I wave at him, and he nods his head. He's an older kid, a year ahead of me in school.

"C'mon," he says, pedaling away.

"Wait." My legs whirl around loose, like I'm in the air. I squeeze the gears, and they make a clicking sound. I go.

"Hurry up, slow poke," he calls.

I'm pumping hard up the road when Bob flies out of my arm, falling on the street. A car is coming. I scream and turn my bike, too quick, and I fall off. I'm not hurt though. The car swings around, missing Bob. It probably thought the brown thing in the road was a rock. I go over and pick up Bob. I punch him in the face.

"You still have that stupid bear?" Thurman says, doing wheelies around me in the street. I stuff Bob in the pocket under the bike seat. His head flops out. "That's a kid's toy. It's for babies."

I get teased about Bob a lot. I just pump. Thurman has to boss somebody, as his little brother moved to California to live with their dad. "At least a stupid bear can't run away like a dumb dog." Thurman's dad also left him is what I'm thinking.

Thurman drags his leg as his bike swoops up, showing off. He's not that much older than me, but he's a whole lot bigger. I'm the next-to-smallest kid in my class. Ernie Fisher is really teeny, plus he wears glasses.

"You OK?" Thurman asks.

"Yeah."

We ride up the road going to the foothills. I stand up on my bike to pump, almost catching up to Thurman. "Where you been today?" he says at the top of the hill. "Nowhere." I want to tell him about Uncle Stan's pictures. Thurman would think the spiky hair was neat. But he's not the one getting in trouble. I tell him about my brother Tucker getting married to Natalie. "My mom's afraid they'll get divorced."

"Yeah. Most everybody does." Thurman pedals faster, up to where the road turns into dust.

"Not everybody," I call after him.

"Anybody can too get divorced." He slows down. "You just have to be married is all." He leaps his bike over a rock.

"Not my grandma and grandpa. They couldn't get divorced." I swing around the rock.

"Could too."

"Could not."

"You go ask 'em."

I hit a hole, and my bike wobbles. "They wouldn't get divorced even if they could. They still kiss."

"You can kiss and get divorced," Thurman tells me, zigzagging along. Tucker knows stuff like this from his own family. I guess I just don't want it to be true, like when you find out that Santa Claus isn't real.

"That doesn't mean my brother has to get divorced."

"Your brother's a goofball. Can you see him having a kid?"

Wow, that was too weird of a thought. "No way." I grin

171

at him. Thurman is a smart guy. "Natalie, maybe her. She'll be like my sister," I say proudly. Thurman only has a little brother. "She'll probably be my stepsister."

"No, dummy. That's when your parent marries somebody who has a kid. Like the dorky son of this lady my dad got married to. Supposedly he's my stepbrother."

"Is he bigger than you?"

"He's a scrawny jerk."

We keep on riding, and the sun is warm, with everything feeling nice. I get up the nerve and ask Thurman, "How'd you know your parents were getting divorced?"

"I never knew." He speeds up on his bike, click, click, clicking it into a faster gear.

"Did they fight?" I call out.

"Nope."

He slows down. He stops his bike and sucks from his water bottle, breathing hard, even him. Thurman lives in a big house. His mom bought him a pool table after she and his dad broke up.

I look down the hill, trying to see my street. The houses look like toy houses. There's mine!

"So, how'd they tell you then?"

"Took us to Disneyland, me and my brother Joseph." Thurman keeps holding his bottle, forgetting it's in his hand. He's just standing there. "Ever been to Disneyland?"

"Not yet. My mom says we might go next summer."

Thurman starts riding his bike, slow this time. "So we're eating at these outside tables they have. I'm flipping ketchup with a French fry at my bratty brother. I should have known something is up as my mom isn't railing on me. She just sits there with this hot fudge sundae and her spoon not moving. She puts on these huge dark glasses. 'Boys,' she says, 'We have something to tell you.' Meanwhile, my dad takes this humongous bite out of his burger."

"Then what?"

"It was like on TV, one of those sappy shows. Probably that's where she learned how to say it, from some soap opera. 'This has nothing to do with you boys,' she says in this tight type of voice. 'Your father and I love you very much.' Like, they're telling us this at Disneyland? 'Explain to them, Phil.'" Phil is Thurman's dad, who is not a big talker. "'We'll always be a family.'"

I reach behind the seat to see if Bob is there, touching where his fur is worn off. It's him.

"My mom sounds dumb saying this stuff. And her ice cream is melting in the dish. She doesn't even eat the hot fudge part, and if you know her, she's a chocolate freak." Thurman likes his mom, but he misses his dad. His little brother too. That's why Thurman plays with a skinny kid like me.

"My dad, he's picking on his fingernail, tearing off a piece of it. 'Damn,' he says. 'What?' He looks up like he wasn't there the whole time. 'That's right, sons,' he says —which he's never called us in his whole life. 'Your mother can say it better.' He never tells us zip and makes her do the talking—when he is the one leaving us.

"By now me and my brother are squirming in our chairs, staring down at the ketchup on the plate.

173

"So, my mom finally says they're having this so-called trial separation. I mean, like, they're splitting up. Me and Joseph, we're going along with this thing, nodding our heads as if we're polite or something. You do the dumbest stuff at times like that."

I ride my bike slowly, hearing all this. I know one thing. I'm not bugging my mom any more to go to Disneyland.

"Hey, but you get all kinds of stuff when your parents split, you know?" Thurman says as he takes off. "Plus, they don't even notice half the crap you do."

We're going down the hill now. I'm speeding faster than ever. Our shirts are flapping like flags on us.

There's my house. My dad's truck is in the drive. He's home!

I'm riding with no hands. Thurman lets out a whoop, and I whoop back at him as we race down the hill, waving at the cars, flying home.

26 Top Cat

I am the top cat now. It's great. I leap up on the table for meals. She used to shoo me off when he was here. A bit of bacon? Tasty. I pat a muffin off the plate, and it rolls along.

She stays home grading papers. I leave teeth marks in some. I get to sleep on the bed every night.

Sometimes I still think I hear him coming. But the sound isn't him. Did he go away because of things I did? I got my hair on his clothes. I peed in his closet.

He was a dog guy. That must be it. He threw stuff for a cat to fetch. Excuse me? When I got on his commode, he tossed me out. All cats do that. If my lady finds me drinking out of her toilet, she swoops me up and lets me sit on her lap in there.

Anyhow, it's great with just the two of us. Guys come around, but they don't stay long. I see to that. This one character jumped when I walked by him. Afraid of a cat.

He brought this package in a shiny wrapper. I leaped up on the table to sniff the food smell, ripping into it. Something sticky and sweet. Nasty stuff. I edged it across the table, tap, tap tap. It smacked to the floor.

She yelled at me for that. Then she went back and sat on the couch by him. He put his big arm around her. I hissed. And what did he do? Just kept on talking.

I hauled up and landed on the couch behind his head, biting into his hair, gnawing down to his scalp.

He reared up, knocking me off. I raced away—with this wad of hair caught in my teeth. I shook and shook it out, with this bald guy chasing me. I dashed in the other room and hid under the bed.

The front door shut pretty quick. She came looking for me, crawling along the rug to me. But she didn't say mad things. She was laughing.

We came out, and she swept me up in her arms.

She is my lady. I am her cat.

27 How To

The storm was over. Limbs lay on the ground. When it rains in Virginia, it rains hard. Now the sun glistened through the dripping leaves down Arlington Boulevard as Abby drove over to Fort Myer, where the community college offered classes.

It was the first day of a mid-spring term. Oh, new semester. The mistakes of the past erased for everyone. She'd always been that happy kid with her book bag laid out before September ever came. She quickly breathed. Who would be in the room this time? What students from around the world would gather on this day?

The guard at Fort Myer was in full uniform, a white band across his navy chest. He saluted and waved her through. Abby saluted him back, proceeding along the tree-lined street of red-brick houses with brass nameplates, here in this haven of order along the Potomac. She liked military students. They obey. They don't come with nebulous personal excuses. One soldier asked permission to be absent because he'd been assigned to protect the White House.

The main street at Fort Myer circles around to a chapel. From there you can see tennis courts. Meticulously kept gray sand courts where the groundskeeper sweeps the baseline with a little rotating broom to make it white.

Soldiers came uprightly down the walk with their heads shaved. Women in the military too stepped proudly along in big-toed boots.

The class was held in a small frame building with the door at the rear. No grand entrance here. Next door to the blackboard was the latrine. Well, she liked this place just fine. Over here where nobody knew her.

She made her way to the front. And what were the students' hopes on this first day?

She faced the room of strangers. At first you don't think you could ever know these people, certainly not like them as well as the last class. But it usually happens.

Many wore uniforms, khaki leaves. They had been laughing and talking when she came in, a gift right there when they already know each other.

Civilians come here too. A young couple, likely Vietnamese, slim in white short-sleeved shirts, shared a chunky dictionary on the desk between them. A fellow on the front row looked up with blue metallic sunglasses. "Hey, Lamont." His neighbor poked him. Lamont remained at military attention.

It was then that Abby saw in the back of the room, his chair pulled away from the others, a man in his late forties, bleached bangs combed toward deep-set eyes. Possibly a Vietnam vet. Angry, detached, for some reason forced to be here. Well, before this class was over, he might be working in a group with the Vietnamese couple, sharing with them what he wouldn't tell the rest of the class. She had seen it happen.

The room hushed, here where the late afternoon light came dimly through opaque windows and the air conditioner sputtered. Yet there they were. Another class, another chance.

Abby said she was glad to be here, admitting about herself that she had a cat, plucking an imaginary hair off her sleeve. That always worked. She got smiles.

After their introductions she suggested a how-to paper this time. "The bookstores are full of how-to's. It's the American way. Recipes. Diet books. Follow the steps to financial, spiritual, personal success."

"Can we write about recovery from an addiction?"

"Absolutely. I'm in awe of people's ability to survive, to triumph over adversity. We have all suffered major setbacks. Loss of a job. A death. How do you make a marriage work?" Her voice rose to an excitable pitch as she strode across the narrow room, arriving at the wall in no time, turning back like a swimmer doing laps. "Well, enough of that."

She lowered her arms. She paused—not to get the attention of the class, for they were quiet and watching her carefully—but to breathe.

"Questions? All right. Begin."

She sank into her chair, reeling from her rousing speech, and watched. Some people stare for a while. Then a pen starts moving. Another. Finally, everyone is writing, with only an occasional paper being crushed or ripped, those worthy sounds of editing, to interrupt. The instructor is forgotten as words on a page take over, shaping the bits and pieces of life into something meaningful.

This was peace. If she could just remain in these rooms. Forget social life. Holidays. The long visit to Utah this summer to help with her nephew's wedding, and to be with the family for a change. They would ask about her life. Well, she was getting along just fine. She'd read every how-to book in print about moving on with life. Not a breath of her past would escape her lips.

Proudly she marched into the next class at Fort Myer with the how-to essays. "Megan, would you read yours?"

Megan, with red curls springing jauntily from under her military cap, was not shy. "Yes, ma'am. It's called, 'How to Annoy Your Husband.'" The girls smiled. The fellows sat up.

"I never meant to offend my husband, Bud. I came home from work and greeted my cat, Anthony, who was rubbing against my leg.

"'What about me?' Bud said, standing there. 'I'm the husband.'

"'Sorry, but Anthony has been with me longer.'

"That evening did not go well with Bud and the cat. So if you want to annoy your husband, here are some tips.

"One. Feed your cat before your husband. Dry cat food will spill on your husband's placemat, sending hairs floating up in his cereal dish.

"Two. Let your cat sleep anywhere. On the bed. On top of the TV. Especially in your husband's closet, on his dark socks if your cat has light fur.

"Three. Put the litter box close to your husband's office. He probably won't change the box. But do get him to carry the litter to the trash so that when the bag pops, the trail across the yard cannot be traced to you."

Megan politely stopped. "You want more?"

"Yes, yes," the class called out with enthusiasm (also aware that their instructor liked this piece).

"Four. Groom your cat on your husband's pillow, combing while he tells you something important about taxes or a deal he's struck. Pull the cat hairs out of the comb and hold them up to the light as he talks. Wad them onto his nightstand nearby.

"If your husband heads for someplace quiet, follow with the cat and clippers to snip his toenails in the silent room.

"Travel? But you can't travel, you tell your husband. Your cat would get lonely. Boarding is for dogs.

"Should your cat become ill, barfing in creative places, or if you're just going to the vet for shots, don't be deceived if your husband leaps in the car to drive you. He might be hoping the cat will stay away overnight. He might even vindictively wish for a serious diagnosis.

"What will knock the smile off your husband's face is the depth of concern you show for your cat's mere sneeze, let alone your grief should he (the cat) ever die.

"These suggestions are guaranteed to annoy any husband of a woman who has a cat. Obviously, avoid this process if your marriage is on shaky grounds."

The class cheered for Megan. They clapped when she got through—applause in an English class.

181

Abby sank back blissfully. She would probably be teacher of the year for this.

"Well, Megan got her *A*," somebody said. "She knows that the teach likes cats."

"I learned from this," one of the girls observed.

"Yeah," Lamont replied from behind his one-way glasses of metallic blue. "Stay away from a female with a cat."

A second writing assignment for the Fort Myer class was to challenge authority. Good idea for the military, no?

Abby stretched on her balcony recliner, sipping wine and giving *A*'s. Why not make people happy when you can? And these students were good. They followed directions.

What? Someone was defying her. The essay was entitled "No How-To."

Here in America is belief you can do anything. Pull up by bootstraps every time. Make million dollar. How to recovery is possible for all mental problems, even sadness, I think. Probably a person can recover from murdering someone.

How-to books say it easy. I read this, and I am feeling glad. But it not always true. It not easy to learn English language. Many how-to books say a thing simple to do, but it is hard to do.

I see the many diet books. Yet American people growing bigger. In the supermarket it say "fat free" foods on shelves. Lite ice cream. In all-you-can-eat salad bar is chocolate pudding. I never hear of this before. In my country the people grow thin, but no how-to books on diet. Small food in small bowl is what I think.

Another book not helping is how to swing golf club. My friend Cuong, he caddy for very nice man who is reading many how-to books. Mr. Emory say excitedly, "I have new grip." He holds golf club with fingers exactly right. Yet he maybe stop smiling that day forever. The ball went flying out into many trees. Mr. Emory's face is getting red and boiling up, and he mutter from his lips. Still, he is gentleman, not shouting curse words.

When they find the tiny ball out from dead leaves, Mr. Emory try to relax as the book say. He swing with whole body, and the ball cracks up in sky, surely to be straight this time. But it goes unbelievably hook as they say and lands in water. Mr. Emory's face grows dark. Suddenly he is mean man. He drags golf bag over and throws it in pond of water, making big splash right there.

Next day he tells Cuong no more need for caddy, as he is finishing game of golf.

How-to book cannot help to do everything. It cannot erase our minds. In my country of Vietnam our ancestors walk in village with us and remind us of our past life. It always in our minds. Memory is something that imprints on human brain and cannot be wiped away until we die perhaps.

Back when South Vietnam was invaded by Communist, sixty people were trying to escape on small wooden boat. My Uncle Luc took his wife on boat. After five days and six nights drifting in South China Sea, food and water were almost empty from the boat, and they are almost reaching Thailand.

Suddenly the darkness is falling quickly, and storms and waves are rising up. Everybody is losing self control. No one can see each other, where the darkness and sea water is all around.

My Uncle Luc is trying to swim and find his wife, but boat is being swallowed in ocean, and the wind continues to blow. The next morning he is holding onto piece of wood and floating in the water. He doesn't see where his wife has gone. He realizes she already sink completely. In some time he is rescued by fishermen and brought to refugee camp far away from here.

Later he came to America. The people know of Luc's bad experience and try to help him. They drive him to shopping mall and Blockbuster store. We even take him to English class. But his actions are sitting there silently, and his tears drop, as if he not know where he is or even who he is in new country after the many things he lost.

It take years for Luc to recover almost fully. Yet he different man. He is acting slowly. Sometimes he is telling me his past when he met his wife, when they got married. Then is the first time I see him smile.

He smile for what he could not forget perhaps.

28 *Love Game*

When memories seep in at dawn, go out. Abby played tennis in the morning, up with the dew and the birds. She played at night, reaching for a yellow ball on a black sky. In the middle of the day, she practiced by herself.

Obsession may not make you a better person, or even more skillful at what you do. But it does give you something to live for.

So what if she lost. She would hit with style. Brush up with topspin. Charge the net. Go, girl. Many a ball sailed by her in this feisty mode. Miss she might, but lunge she would.

She hung out with others addicted to the game. And most tennis players at least appear to be fine folk. They show up at family functions, particularly in rainy or icy weather. However, *their minds aren't there.* Somewhere out on a court, they are replaying the overhead they slammed into the net. Their nearest of kin would not want to hear their court-side conversations. "What will I do when my mother comes to town?" says one. Another relates how she forgot her son at McDonald's for three hours while she played in a pickup game.

Tennis addicts are most abusive to their nonplaying

spouses. They with their suggestions of alternative activities —taking a walk, an ocean cruise—which are greeted by a perplexed stare from one who dreams only of being in the zone. And should the nonplaying spouse make the mistake of driving past a tennis court on the way to anything else, his buckled-up mate will sigh, possibly moan out loud, then in sullen silence stroke the dwindling callous on her palm.

Yet this same person is suddenly graciousness itself in regard to her tennis associates. Phone calls are answered immediately with a bright new voice, schedules rearranged with stunning speed, travel cheerfully incurred for exorbitant distances if a game awaits.

The sins of the sports junkie are many. Yet nonplayers too have their fatal flaw. They never ask about your game, although they can go on all day about other matters. World affairs. What's for dinner. But the closest blood relative will fail to inquire, "What is your favorite shot? Your finest moment on the court today?" Otherwise sensitive souls muster only the most mundane of queries here: "Did you win?" Then when you bound in the house after your greatest triumph, they forget to ask that.

Thus the tennis friend, who understands all, is to be gathered to your heart. Such was Marge. And this dear woman was available to play on weekends. One's own divorce can be such a handicap; that of another, however, can be quite a benefit to you.

It was a warm spring evening. The air was soft. No wind at all to blow the ball. This time Abby was meeting Marge at a Fairfax County park with a newly surfaced court, clean green on red. This one was surrounded by a golf course. Mounds of soothing grass for as far as you could see. Here a tennis player might gaze in bemused amazement at golfers trudging into the trees looking for their tiny balls, their scores adding to infinity. Tennis is a kinder game. The worst score you can have is 6-0. Then you get to start again. Yet surely these golfers too would rather be in this park tonight than anyplace on earth.

Saturday night brings out a special crowd of lonely souls and fanatics as the family folk are off attending to social duties, with only the occasional married ones sneaking out to play. She and Marge sat on the grass, waiting for a court. They spied two men they knew going on. Sung was a small man who wore a leg brace and and hit with slice. Cooper powered every shot with a contorted wristy stroke, which he practiced faithfully against the wall, a familiar figure there in his black biker shorts.

Maybe these men would play doubles. That would be better than waiting.

Sung nodded yes, and Cooper grudgingly agreed to share his court. At least he wouldn't have to lose to Sung, this smaller man who beat him regularly. Cooper eyed the women, trying to decide which one should be his partner. But Abby and Marge chose to play together. Cooper shrugged and went around on Sung's side of the net.

For every point Cooper lost by overhitting, Sung won his with touch. His drop shots floated over the net, sinking, as Abby charged in and missed. Or at the last minute, Sung let his arm go easy, soft as an old rubber band, and lobbed.

She and Marge lost that set.

After that they hit to Cooper. And the more errors he made, the more he hogged the court, lunging in front of Sung and shouting, "Mine." Then he'd blow the shot. Yet Sung never once showed the least homicidal reaction. Good partners are like that. They look beyond your mistakes to the better game they know you have.

Gradually she and Marge found their rhythm, knowing where the other would be. Their ground strokes started going in the court. They put away their overheads. How nifty, how neat, to do it right. They went ahead 5-4.

This was it. One last game before their time was up.

"Now," Marge whispered as a short ball came, and they moved together to the net. Cooper loomed up and pounded the return at Abby. She held out her racket. The ball bounced off the handle, landed on the tape, and dropped to the other side at Cooper's feet. He teed off and smacked it in the net.

Forty-love for her and Marge with that bit of luck. It is luck when a let cord goes your way, although it feels like a benediction.

Marge was serving to Cooper. Abby knew what to do. Poach. Go. She imagined where the ball would come. Her strings met it there, crisply volleying into the alley, away.

That's what you live for out here, hitting the sweet spot. After all the mishits of your life, find the true center once, and it will change you.

They won that game at love—and the set—with Abby's

magnificent volley. It felt like championship point, although it only meant that they'd split sets. No time to play a third. This often happens in social tennis, generous game that it is, letting you all go home as equals.

Sung gave a big smile and reached across the net to shake hands. Cooper grunted and stepped aside to practice his swing, swishing his racket wildly. He demanded a rematch. They agreed on the next week. As he walked off with Sung, Cooper spoke in low intense tones, no doubt planning his strategy.

Abby's step was light as she went out to her car, a new white VW Cabriolet, luminescent in the glow left in the sky. People's tennis clothes coming through the parking lot were bright. Their skin was gold.

It was then that she saw him. Short, getting out of his car with those stocky legs of his. So, he wasn't driving the Cherokee anymore. It was a Subaru Outback. Abby had wondered what she should watch for along the roads.

Her first thought was to run—to flee as she had from his image in every mall, lobby of a theater, aisle of the supermarket. She had her escape route ready to the nearest dressing room, toilet, hallway to an exit. The key to avoidance is to spot the other person first. He wouldn't want to see her either, would he.

She had seen Stan once at the tennis club. He was playing on the end court where she was scheduled to go the next hour. In minutes the buzzer would sound. They would meet in the single corridor leading to the courts. It was the only route. She started in that direction. Then like a crazy woman, she swooped under the curtain out onto a court where people were playing, crept down the sideline, and snuck behind the curtain at the far end. There she hid, flattened against the wall, hyperventilating, grateful to be spared.

But tonight after hitting that fabulous winning volley, she did not need to run away. Certainly, she could talk to a man she had been married to once. After all, it had been three years.

And there he was, alone on a Saturday night, maybe even lonely—

Abby stepped toward him, the sweat cooling on her clothes and her heart big. Maybe they would be friends, do you think? Her blood was pounding in her madly, with a frantic joy. All would be well. All would be well even yet.

He was getting his racket out of his trunk. He flung the tennis bag over his shoulder and headed for the courts. She was about to call out when his legs grew longer, not so muscular as she had remembered them. And Stan didn't hurl his tennis bag on his back like that. He held it reverently in his hand.

This person wasn't Stan. So she didn't have to face him after all, although sometime, somewhere, surely she would see him again.

Her breath shrank back to normal, and her step grew regular as she walked out to her car. But the thing was, she *would* have spoken if it had been Stan. She would have been calm, charming, knowing exactly what to say on this fine night.

As she drove off in her convertible, her moist hair flying in the Virginia air, she hummed a triumphant tune. Now she could handle anything.

29 Shenandoah Street

Abby sat grading papers in her cubicle at the office, which was practically deserted on one of those spring after- noons, unusually warm, when everyone is restless. Soon she too would leave—drive away, be free. Yet she would miss this, her classwork. Her vacation to Utah would be long.

One more essay to go. She had put her favorite on the bottom of the pile. Angie Kim was a shy Korean girl who rarely spoke. But her writing did.

Where I Lived

I don't think of it often. But the picture of my home comes back to me, on the street that I knew, the place of my root. I can see it again as if I were there.

It is a small road covered with rough cement and two- story houses, where the laundries hang out and wave in the wind. The big house in front is shiny from tiny bits of stone. The roof is blue like a sky, built in the special Korean manner, shaped gracefully. Behind this is our small house.

The street is empty. Nobody is going there because the high noon sun melts the street as if it were ice cream. I start to walk very slowly. A tower belches black smoke. It comes from our town's public bathtub. During the summer people don't go there to take a bath. The thought of putting your body into hot water makes you weary. The owner probably wears a tearful face because of the slow business. The empty tub may be lonely.

Around the corner is a little tavern, or just a few chairs under a big umbrella. When the hot summer day is almost over, the men in the neighborhood come in. They have already finished dinner with their cute children and passive spouses. Here they gather to talk and drink and tell stories of their lives. Sometimes they argue loudly about social and political issues, but they also listen to each other well most of the time. When their faces start to become red by the influence of liquor, the evening glow also reaches its summit. Soon dusk comes with a cool whiff of the wind. They stay and stay, not wanting to go home. Maybe this is their favorite place, such a small tavern with its big umbrella. This spot is their root.

In Korea people have a tendency to pull back to their root. I am physically many thousands of miles from my root. But my blood veins pull me toward my little country, toward my little town, and toward my street. It is my heart that leads me to the place.

It takes me back to that familiar street, as if I am there again.

Angie's words were swirling in her as Abby left the office and drove down the hill toward King Street. It goes north through Bailey's Crossroad and was the easiest way home to

Fairfax County, but she automatically took a detour to avoid her old neighborhood. In these three years she had not been back to Shenandoah Street.

Today a blinking arrow of orange bulbs nudged the traffic into a single lane, funneling it onto King Street. Her side-street exit was closed, under construction today. There behind the barricade, workers in hard hats leaned into drills and broke the road in pieces.

Well, then, if she was forced to drive past The Commons where she had lived, she would look away. However, King Street along here had changed so much that she hardly recognized it. There where the dry cleaners used to be, where Stan took his suits, was a Jiffy Lube.

Shenandoah Street would be changed too. Maybe she should drive by. Dispel the myth. It wasn't as if Stan lived there anymore. She knew that from the phone book. He had moved to a nameless street, somewhere in the area. No, she had not dialed his number (although she almost did). Grown-ups do that. Not just silly kids. Is it to hang up on the person? Probably just to hear the voice again. Don't many of us, when we answer the phone and nobody is there, imagine that it might be an old love of ours?

Here came The Commons on her left, the name carved in stone. She didn't need to do this. But her car was signaling. It was turning in, onto a hushed street of shade, where out of the shadows, flowers glowed in the roundabout. She passed the mailbox that tilted the way it always had.

She drove around and naturally took the right turn onto Shenandoah Street. It seemed brighter than before. Stark. A tree must be gone. Yes, the big oak near the curb had been cut down. The sun blazed onto the parking place by the bus stop where Stan had parked the Cherokee so he could wait there when it rained. She thought of him up on his seat in a storm, reading the *Washington Post*.

She should not have come, should she. Abby thought of the day she drove away from here, and she could hardly breathe. She remembered the pollen that had collected on the windshield. Green fur. She heard again the cry of her cat.

She faced forward and drove past the entrance to her place, quickly in her new convertible.

But it was too much to ask. As Angie Kim wrote, your root calls you back.

At the end of the block, she pulled to the curb with a great welling up in her for this place that had been her home. She had nearly fallen on this sidewalk. It was hers.

She got out and was drawn up the street, past the Virginia, red-brick buildings that are ridiculed for looking so much alike, into a certain parking lot, over to a doorway like no other.

There was the front window where Dwayne had sat, his big tabby body filling it, hissing at strangers going by. Now there were curtains, ugly beige drapes tied back with ropes. She smiled, thinking how Dwayne would attack those tassels. She and Stan had vowed that they would never own a curtain. They had kept that vow.

She went around and peered into the guest room. The shutters were closed. At least the current residents had the good taste to retain those shutters. If you left them slightly open, they made a ribbed pattern of light, there where she and Stan lay on the bed. Faintly Abby held to the windowsill.

Now away. Somebody would report a peeping person here. Be gone, you fool.

She had her car key ready. But one more path to take. It went behind the common building, back of the small enclosed yards. She and Stan used to snoop around here, looking through knotholes in the fences to the profusion of shrubs some neighbors had. Or sometimes inside a wall a place had gone to ruin.

It wasn't until she approached the familiar gate out back that she thought of the tree her father had planted on that hot August day. She feared for it. New trees die. Or maybe these tenants had replaced it with something they liked better.

She looked up. White bloom lifted above the little wall, branch after crooked branch of the dogwood tree. Such white blossoms in the shade back here, seeming to grow randomly on air, yet orderly, as if laid out on a plate, their four-square petals looking up.

There is a legend of the dogwood tree. The story goes that it once was as big as an oak and other forest giants. But among all the trees its wood was the strongest, so it was chosen as the timber for the cross. The dogwood was so grieved at its job that Jesus, sensing the suffering of the tree, said that never again would the dogwood grow big enough to be used this way. After that it grew slender and bent and twisted, with only its blossoms forming a cross, that all who saw it might remember.

She looked long at the lovely tree, feeling an unexpected sweetness, which stayed with her as she turned away, remaining as she made it down the familiar walk and out to Shenandoah Street.

30 *Going Home*

The plane lowered into Utah Valley, and there were the mountains of home. Purple rock with white on top rose clean against the sky. The ocean calls people back, so it is said, for the sound of its water, the smell of the air. A mountain comforts with a familiar shape, a profile laid down in the soul.

What else remains? The tallest building in town sinks to its knees with the touch of a switch. Rivers change their course. Yet in all its lights and seasons, pink snow cliffs to a green hem, a mountain is there for your whole life.

Here came Mount Shoshone with its Indian lovers lying along the top, at rest after leaping to their death when the jealous god of the mountain separated them. The maiden at one end, her hair flowing down—her brave at the other, in his headdress.

Back in her fearless days, Abby hiked there once, along that slim spine at the top of the world. She and Arthur barreled down the glacier and jumped in the turquoise lake surrounded by ice. Not a wise thing to do, but nothing bad came of it.

The plane dipped, showing the scar on Shoshone from last summer's fire, started by kids playing with a cigarette lighter. The red snake along the mountain stayed for days, sending ash floating into town, specks on your clothes that looked like gnats. The smoke got so thick that you couldn't see the mountain, leaving their town of Sharon an ordinary place without its magnificent backdrop. Just another town along the freeway, where people look for exits to Burger King instead of up.

But you know the mountain is there. It disappears in a storm. Then it comes back, sometimes clean with snow, that rock against the sky.

Utah is a state of clarity. The streets are straight. They go around the block and bring you back where you started from, unlike the meandering ways of Virginia that could take you anywhere. In the west, summer days are hot, the nights cold, whereas midnight in the south can be as warm as afternoon. Pioneers marched across a desert and grew crops out of dust. Utah assumes success. Virginia is acquainted with failure, placing a cemetery at the heart of town, where lush green grows as a gift.

Well, she was in Utah now, where you're supposed to be happy. And after three years of being rotten to her family, it was time to be decent. At the time of the divorce, nothing they did was right. Her mother left her alone, and Abby barged into the family room, "Am I that much of a plague?" When her father showed slides and Stan popped up on the screen, she got up and left.

She refused to discuss the divorce with her sister, this friend who might have helped.

"Abby, admit it. He was a bastard."

"You know nothing," she replied haughtily. "He's a fine person."

The family's affection was irrelevant. Her parents would have loved any child they had. Elizabeth would have doted on any sibling.

A husband was different. He had a choice.

On her visits since then, the family were not allowed to mention it (the divorce). Related subjects—news about couples, their darling children—were also taboo under the quarantine of Abby's misfortune. She used it well. The inconsequential problems of others, such as Elizabeth's marital woes, were forever trumped by Abby's card, divorce.

This time she must be a nicer person.

She took the last swallow of her Bloody Mary as the plane came down. All right. Still, she needed time, more time, before family intimacy. Why couldn't this flight be diverted like so many others? Once when Salt Lake was in a fog, the plane landed in Durango, Colorado. And when you put airline passengers on a Greyhound, they turn into different people. The gentleman who'd made witty remarks to the flight attendant now growled at his wife, who stared out at the sagebrush and didn't say a word.

That word *divorce*. She must learn to use it. "I'm Abby Hopkins, and I'm divorced," she whispered. Louder as the plane bumped the ground. "Divorced, that's me, divorced."

The man sitting next to her moved his arm away.

It isn't the worst sounding word, *divorce*, if you don't know what it means.

The passengers began moving down the stuffy aisle, the couple in front of her holding up a baby to the beaming grandma pushing to the front of the waiting area. Well, Abby had a Virginia ham in her backpack for her parents.

And there they were, the faces she knew in all that crowd. Her mother saw her and gave a mother's smile as if she'd seen the greatest sight on earth. Her father, wearing the Christmas tie Abby had given him, held out his arms.

The next morning her mother wanted to go for a walk. This was new. But she was dressed for it in a hot pink warm-up suit and the latest jogging shoes. So, they set out in the cool morning air, where sprinklers sizzled down the block, getting the job done before the day got hot.

"It's good having you, dear."

"It's good being here." Abby picked up the pace. Behind the innocent statements of mothers, questions lie. How are you adjusting? Are you happy? Do you ever see him? If she were the mother, that's what she would ask.

Her mother was smart. Instead of risking the outright question, she provided the answer herself. "You do have a good life."

"I do."

"Have I told you about the happiness study?"

"Tell me again."

"Well, married men are the happiest."

This was supposed to make her feel good? Yet how could someone whose husband stays know what it's like when he goes?

Her mother was used to solving problems.

"So, listen to this, Abby. The second happiest group are single women. You have a career. You know how to live alone. Many people are afraid of that."

"I'm not *that* alone. I have Dwayne."

"Dwayne?"

"My cat. He sends you birthday cards." Her mother also had been given a framed picture of Dwayne, which she had not placed on the mantle with the photos of her grand-children.

"Does your cat still hiss at people, dear?"

"Yes. That's what he does. Haven't you ever wanted to hiss?" Abby whirled around, making that gagging sound she had learned from Dwayne. Her mother gave a slight shudder but didn't say a word. "Sorry. I'm just having fun. In the musical *Cats* they hiss. You're a theater person."

"I like cats."

"What cat?"

"One that sits on your lap."

"Dwayne does that," Abby lied. Well, he crouched nearby.

"Back to this happiness study. Single women are ahead of married women."

"So, that makes me happier than you."

"In some ways, yes."

With a wave of affection, Abby thought of her life in Virginia. It was true.

At the end of the block, they hurried past Bernadette's house. She would come out and whine about how her husband didn't care about her, preferring his coaching, his fishing, his pickup truck. Because she had a divorced daughter too, last summer Bernadette insisted on going to lunch with Abby and her mother. Before the bread arrived, Bernadette announced that her Heather was remarrying, naturally someone who would make a better husband than the first.

Remarry. Abby detested the word. You retread tires. Restring a tennis racket. You do not restart a marriage by plugging in a new spouse.

The news had come a year after the divorce in a small white envelope that looked like an invitation or a thank-you note. When she saw the handwriting, Abby thought for a crazy minute that Stan was writing to say hello. After all, he was another single person out in the world, since marriage wasn't for him.

Then she saw the unforgettable words. *Ever the optimist, I plan to remarry in the spring.*

She never learned who the woman was. It would have been too painful to find out how remarkable, lovely, and nice she might have been. Or perhaps that she was nothing special at all.

"There are many ways to be happy," her mother said.

It was true. Abby looked up at Mount Shoshone, where the burned places were filling in with green. She took her mother's arm, suddenly glad to be walking here. She could hike the whole state of Utah and never see that man.

She broke into a run toward the house where she had been a happy kid. Her mother jogged along too. Then she was down, catching her big shoe on the sidewalk. There she lay. She held up her hands, red on the palms where she had caught herself. "It's all right." For somebody who didn't fall often, her mother did it very well. "Just clumsy. I didn't twist anything."

Abby knelt to her. "I am so sorry."

"I'm fine. Here, help me up."

She looked into her mother's eyes. "I'm sorry I've been so—distant."

"No, dear. No." In those hazel eyes was the utter caring of a parent. There's nothing like it. Abby liked to imagine that she too would have felt that way for a child.

There is a line in a Mormon hymn, known to anyone in the valley here, and perhaps to some outside. The song is "Come, Come, Ye Saints." The words are "all is well." Spoken after a long journey.

She and her mother stood. And for a moment it seemed true. All was well. All was well.

Abby's sister was a great cook. Elizabeth could make any kind of bread. Shiny braids with bits of salt on top. Loaves with Parmesan cheese woven into them. Elizabeth's hot rolls rose to perfect lightness, requested around the table many times. Yet that same roll recipe didn't work when Abby tried it. The dough stayed folded in gray lips at the bottom of the pan. The only dishes that succeeded were the ones that Elizabeth never made, calling for exotic spices not mentioned in Utah cookbooks.

She found Elizabeth today in her kitchen, where she went for solace and fortification. She would make anything you ordered. It didn't matter when. Elizabeth might jump up after a meal and head to her pantry. Many a lagging after-dinner conversation was enhanced by the hum of her Mixmaster as she whipped up a nightcap of brownies or even sticky buns.

Today she was baking Abby's favorite oatmeal cookies, made with nuts. "These are good. What recipe?"

"On the oatmeal box. Anybody can do it." That's what good cooks say, but they know it isn't true.

"Nope. You're a cooking genius."

"I'm a failure as a mother." Elizabeth rammed a sheet of cookies in the oven and let the door slap shut. "My son has no ambition. What will Tucker do getting married at the age of twenty?"

"What will he do if he's single?"

"Couldn't you warn him or something?" Elizabeth wiped off the counter, over and over in the same place.

"What, tell him to wait until he's thirty?" Abby took a hot cookie and bit.

"You must have learned something."

That's what was wrong with her divorce. She hadn't learned squat from it. Certainly not that communication is the key.

"And guess *where* they're getting married." Elizabeth covered her eyes.

"Let's see. Up on Mount Shoshone. In the cave. Candles would look great in there."

"You wouldn't joke if this were your son. But it's worse. Try Aspen Hill."

"The cemetery?"

"Yup." Elizabeth shook a cookie off the spatula onto the cooling rack. Another, another. "It'll be humiliating."

"Humiliation. Poof. There are worse things. Tucker and Natalie are brave starting a new life in the presence of death. You could wear black to a cemetery, Elizabeth. You look sexy in black."

"No doubt she'll wear something dreadful. What is it with these kids and black?"

"To avoid laundry?"

"It's her father's business. He's an undertaker. Farmer's Funeral Home. That's why they chose a cemetery, to drum up business for him."

"Well, Natalie is loyal to her family."

"Some family. Her parents don't speak, not since her mother left the day after Nat's graduation. She'll be on one side with her current boyfriend, the father on the other with his third wife. In a cemetery." Elizabeth's voice shook. She looked really sad.

"Think of the free flowers up there. At least be glad that Tuck cares enough to marry someone."

"It won't last. Oh, Abby, I don't want him going through a divorce."

Abby wiped a crumb off her lip. She wiped where no crumbs were. "No, of course not," she said softly. "What does Jack say?"

"He's all for it. He tells Tucker that marriage is great. How can he say that after the way we are?"

Here it came, the litany of Jack's failings. He smelled of

paint (he was a house painter). Jack swished coffee in his mouth at the breakfast table. He watched television. "What crime now?"

"He's decided he wants to cook."

"That is ugly."

"OK, so I'm a rotten, selfish person. But, Abby, the kitchen is mine. Cooking is the only thing I do well. You have a profession. You get respect."

"You never wanted a job. You like staying home."

"I know. But not with Jack there all the time. When I come in and he's frying his stuff, I get violent. And he competes. Friends were coming to dinner, and I mentioned I was making a lemon meringue pie. So, Jack had to make a pie too. Great, the guests could take their pick, his or hers. He baked a pumpkin pie—and it was summer. The barbecued ribs in the oven were smelling great, and I went upstairs to get ready. When I came out of the shower, what did I smell? You'll never guess. Popcorn. Jack was making popcorn, stinking up the house like a movie theater minutes before the people came. When I asked why he did this, he said he was 'in the mood.'"

"So, you hid the popper."

"You have all the answers, don't you."

"Not any. But I know that Jack adores you."

Elizabeth flung a spoonful of dough onto the cookie sheet. "You always looked down on Jack. And you were right that I wasn't wild for him. I envied the way you felt, Abby. Even now. How could Stan, that bastard—"

"Something awful was happening to him. Anyway, you

and Jack have more than you know."

"He puts up with me. I'm such a shrew."

"We like you that way." It was true. When the older sister has a temper, the younger sister appears to be sweet.

"How are you, anyway?" Elizabeth asked. "Are you going with anyone?"

"No. Lonely people. Desperate ones." There was the vice chancellor of the college, recently divorced and wearing a toupee. Dwayne took care of that. "Dating is ghastly. Would you want to do that again? In the words of a student, 'I'd rather have pins stuck in me than go on another date.'"

"I've lined you up."

"You wouldn't. Not without asking me."

"You'd just refuse. It's only lunch. Go. Show that it's no big deal."

"Well, all right," Abby said, using her fair teacher's voice, which can come in handy in family situations. How weird could one lunch be?

"He's a psychologist in Salt Lake. He has his own family practice."

"You lined me up with a marriage counselor?"

"You can learn something. And he's been divorced. But that was years ago. We all know what a mess people are at first."

Abby let that pass. "I'll go, but not if he left his wife. I'd spill hot soup on him if he did that."

"Nope. In fact, Michael was devastated."

Michael. It was a good name. A fine, sensible name.

31 *A Funeral*

The next week Bernadette's husband died. The high school football coach beloved by all was gone. Buck had finished his breakfast of granola and set out for his morning jog, a familiar sight along the street, this coach with the unathletic body, round in the middle with skinny legs. He jogged past the Hopkins house and on up to the foothills, where a hiker found him on the path, dead of a heart attack.

The day was too sunny for a funeral, the sky too perfectly blue. Utah is a place more conducive to a picnic. In the winter people are jolly as well, roaring off to the ski slopes in vehicles with tires so huge that they cannot slip even in the deepest snow. Today the usual strollers piled with children merrily rolled into the crosswalks in front of your car. On the sidewalks, young biker fathers jauntily pulled the current baby along in a covered cage.

You don't want to be single or sad or any of those things out here.

Farmer's Funeral Home did considerately reside among aging trees with peeling trunks that gave a certain comfort. Abby and her parents parked in the shade and went in to the dark air-conditioned foyer, following the arrow to Buck. He didn't look ready to be gone. His black eyebrows stood up crisply as if to ask, "Where're my boys?" "When is the game?"

Bernadette presided over Buck in pink. "He liked me in this color," she murmured, touching a perfumed handkerchief to the corner of one eye. Although it came away damp, she was amazingly upbeat. She became downright animated, in fact, urging everyone to come over and look at Buck. "Such a wonderful husband," she said, patting his hand. Every compliment to Buck was bettered by Bernadette, who never said a good thing about him when he was alive. Now she expanded on her deceased husband's generous nature, the sensitivity he showed to a family of women, with five daughters. Even at the mention of Buck's professional dedication, Bernadette nodded vigorously. After all, never again would she have to wait at home jealously while he practiced with his team.

"I am so sorry," Abby said (guilty for her shoddy thoughts about this woman). "I do know about loss," she whispered. Though their situations differed, grief is grief. But when the person behind her said, "Poor Bernadette, a widow with all those daughters," sympathy modulated to envy.

A widow is the lucky one. She's referred to as a survivor in the obituary. People bring her casseroles. Nobody brings you a cracker when you get divorced. You get questions. "What happened?" "Did you go for counseling?"

Abby took a seat by her father, eyeing the glossy casket where Buck was shut away in the dark for good. Never again to jog along in his black and gold school colors, chugging up the hill looking like a bumblebee moving up a stem.

What did he think about as he ran? Did Buck ever want to keep on going? Most married people dream of escape at some time, Abby had read somewhere. She just hadn't been one of them.

Bernadette, on the front row, whispered to a daughter on one side, then the other. They laughed at something. Who were these people? In her fuchsia outfit, Bernadette looked ready for a party. Yet a closer look showed that her makeup had slipped on this day, applied by a hand that must have trembled. The blush on her cheek had gone too far, turning her hair pink.

Still, Bernadette would probably do just fine, thriving the way certain women do with an unaccustomed freedom. She would stand tall at Buck's grave, taller than she ever had.

That's what Abby wanted—to go to Stan's funeral. She would be magnificent. Not that she wished him a painful death, one of those lingering cancers that make you scream in the night. Something quick and painless would do. A freak accident. A boulder falling on his car as he drove through Rock Creek Park. One of those things that simply could not be avoided. It has nothing to do with you.

She would bow at his coffin, seeing that excellent face once more, the soft distinctive lips, never to speak or kiss again. She would weep true tears of loss. She could share her sorrow with Fred and Edna, be one of the family again. And she would visit Stan's grave, where she might place a tender daisy against the stone or, in a certain mood, drop choke cherries on his head.

The eulogy for Buck was offered by an old football buddy, still with a linebacker's body, neck sloping from the ears. "Buck was the guttiest quarterback you ever saw." He gripped the pulpit with his sizable hands. "They'd blitz him, and he'd scramble. You'd think he was sacked, and Buck got off a bomb." The big man's voice faltered. "This game ball is for him." He swooped up a football, put it on the podium, where it wobbled, rolled to the edge, and sat still.

Just then there was a clicking sound outside. Here came Buck's boys, suited up in black and gold, trotting down the aisle of Farmer's Funeral Home with their helmets in their hands. They came from the past, hair gone, stomachs stretching their faded jerseys. Young players came, second stringers, looking scared. Here they all came with their helmets in their hands.

The last person in line was Tucker, who had spent his high school years on the bench, looking lost in those big shoulder pads. But this coach changed his life somehow, making him "want to try for stuff." Tuck slowly jogged down the aisle, his dreadlocks rising and falling with his steps, the hairdo his mother hated. He did not wear beads in his braids today. They didn't make a sound.

Tucker reached to wipe a tear off his chin.

Buck's boys gathered in a huddle, muttered a final audible, then rose up with a final cheer for their coach.

32   *Blind Date*

A funeral is comforting compared to a blind date. It can make you sick. But why nausea over a stranger? A meeting with someone you care about, sure. Not Dr. Michael Dupre for lunch.

Well, possibly he was gay. A man who could be a friend. Abby glanced out the window for someone relaxed coming up the walk, free of the tension that women cause.

Or maybe he wouldn't show up.

But the knock came precisely on time. And she felt a sudden warmth for the person who doesn't make you wait. To be this prompt coming from Salt Lake, he must have gotten here early and waited down the block. That would have seemed dorky once. Now it was nice.

"Hello, Michael." He didn't look like a blind date. Good skin. His own hair, light brown and crisply combed. He was a height most women like, six feet at least. Only his nose was slightly out of line. Not unattractively so. Just enough to make you wonder what hit him. Abby checked his navy polo shirt for cat hairs (perhaps that was asking too much), found none, and concluded that he wasn't a dog guy either. His pressed khakis definitely had not been pawed. He wore shoes

213

with tassels, dressed for success.

They went out to his antique yellow Thunderbird, polished and parked away from the other cars. The beige leather seats were worn to softness but without a crack. And no accessories had been added to mar this vehicle. Not a cup holder in sight. No CD player plugged in here.

Michael had made reservations at a restaurant in Salt Lake, the place, a surprise. How thoughtful, for lunch. So they drove north, leaving the green of lawns and then the farms behind, out to the gray Point of the Mountain, where hang gliders float down from the bald hills like giant dragonflies across from the Utah State Prison.

Rather, "correctional facilities." What corrections were those? Minor tune-ups to remove bad habits? Or might one hope for that miracle, a change of heart? We all know that hearts do change.

Driving by the prison tends to silence you, even if you don't look over at the concrete apartments, where within those walls the tenants have time to think about their lives. Or perhaps some are clever enough to forget, even as they look out at the blue skies which are no longer theirs and the expanse of dust that is.

Once you get past the prison, you can look forward to Salt Lake City, where the buildings are taller than to the south, but the mountains are not as high. And none are as beautiful as Mount Shoshone.

Good restaurants up here. So, what exotic place had Michael chosen? He was a stylish fellow. Thai food? But then he pulled off the freeway into a strip mall, stopping at a stucco place called Los Amigos, which you wouldn't think even took reservations. Well, he lived up here; he must know what he was doing.

Michael sprinted around the car to let her out. Hungry? Or was he enjoying her company more than she had noticed? Buoyantly he guided her into the little restaurant over to a particular window seat. Sure enough, a three-by-five card said that the spot was reserved, although it was hardly necessary with only two other people in the place.

They were a couple in their fifties, sitting in a corner booth touching fingertips across the tile tabletop. You often see such a pair in out-of-the-way places at lunchtime. She wears her best blouse to the office that day; he puts on cologne. Afterward they give a furtive hug in the parking lot, go to separate cars, and drive stiffly back to their lives.

Michael ushered her to the chair facing the window, a thoughtful move even though the view was a parking lot. On one side was a dented Bronco, on the other a shiny Grand Cherokee.

"What? Sure," she answered when Michael ordered a strawberry margarita for each of them. She couldn't remember being with a man who took that initiative, certainly no one she had seen more than once. Oh well. She did like a good margarita.

"My wife and I came here." Michael gazed at Abby's chair. "I hope it doesn't bother you if I mention her. It turns some women off."

"Of course it does." Abby smiled. She laughed, her nausea gone.

"Michelle was the love of my life." Michael announced, looking at her with honest brown eyes through glasses whose slim burgundy rims reflected specks of gold. And she believed him.

Michael and Michelle. The morphology of their names, as well as the destiny of alliteration. David meets his Donna in high school, and they bond for life. Jennifer may take years to find her man. But somewhere in a singles bar, the moment Josh speaks his name, she knows he is the one.

"Michelle and I got married after my mission. I am a Mormon, you know." Abby did. "It was my best year."

"The first year of your marriage?"

"It only lasted a year." Michael drank his water, letting the crushed ice in his margarita melt.

"I'm sorry." Abby tried her drink and found real strawberry seeds, although it did lack the tingle of alcohol, being a virgin drink, after all.

"Michelle was a good Mormon girl. You're not Mormon, Abby, right?"

"That's right."

"Anyway, she was everything I could have wanted in a woman. She had long red hair. Her real color too. Michelle never would have dyed it."

Abby flicked back a strand of her hair, tucking it behind her ear. Hair of a new ash-blond shade that she thought looked particularly natural.

"Michelle was young," Michael said, with a caress to her name each time he said it, which must be several times a day. "She didn't realize what we had."

"I'm sure she didn't." Abby watched out in the parking lot as the Grand Cherokee drove away.

"She suffered from depression. But with the medications we have today, Michelle and I would still be together."

"A drug can do that?" Wow. Maybe something slipped into Stan's coffee would have helped. "How long have you been divorced?"

"Seventeen years. That sounds like a long time. Still, the shock of it—"

"I know. I, too—"

"Michelle was happy at first. I know she was. Would you like to see her picture?" Michael whipped out his wallet, the way a person might light a cigarette while he asks if smoking bothers you. He pulled out a laminated picture and handed it to her. It was a couple in bed. The man's chest hair curled darkly over the top of the sheet, and there were Michael's eyes. But he had a different smile. Joyful and awestruck. The one he used now was pleasing, quick to come and quick to go, no doubt useful in his profession. Yet the light had gone out of it.

Michelle was not looking at the camera. She lay on the bed staring up, her sparse red hair spread on the pillow. She was not a glamorous girl. Freckles dark as beauty marks, however, gave an intriguing aspect to her face. And you couldn't help but wonder what lay behind her lovely distant eyes.

"This was taken on our honeymoon," Michael explained, retrieving his photo and replacing it under his American Express gold card. "I know I shouldn't be showing this. But you seem like someone who might understand."

"What would you tell a patient who did that, Dr. Dupre? Do you mind if I call you that?"

"Fine." He sat up straighter. "Obsessive compulsive, certainly. Psychologists don't claim to be the sanest guys in the world. But this relationship wasn't a fantasy. Michelle was my wife. We were married in the temple for eternity, so we'll be together in the next world. By then the problems of this life will look small." Michael's eyes were bright, and he spoke from his soul. "Michelle was a good Mormon girl. She made the same vows in the temple that I did. Nobody can take that away. She did get married again. But it was just a civil ceremony, for this life. We never got a temple divorce. We never will."

"What an amazing belief." The implications were so stunning that Abby could hardly swallow her drink. Yet who was she to say what might be possible in another world? If you can believe in one miracle, why not another?

"So, what happened to your marriage, Michael? You're a therapist. Tell me. *What goes wrong?*"

He smiled a modest smile, and she saw a faint blush there. "I could give you all the standard answers. Marriages break down because of abusive behavior, addictions, lack of communication, selfishness. People change with employment status, health problems, family tragedies. Yet to this day I couldn't tell you what happens to the human heart, how love goes."

"Oh." She wanted to clutch Michael's hand and kiss his knuckles.

"I still ask myself, every day, what happened, why—?"

"I know, I know," she said.

Michael was silent then.

"How did yours end? Tell me about your last day," Abby asked, for he would remember it, the feel of the air tightening in the room, the altering shapes of things. Those details would be his for all of his eternity.

"It was Thanksgiving week. They gave us a turkey at Sears, where I worked while I was getting my business degree. I was coming up the stairs with it cold in the sack, a frozen turkey. We lived on the second floor. Usually I could hear Michelle practicing her flute. On this day it was quiet.

"I went in, and everything was gone. All the furniture, TV, the VCR. Pictures of her family were gone off the walls. I miss her family, I still do. The only thing left was the stationary bike.

"There was a note on the counter rolled up in her wedding ring. It said she was sorry, but she couldn't take it anymore. What? The marriage? Me? I was afraid she might be suicidal, although a person in that state doesn't usually clean out a place and move that way.

"She had gone to her mother's, and she wouldn't talk to me. She wouldn't have anything to do with me after that. Not even to tell me why."

"I am so sorry."

"Well, I guess something good comes out of every experience. If Michelle hadn't left me, I never would have gotten my doctorate in psychology." Michael gave a quick smile. "I like my work. And the practice has done well." He took a bite of burrito, no doubt the same shredded beef he ordered when he ate here with Michelle. "She was losing her faith when we got divorced. But she can come back. You always can. You always get another chance."

"You are patient," Abby said, dumbfounded as she cut her chicken enchilada. "What will you do in the meantime?"

"Sure, I get lonely. I'd like to find a companion for this life. Plenty of women want to get married, I will say that. But she'd have to understand about Michelle. I couldn't deceive anyone about that. I think a non-Mormon would be best, someone who wouldn't want a temple marriage herself. I just don't meet that many around here."

Abby nodded, chewing slowly.

"This has been great, Abby. Most women think I'm crazy."

"Many of us are."

He smiled his quick and pleasant smile. "Seriously, I've really enjoyed myself today."

"I have too. We have something in common, Michael."

33 Avalanche

Most dangerous of all snowslides are the slab avalanches. Their potential exists when the snow on top is not well bonded to the layer beneath. The upper slab experiences the stress of supporting itself on the slope, and release comes like a pane of glass shattering under its own weight. The trigger may be a storm, a change in temperature, or the weight of a person.

Abby's father, ever a reasonable man, got up from the table to do something useful, leaving his wife and daughters to discuss vegetarian hors d'oeuvres for Tucker and Natalie's reception. Her dad did yard work, cared for his tomato plants and a prized raspberry patch, where he picked the single berries until the cup around his neck was full, harvesting enough for ice cream sundaes.

Outside the mower started up, a cough, then another, and it got going. His route brought him past the window, wearing his straw fishing hat with the license pinned to it. He could catch the fish or not, accepting his fortune with the natural cheer that was his. He laughed at everything. When a microburst split their maple tree, he shrugged off the mishap with a smile. This is the father you want to have when you wreck the car. But when you come in with a scraped knee, a laugh is not so welcome.

It was an automatic response, nothing cruel. Yet after he'd learned about Stan leaving, the hasty laugh over the phone had sounded heartless. Silence then, which wasn't much better. Finally, her father said, "Well, he must have had his reasons."

So she had been cool.

Her father was also the person who taught her how to be with a man and not talk, a practice that had seemed relaxing and harmonious at the time. But maybe it is fatal.

As he passed the kitchen window, head down in the heat—this man in a family of women—he looked lonely. So when he came in to get the list for the marketing, Abby jumped up to go with him.

"You hate the Food Barn," Elizabeth called as they went out. But their dad didn't seem surprised as Abby hopped up in his Isuzu Trooper, although surely he knew of her horror of food warehouses, with their looming cartons of bran flakes, toilet paper, the obscenely crammed shopping carts wobbling down the aisles. No single portions here. "Good to have you," he said.

For him the Food Barn was a challenge which he met with speed and efficiency, shuttling past gallon jars of mayonnaise, blocks of cheese the size of a car battery, to the exact brand of cake mix his wife desired.

Her father liked mild food himself. But if the family ordered something spicy, he would get it, hot salsa by the quart. He did not like vegetables, yet here he was stocking up for tonight's barbecue with Natalie in mind, selecting egg-plants—which Elizabeth contended would look like beef on the meatless shish kebab—and adding yellow peppers for color to their cart. Fruit is what he liked. He could heft the cantaloupes and know which one was sweet, with a touch of his fingertips detect the grapefruit with the juice. And he was a happy man getting the bargain bananas.

As they left the store, with Mount Shoshone rising ahead of them, still with cooling fingers of snow on the higher slopes, Abby suggested that they take a drive up there. Her father had helped build the trail to the top. He even carried his pet pigeon the eight miles up, getting his brother to clock how long it took the bird to fly home.

The canyon wasn't far. Soon malls and churches were behind them, and the air grew cool. The river bounded along beside the curving mountain road, running high this year and requiring fishermen to stand in the chilly waters to their hips, catching the fish that these days they threw back. Kids used to ride the river on inner tubes, pushing off from boulders. Abby did that. Then someone got killed, and the practice became illegal.

In the canyon her father usually drove all the way up to where the aspens grew, their leaves quivering silver in the sun, the names of lovers carved in the papery tree trunks, becoming thick and black and illegible with time.

Why was he slowing at the turnoff to Deer Lodge today? Surely he didn't think that she would want to go there. Was he so insensitive that he didn't understand anything?

But saying something would be worse. So Abby kept her mouth shut as the Isuzu gulped to the lip of the hill, turned where the rock sign said Deer Lodge, and down they went.

This road did continue past Deer Lodge, up to mountain cabins. Yet how could her father drive by as if nothing important happened here, not remembering the night he walked his daughter down the aisle toward the glowing fireplace? Icicles as big as swords gleamed in the windows. Yet nobody at the time worried that they might fall.

Today he did slow down more than was necessary for the bumpiness of the road. But he didn't say a thing. They continued on to where the road narrowed in the shade, and Deer Lodge was left behind them in the tall fir trees. He asked if she wanted to see the Anderson cabin that had been hit by an avalanche in the spring. She did.

More a mansion than a cabin, it was built on the grandest site in the canyon. The structure had taken three years to finish, complete with every luxury, including an elevator shaft and a balcony off the master bedroom that sat up like a gondola so the occupants could see Mount Shoshone with nothing in the way. The Andersons had finally moved in at Christmastime, bringing up gifts and guests by four-wheel drive. However, they were on vacation in Hawaii a few weeks later when it happened.

How long does an avalanche prepare to make its move? Does the snow separate gradually before its devastating slide? Or might a sudden change in temperature make it happen overnight? But for a bit of bad luck, would the mountain have held?

Snowballs roll on ahead of an avalanche, it is said, building to great wheels as they pound down the mountain with their news. Then comes the unearthly thunder, whips cracking as the air sucks in to fill the space.

Should the Andersons have known not to build on that spot, warned by the path carved by a glacier in some other age? Yet surely we would forgive nature one such deed. And on the sunny day these visitors came from California (leaving their earthquakes behind) to find this lovely place, it would have been unseemly to dwell on disaster.

There it was, up on the hill, the wreckage of a great house. Wood beams were split, chunks of concrete tossed aside. Cords of twisted steel reached out of the foundation, huge arteries cut. Only the elevator shaft stood intact, with a metallic eagle pinned to its concrete side.

Her father, not known for breaking the law, on this mountain, on this day, stepped over the yellow tape with its No Trespassing signs. Up the paved drive they went, past a neighboring cabin, its timbers stained by time but left untouched by the avalanche. Squirrels chased across the porch, oblivious to the close call they'd had.

A plank led into the ruins of the mansion, and they hiked up to it through the powdery mountain dirt that colors shoes and socks with the same charcoal dust. The air smelled of stinging nettle, a pretty weed that looks like mint but makes welts on a bare leg.

A portion of the kitchen wall remained, with stainless-steel ovens clinging to it, ready for the grand party that would never be. A chunk of granite countertop had gouged the hardwood floor, cherry perhaps, still with a tint of rose.

An immense window facing the avalanche was boarded up. In front of it was a Jacuzzi, cracked down the middle. A navy blue Jacuzzi. Not a bad way to go, reclining in your lover's arms in the swirling waters, gazing up at white cliffs in the moonlight, never dreaming they could collapse.

But nobody was home at the time, not to hear the unearthly sound of the avalanche arriving, or for that frozen moment to see the tsunami of snow rising before the glass.

And which family member was it who drove up this road to discover the destruction?

A stairway to the master bedroom had new treads, and she and her dad went up, past what remained of a child's bedroom, faintly decorated with teddy-bear wallpaper. So that person who would have grown up hiking these hills ran on a beach instead, since the Andersons had returned to California.

Abby stepped out on the balcony—a capsule in the air. Far below, aspens were bent to the ground. Ahead, nothing interrupted the sight of Mount Shoshone. Not a roof in sight. No smoke signals here. Only the mountain, its mighty limestone cliffs rising from a glacier that never melts.

She stood and watched her father going down the hill, growing smaller, to where he would have vanished into his Trooper. Then she followed, sliding, finally galloping inevitably to where he was. "Daddy," she called, catching up with him.

He turned and chuckled. He didn't ask why she stayed

up in the rubble. He didn't tell her to be careful as she ran down. He was simply glad to see her when she came. She felt a rush of joy for all that is possible without words, elation that she hadn't said every mean thing, words that put spikes in other people and the person who says them.

He waited with the car door open, this generous, un-threatening man who would care for her all his days. Maybe he hadn't noticed how cool she had been these last few years. Or if he had, he was too kind to mention it.

When she was a kid, he told her something. It was a genius remark of a parent, words that you hold to in dark times. She hadn't done anything special that day. No stellar report card. No decent behavior to a creepy neighbor. Out of nowhere her father said, "You are a good person, Abby." She had taken it to be the truth for he was an honest man.

"Thank you," she said.

"Guess we better get the groceries home."

His face was warm and pulsing as they got in the Isuzu. And she felt a burning shame for the August day when he had planted that tree, in a yard where he thought his son-in-law still lived, long after he had moved out.

"Remember the dogwood tree you planted in Virginia? On that hot day. Too hot. Stan had left by then, Daddy. He had been gone for some time."

Her father's hands wrapped around the steering wheel. He did not laugh this time. "I wanted to do it."

"The tree grew. It's alive! The blossoms come over the wall. I thought I could never go back to Shenandoah Street. Now I must."

He laughed this time, and she was glad. And he didn't say a thing, no suggestion that she was a fool for being bound as she was to a certain tree, in a certain yard, where once she had lived. Abby laughed too.

So they drove happily down the canyon in the Isuzu, with its intermittent gasps after the accident it had in the Meineke shop.

"Why did you get an Isuzu? You wanted a Cherokee."

"I thought you knew," he said, turning to miss a rock in the road. "That's what he had."

"You didn't get a Cherokee because Stan had one?" Abby smiled all over. This was the man who studied a product and made his purchase based on facts.

"I've liked the Trooper." He had become even more endeared to it after Meineke dropped it off the lift. Yes. Her father was in the waiting room when he heard the crash. The mechanic appeared gray-faced with the news. Meineke did fix the car to ride as well as ever, except for the occasional gulp it made, no doubt resulting from its fall.

The Trooper recovered from its hesitations, and they rolled on down the road, out of the canyon into the bright sun, driving in perfect silence home.

34 *Reunion*

Only stars and fools go to class reunions. The stars return to shine. There the cheerleader will be viewed with awe even if she's become a bag lady. Why outsiders attend is a mystery. The fellow who owns a football franchise is still the person who couldn't make the team. The girl who wasn't invited to the prom, though she might have since walked on the moon, will forever miss that dance.

Abby had not been a star. Rather, she was that anomaly in a Utah school, a non-Mormon. Not that her classmates were rude. Mormons are exceedingly friendly, hoping you will join their church. They can't help themselves. It is in their nature to hope, hope, hope and never stop hoping.

They do have a wonderful saying, "Man is that he might have joy." It may apply to women too. Their concept of eternal marriage was the best. Maybe she could have had a marriage that lasted. Yet it would be to a different person. Why would she want to spend eternity with anyone else?

But there is a clean look that is stunning. Drew Atkinson in her class. You couldn't find a better person. Here was a man who wouldn't leave his wife, no matter how disappointing she turned out to be.

As it was, Abby hung out with the heathen crowd where she belonged, although even here she was somewhat embarrassed by her lack of religious belief. Sandy Johnson, who would have been a queen in any other school, tan without a strap mark, sang in the Lutheran choir. Anna Matthews was so lifted up by her Catholic mass that she appeared to have had a perfect meal. At least there was dear Arthur, with his Buddhist personality and no church affiliation either. Then he moved to California.

"Why would you go to your high school reunion?" Elizabeth asked, up to her elbows in dough for cinnamon rolls, flour wafting up to collect on her dark eyebrows. Jack had given her an automatic bread maker, but she liked to knead the dough herself.

"I can be social. I went on that blind date you organized."

"Are you seeing Michael again?"

Abby gazed at her sister.

"OK, I've heard he's a little odd. Fixated on his marriage."

"Being fixated isn't *that* odd. And he is an honest man. But no, Elizabeth, no."

"You were always picky So why this class reunion?"

That settled it. "My high school wasn't that bad," Abby answered, feeling a surprising tenderness for those days. She and her fringe crowd had fun.

"Whatever," Elizabeth said, chopping walnuts for her buns.

The reunion was held in a deserted roller rink, where a section was roped off for people bringing Rollerblades. Abby had hers. She had taken lessons from her nephew Roy and felt confident doing her dips now that she had knee pads. The far side of the rink was decorated to commemorate their senior prom, Some Enchanted Evening. Paper palm leaves fluttered in the breeze from a fan, and a sunset was pasted on the wall. She had gone to the prom with a shy fellow named Dan, whose face she could not remember. They went to Baskin-Robbins afterward.

Name tags included a yearbook picture, pinned to a shoulder for identification against the weathered face above. A few people had surprisingly perked up. Not most. But they were nice folks, almost all. They didn't shoot their teachers or each other. Otherwise, theirs had been a high school like anyone's, with its sweaty smell from the gym, the band feverishly practicing down the hall to help the team win.

A scratchy sound system came on, and Ezio Pinza sang as he had then, "Some enchanted evening." Find your true love and never let him go. These people had believed those words. She had too.

"Abby Hopkins," a nasal male voice called. Here came the class nerd, Clifford, tall and bent, with big teeth and a big smile. Although he had grown an extra chin, time had not tamed Clifford's hair. It still looked like mowed wheat stepped on. "You're Abby Hopkins," Clifford announced.

Because they had been cruel to Clifford then, Abby went over and hugged his loose-jointed body, which no girl, including herself, would have willingly touched in those days.

He pulled back. "I'm married now."

"Oops, sorry."

She put on her Rollerblades and was gaining speed around the floor when Rick Davis glided by, Drew Atkinson's best friend. With graceful swoops she skated up to him. "How're you doing?" She did the usual chatter, blah, blah, blah. Then she asked if Drew had come to the reunion.

Rick kept up his stride, but he didn't look at her. "You don't know? He died in a car wreck three years ago."

The floor rolled under her. Not Drew. The finest of them all, meant for success. He'd planned to be a surgeon since the tenth grade. "I didn't." Her skates felt lumpy, and her knee pads were tight. "I live in Virginia and don't come to reunions. How?"

"His wife was driving. Just them. She was OK."

No, she was not OK. She would never be OK again. Abby skated faster, feeling the nicks in the floor as she whirled around the room. Did Drew's wife close her eyes for a second in the desert? Many do. Darkness then or did horrifying headlights come at her? After the crash, in the quiet, did she lie next to Drew knowing that he was gone? Possibly she didn't remember the accident at all.

Yet all the mornings of the world afterward, she would.

Abby skated on around the blurry floor.

Then, damn. Ahead of her was Cheryl Smith—Miss Dairy Queen with the creamy skin, teeth whiter than marsh-mallows, a brain made of Cool Whip.

Cheryl's forte was a pathological friendliness, an oozing compulsion to be intimate with every mortal in her path. If you did not escape, you'd be attacked by her anaconda hug, bathed in her perfumed kisses, assaulted by her lascivious questioning.

"Abby Hopkins, I see you." Here came Cheryl on the move. You could truly say that she hadn't changed. Abby skated on, pumping her fists. Rats, she hit a crack and went down, skidding to the side.

Here came Cheryl in high heels.

Abby waved her off. "Not in here with those shoes."

Cheryl forged on, crouching down to Abby, squinting at her name tag. "Back to your old name, I see. Well, take off those skates, Abby Hopkins, and let's have a chat. Don't be ashamed about your divorce," she said in low tones. "We all know people who have been divorced. Decent people! So, tell me, what happened?"

Abby tugged off a skate, peeled away a sock, and held it up to Cheryl. "Guess he realized that I'm a bitch and left."

Cheryl gasped. "I wouldn't call you that."

"You don't know me."

"You were one of my best friends."

Up and barefoot, Abby two-stepped away from Cheryl's grasp. "I don't like you."

"What?" Cheryl's face was astonished, though as pretty as ever. Not a mark of anguish there. "I've never done a thing to you. Why, you just think you're better because you moved out to Washington, D.C."

"Virginia," Abby softly corrected her.

Cheryl dropped her arms. "No wonder your marriage failed if you don't like being touched."

"Gotta go," Abby said, hoisting her skates. Anywhere.

"I still care about you," Cheryl trilled as Abby took off across the floor. "Call me."

She got a glass of punch, testing it with the faint hope that it might be spiked. No luck. She took her Kool-Aid and sat under the furthest palm tree, resting against the South Pacific sunset, breathing peacefully.

She had been there awhile when a slim male shape appeared across the rink. The fellow was strolling her way. Arthur? But he'd moved to San Diego the year before graduation. Could it be Arthur Shue?

Here he came. Yes, it was easygoing Arthur. A friend.

She went to meet him. He smiled, and a front tooth was chipped. She rested her forehead on his chest. "It is you."

"Yup."

Abby stood back and looked at this grown-up boy. They used to go swimming together, hiking, before the age of dating. That business. Arthur was simply there. In fact, he was so easy, you almost forgot that he was male.

His blond hair was mostly gone. But my, he did look good in his clothes. He had one of those sleek bodies that you can't imagine getting fat, looking fine in stonewashed jeans that fit close on his narrow hips. Except for the damaged tooth, his easy smile was the same.

"I've missed you, Abby."

She must have missed him too, although she hadn't thought about Arthur for years. Not until she looked up at Mount Shoshone the other day.

"Remember our hike?"

"Best summer I ever had," he said.

They'd climbed the eight miles to the top as if it were nothing, sliding down the glacier strewn with lost gloves, abandoned walking sticks, brown-bag lunches flung to the side. Then that wild leap into the icy lake. Down they went into a cold that cut like knives, sunlight growing dim. But they bounced out like a couple of corks, bounding on down the trail to brag about what they'd done, heedless of the dust collecting on their chilly clothes.

"How's your life?" she asked.

"I got divorced."

"So did I." Abby tried for his casual tone, but Arthur knew better.

"You?" His dark eyebrows lifted slightly. He had never been one to show strong emotion.

"He left."

"Dumb guy," he said.

"Thank you, Arthur. And you?"

"Isabel wanted her life."

"Which presumably was waiting on the doorstep. Did you have any idea?"

Arthur shrugged. "I figured we'd break up."

Once Abby would have asked how a person can live like that. Now she didn't know what to ask, or to answer, about such matters. "Children?"

"Two." Arthur did not bring out their pictures. Wow. "Danny lives with me. He's thirteen. Susan is nine, with her mom in Long Beach."

"Good for you. A boy and a girl."

She and Arthur had fun. They drove around doing nothing, visiting the ruins of their high school, its yard gone to weeds where they used to stay and talk until dark.

They went biking again, which she hadn't done in years, this time wearing helmets. One warm afternoon they took a path down by Utah Lake, far enough from the mountains so you could see them whole. The outline of the Indian lovers on top of Shoshone was but a ripple. Yet if you knew they were there, you could see them.

She watched Arthur pumping on ahead of her, moving as one with his bike. An athletic fellow, but he had never cared for competition. Most of their classmates had serious ambitions. Arthur was the lost one.

He sat waiting for her now, helmet on the ground, chewing on a piece of grass. Abby lay down her bike and found a place by him in the dusty weeds, under the blue Utah sky. The bees were humming. He leaned over and kissed her on the lips. "We could get married."

She laughed. "Just like that." Yet people do it. Leap into marriage as if it's nothing. Some even stay together.

Arthur smiled, and his broken tooth was just fine. She'd been thinking of suggesting a cap for that tooth. Instead, she reached over and touched his lips.

"If you didn't like it, we could get divorced." Not a funny idea, but she smiled. "But I'd never want that, Abby." Well, everyone feels that way at first. "Why be alone?"

"You'll marry somebody, won't you." He had been divorced six months. "I give you a year."

"Could be. But you're my first choice."

236

Her heart was beating strangely. Was it possible that she could marry Arthur Shue? They wouldn't make each other suffer. Not major suffering. There are many ways to be happy. Her mother was right about that. "What brought you back to live in Utah?"

"Mountains, I guess. I like the desert."

That's right. Arthur actually enjoyed those dreadful drives without a stick of green, a capacity she supposed could be seen as an asset, not a blind spot.

"My parents moved back," he said. "Meet the new manager of Shue's Lumber."

"Congratulations." See. Arthur was a responsible person. And she loved the smell of wood.

"You must like it out in Virginia."

"Yes. The trees. Soft southern nights. Fireflies. Nobody asks what religion you are."

"What do you believe?"

Abby looked off in the distance to Mount Shoshone, recognizable from anywhere. "God, the maker of mountains. Cats. Not the jealous biblical version. He is so cranky. Testy all the time. You'd think he was going through a divorce."

Arthur grinned. "Guess she left him. Too domineering."

"Good point. With all his powers, he couldn't make a marriage. God must be lonely. So lonely."

"Like I say, Abby, why be alone?"

Arthur wanted her to meet his son. She said it was too soon. He laughed and informed her that Danny met all his father's girlfriends.

Girlfriends. Wife. Children. These were actual people in Arthur's life, weren't they. Yet it wasn't until they drove up to the house with Isabel's white curtains in the window that she became real.

Isabel was in these rooms, wasn't she. She always would be.

Otherwise, the place had reverted to the look of a bachelor's quarters, with the determined temporariness they have. The carton for the TV sat open in the corner; a black futon was ready to fold. Only the couch revealed a history, indented where particular people sat, threads dangling from the upholstery where it was badly scratched.

Music thudded from upstairs, and Arthur went up to his son. Abby sat on the edge of the futon, looking for a way out. She and Arthur had nothing in common. They had climbed a mountain together once. This was dumb.

Yet would it never be possible for her to change? She wanted to relax and be part of the world. Live in a neighborhood such as this, with kids running in and out even if they weren't hers. Not expect so much.

At least she wanted these things when she was in a certain mood. At the moment she wanted out.

But maybe being a stepmother was to be her challenge. Any woman can love her own kids. Caring for someone else's takes character. If they're teenagers, saintliness.

She knew the rules about steppersons. Her students had taught her that. They are disgusted by the women their fathers bring around. So expect nothing. Don't butt in. And never wear strong perfume.

She could handle that. If only she didn't have to be in the actual presence of the child.

Meanwhile, any moment the little gangster would appear.

Abby was calculating how far it was to walk home when she sensed a presence in the room. The sound of a sneeze. She looked up. Draped on the mantle, possibly stuffed although it might be alive, was a black and white cat. Huge.

Carefully she went over and reached to touch the large soft head. The cat didn't purr. Nor did it hiss. Then the slitted yellow eyes narrowed and sank back into fur. Alive!

Arthur came in the room and put his arms around her. "Danny wants to go for pizza."

"You have a cat." She turned and kissed Arthur on the mouth.

"It's Danny's." Then Danny must be a fine, sensitive boy (assuming he didn't own the cat for the purpose of torturing it). After all, he was Arthur's son.

Danny came down the stairs, resembling his father at that age. He had the same lean and relaxed motion, dark straight eyebrows, and blond hair, although Danny's was long and draped over his face. His mouth was where he differed: full lips, with a sharp definition to the upper lip. So, there was the mother.

Abby rushed forward with her hand. Danny walked past with a nod as Arthur introduced them.

"I like your cat," she called as they went out to get in the pickup truck, breaking her vow of silence. It was the teacher in her. It's your job to ask and ask more questions, even when answers don't come back. "What's his name?"

"It's a her. Roseanne."

"Good. Good name."

"She's a useless pile of fur."

Cruel child. Yet he did have a way with words.

However, Danny did not deign to use them again. Not at Pizza Hut, where he hid behind his hair, pointing to his choice of toppings on the menu. Pineapple. Ugh. His father went along with it, not asking what she liked. Well, Abby happened to detest pineapple embedded in cheese.

She went off to the restroom. On her way back, seeing Danny and his father laughing by themselves, she understood what makes a wicked stepmother. The evil welling up in her would flourish the more she comprehended the situation. Not that she questioned why the kid was a brat. She would be too if her father brought around some other woman.

She thought of all the stepparents these days, heroically trying and trying to be decent, to be wise, to be lovable, when the kids only want their folks to be together again.

However, Danny was thirteen, so he should leave home in five years or so. Sooner if he was unhappy. She could live in Virginia until the boy moved out and then get together with Arthur. Ah, but he would marry somebody else, wouldn't he.

She slid in the booth next to Arthur and helped herself to the nasty pizza, picking off the pieces of pineapple and lining them up on her plate. No, this is not the way to bond with someone. You mimic his body language. If the person interviewing you puts up his feet, put up yours.

Danny flung back his hair and attacked his pizza. Abby flipped her mane and gnawed her crust. Danny sucked on his straw, and she drained her Coke, rattling the ice cubes the way he did.

He kept on chewing.

"Ever wonder about your dad in high school?"

Danny stretched a piece of cheese up off his plate and wrapped it around his tongue.

"Well, he was fun. When the football players strutted off to practice, taking themselves so seriously, here came Arthur in his Jeep to give us rides."

"A real nobody," Arthur added, but he looked pleased.

"The girls liked him."

Danny stood up. "I'm out of here. Dad, we are still going on that trip." He spoke the words over Abby's head.

"Sure, son." How odd to hear Arthur use that word. He did say it very nicely. "Danny has a job on a ranch in southern Utah for a couple of weeks, and I'm driving him down." Arthur patted his son's arm as the kid left. Right. Let's reward rudeness.

"Good luck," Abby called as Danny sauntered off, thumbs in his pockets.

Arthur then invited her to go on the trip with him and Danny, which she thought was brave. However, she declined, most graciously.

She did begin to see possibilities in this situation. If the stepperson isn't supposed to butt in, she could avoid all unpleasant activities and decisions. This way she could appear to be sensitive but actually be lazy. Free!

As she and Arthur kissed goodnight in the shadows of her mother's garage, furtively, as if Danny were waiting (although who knows where he'd gone to act out his hostility), Arthur joked that she better not find somebody new while he was away.

Go, silly man. No problem there.

35 The Box

Abby lay about in bed, watching the sun spread across the room. Sloth is one of the finer benefits of the single life. The mattress was soft, all hers, and she sprawled to its far corners. Meanwhile, somewhere in the desert Arthur and his teenager were dragging out of sleeping bags. This stepperson thing could be great. You don't have to go on gigs. If the child hates you, there's an excuse. If he goes to jail, it's not your fault.

The house was quiet. Her parents had gone with Elizabeth to find a canopy for the reception, which she was hosting since the mother of the bride wasn't into entertaining. Abby's job was to clean her stuff out of this closet, a fair enough request to the offspring going on forty.

All right, she could throw things away. Cleanse herself in the new millennium. Blouses pushed to the back of the closet were bagged for the Salvation Army. Shoes with pointed toes waiting for their style to return might as well wait in the secondhand store. A plastic garment bag that crackled at the touch showed turquoise through its murky window. It was a strapless evening gown that had felt like a bandage around her chest. Bye-bye.

She did pause with a pink chenille robe, remembering how soft and lovely it was the day she brought it home from the store. When had its magic gone? Did it go out of style with the season? Or was it overnight that she stopped liking it? With a certain shame she folded the robe to go. Maybe someone even yet would choose it.

Here was a wooden tennis racket in a dusty case, heavy after the titanium rackets of today. She slid it out, fingering the fraying strings. Would anybody buy it even for a dime? Worth far more if it were used to hit a single ball.

In the back of the closet were cartons she had stored here when she moved from Shenandoah Street to a smaller place. She took out a Nike shoe box tied with a string. As she undid the knot, the contents expanded as if alive. She did not need to look inside to know the contents. Letters from a certain someone as they are saved in boxes tied with ribbons in basements, attics, anywhere. Perhaps they are meant to be read by posterity. Or the right day never comes to throw them away. In seclusion they await their moment, their paper growing brittle, their ink pale.

She could do it. Dump these relics now.

She got out to the trash can with her box before her recycling conscience kicked in. Today's students teach you that. Anyone with any integrity will recycle. At least paper. The elementary school down the block should have bins.

The sun was staggeringly bright as she ran across the hot street clutching the Nike box, its contents thudding against her side. Up the grassy slope to the school she went, past tricky bars, a seesaw, over to the brown bin for paper.

She was holding up the warm lid to make her drop when she thought of Laura, the student who threw away her journals and felt like a murderer.

Laura was getting married the next day. The man she was to marry wanted her to start a clean new life as his wife, which meant getting rid of the records she had kept since she was a child.

So on the eve of her wedding, Laura went to the trash chute in her apartment, lifted the metal door, and let her journals go. She heard the thumping sound they made against the walls, going the five floors down. She did not hear them land.

At the moment Laura got rid of her writing, she felt she had gotten rid of her best friend. Only her journal could recall exactly the winning goal Laura had kicked for her soccer team, the smell of the grass that day. Her journal told of her first kiss on that warm summer night, the feel of the boy's lips against her own, which she was required to forget when she became a wife.

The next day Laura got married, free of her past.

Abby lowered the lid on the bin. Not that she intended to wallow in Stan's letters. But they deserved better than being tossed in with newspapers. The recycling people might discover them, reading words that were meant for her alone.

She would give them an honorable burial. In her parents' backyard, out beneath the lilac bush.

She went back and found a spade in the shed, plunging it

at the dry ground. But it wouldn't give way as the moist earth of Virginia does, so conducive to digging graves. She sat back on the grass. The day was hot, that part of the afternoon that is usually dead. Not today with these letters close enough to touch. Maybe just a glance. She might learn from them. Was she such a coward that she couldn't stare down words written years ago? This time she would be objective. The key to her failed marriage could be right here.

With trembling hands she opened the box. There was Stan's handwriting, which even now took her breath away.

His last letters were on top, the yellow memos.

Close the box, Abby. Close it now.

But she was an English teacher; she had reverence for the written word. And now she would take a scholarly approach. Explicate the text, place the document in its historical perspective, discern the subtext.

Abby,

The marriage simply isn't working out for me. I can't say why this is, but it is something I always feared.

Down, down she went again, as she had then. Perhaps she wanted to, didn't she, glad that her feelings had not died.

She did notice how clear Stan's message was. He had a main point. *The marriage simply isn't working out for me.* Why had that been so hard for her to grasp? He had simply made a mistake in marrying her. Those things happen.

Let the man have a mistake. You can't blame someone for not being in love with you.

246

I tried, I really tried. I just couldn't seem to adjust. There is nothing you could have done differently that I can think of.

I'm sorry, very sorry to put you through this. I have never done anything more difficult nor have I ever felt so much pain. But I had to have a release. As I have mentioned, I had the feeling I was in an iron lung.

His suffering was real. It hurt her heart to know this. Stan had to leave. His message made that obvious.

Now enough of this shit. She tore into the yellow papers, ripping them, shredding them with her teeth, spitting the soggy pieces to the wind. She dragged out the hose and sprayed the remaining bits across the grass. In terror they scuttled off into the shrubs, lodging there like dying bloom. She sprayed and sprayed, drowning those hopeless words.

Then she stood on the grass, dripping and smiling and feeling good. She could get rid of Stan's letters in a minute if that's the way he felt. Burn those suckers. Or put them out in the garbage to rot.

The door to the garage was opening. Her parents were home. Abby snatched up the last wet blobs of yellow paper on the lawn and slipped on into the house to secure her box for the moment. She might read just a couple more letters to give perspective. As any student of literature knows, you can't judge a writer by one selection.

Going down through the box, working back in time, the letters would get better. As she preached to the students, not

247

everything should be organized in chronological order. Use your imagination.

Plus, the worst was over. No more of those damn yellow memos ever again.

Abby dashed upstairs, zipped open the emptied garment bag, and stashed her box, mail for another day.

36 *Sweet Spot*

Her mother found her reading in the closet. "Dear, what is it you do in here?"

Abby looked up from her letter, smiling. "You said to clean this place."

"I didn't mean a major job. Arthur's on the phone."

"Arthur."

He was calling from a pay phone down by Moab. She could hear the trucks at the Maverick station. The trip with his son had gone well, but it was cold sleeping in the desert. Danny had been delivered to a ranch just seventy miles out of town. Arthur would be back tonight.

So, put these letters away. Just one more.

This one was a note from Edna, thanking Abby for dinner and saying how good the food tasted when she cooked it. You get a great mother-in-law or you don't. It isn't anything you do. And Edna was the best. After the divorce they simply hadn't known what to say to each other. They lost touch except for a card at Christmas.

Then this past winter Edna wrote to say that Fred had died of a heart attack. He danced with every woman at the party that night, and he was gone. Edna wrote that if she had one wish it would be that "you would come and visit me."

So Abby drove across the aging Woodrow Wilson Bridge one more time, hoping that Edna wouldn't mention Stan, just as she humanely omitted him from her Christmas messages. Or as Abby fantasized, maybe Edna would say something wonderful. "Stan made a terrible mistake divorcing you. Those were his exact words. You were the one he loved." She could hear Edna blurting this out. She told the truth. You had to believe her. "Stan only got married again to prove that he could."

Why couldn't that be true?

Or how sublime it would be to learn from anyone, "Did you know that Stan is getting divorced again?"

Edna's yard looked different, barren even for winter. Fred's pink flamingos, standing with their stick legs in the pale grass, brought the first chill of his passing. Fred was fun. Always that. He was also someone who didn't see his son's divorce as particularly sad. Fred called shortly before Abby moved from Shenandoah Street. When she answered, he said, "Who's this?"

Edna hurried out to meet her, and they hugged awkwardly after three years. Edna chatted about the mild winter they were having. She introduced Abby to her next-door neighbor, Alberta, sounding proud. "This is my former daughter-in-law." That was nice to hear.

They stayed out in the yard for a while, as if in the open air they could keep from talking about Fred.

When they were inside, Edna said, "It's quiet without him."

"It is."

"Everybody misses Fred. Even when he was retired, all the secretaries from his office came to the funeral." Edna wiped away a tear. Then she perked up. "But now I play bridge every day."

They recalled card games with Fred, remembering how he forgot to say "Uno" and lost the game. Skillfully they maneuvered the conversation around that fourth person at the card table.

"I should be leaving."

"I don't like my new daughter-in-law," Edna said.

Dear Edna. Honest Edna. Abby sat back down.

It might have been satisfying to pursue the negative details about the person Stan had married. Yet even they would make her real.

Time to go. But Abby had to ask, "Does Stan have—?"

"Yes, a little boy. Six months old."

Well, then. "Congratulations, Grandma."

Edna let out a big breath and beamed. "His name is Stephen."

"Let's see his picture."

It wasn't far to find. Edna hustled in the other room and brought back a large photo in a silver frame. "Here." Abby looked for a familiar trait. Not the eyes. The child's were round and dark. Eyebrows? Too faint to tell. Then in the carved shape of the little mouth, lips she knew.

"Stephen Swan. Nice name."

"I spoil him."

"You spoil us all."

"Will you come visit me again?" Edna asked from the porch as Abby went out to her car. She said she would. But she had not been back.

As she drove away from Edna's that last time, Abby was surprised to find that she liked the child in the picture just fine. Stephen Swan, whose father surely cared for him more than he'd known he could. Stan would teach the little tyke to grip the racket with that same firm wrist, to hit that beautiful backhand down the line.

Abby put away the note from Edna. Now just one more letter from Stan, and she would stop. This one had come to her out here in Utah.

To the dearest wife imaginable,

How I miss you when you're gone! Perhaps I haven't said it enough in our marriage, but I appreciate having you in my life. You are all I could have ever wanted. I am so lucky.

The days drag by without you. I miss our talks at the breakfast table (and of course I miss you at night). Our morning ritual may be a small thing to some people, but I can't think of a better way to start the day than by looking at you. With you off in Utah, I avoid coming home to the empty house. So I find myself driving around, even going to movies by myself. Anything but the lonely feeling of walking in and having you gone.

See, it isn't all about sex, although the longer you're away the more I obsess on it and crave your voluptuous body. It's awful to reach out in bed, and you aren't there. In the kitchen I envision you in your gown making the morning coffee and myself reaching under the soft fabric to your skin. I can't take a shower without wanting to touch the curves of your body, let my hands slide down all of you. Oh, my lovely wife.

"Abby? Are you still working in that closet?"

"It's OK, Mother." Abby took her box and escaped to the basement, with its musty smell, ivy spilling out of the window wells, the lumpy couch. The first time Stan visited here they made love on those lumps, ever so quietly, with her parents upstairs.

Hearing Elizabeth upstairs now, calling to Roy, Abby progressed to the privacy of her dad's workshop. Here were his pliers and drills, twine draped on the walls. Every size of nail. Her father picked up nails off the ground and straightened them. Whatever you brought here he could fix. But no place to sit.

She went back through her mother's fruit room with its rows of shining jars. Cherries glowing in dark juice. Peaches cupped together. Single raspberries floating in red.

Ah, the root cellar. It had a bench. She stepped in and sat by the trough of potatoes sprouting fat white roots, onions sending out golden shoots. The light was a dangling bulb that shone faintly through caramel-colored drops. But it was bright enough so that she could read.

I had a dream about us. We were walking nude in a grassy place (maybe because I had been watching golf on TV). But this was our own place. The amazing thing was how comfortable we felt walking naked like that with no inhibition. We were just holding hands and talking about daily things, though of course excitement was building in me. No, we didn't make love on that lawn. But as I said, we felt no embarrassment being nude with each other, although people were outside the fence looking through.

I believe this picture indicates how well suited we are for each other, Abby. It is something I have felt from the beginning. The conviction grows with time, especially the time you are away, it seems. If I were to write the details of the erotic scene that followed, it would steam up the hands of the mailman delivering this letter to you in your parents' home. Suffice it to say that in the dream, anyway, we culminated our love in the most delicious fashion possible.

Yet no dream can come close to the reality of our love.

Now I've worked myself up into a state.

I need you, my wonderful wife. Hurry home—

The door to the root cellar creaked open, and in came Roy. "Close that. How did you find me?"

"Phew. It smells in here. What are you doing, Aunt Abby?" Roy sat by her on the bench, swinging his pale legs in the ghostly light.

"English teachers are always reading something, aren't they. Pull that door tight."

"Why are you in here?"

"Call it the ambiance," she said with a wave of her hand. Roy giggled. He peered at her reading material. "What's that?"

"Oh, just something from my past. Memorabilia, as they say." Roy liked big words, and he slowly repeated this one. Abby glanced back at the letter on her lap, which still warmed her body in several places.

Roy's teeth looked big and white in here. "What's memorabilia?"

"Call it a person's baggage. Those things we carry through our lives. Your teddy bear there. Hi, Bob. He is more than cloth and plastic eyes."

"I've had him for my whole life."

Abby shook the bear's hand. "Good for you, Bob. And you've had a tough time." He was stitched down the front. "Heart surgery?"

Roy laughed gleefully. Nine years old may be the perfect age for a human being. "My mom sewed him up."

"Elizabeth is a good mother. So, why aren't you outside playing on this nice day?"

"Nobody to play with." Roy yawned and stretched his arms. "My friend Thurman is in California visiting his dad. Can we play tennis, please, please?" He pumped his legs. His eyes were bright.

"Last time you threw a tantrum."

"I was just a kid. I'll be better." Roy grabbed his bear and squashed him.

Maybe Roy had been a bit young when she dragged him out on the court to develop a playing partner for herself.

"And I was in a bad mood that year myself."

So out they went, Roy running ahead through the park to the tennis court out in the bright sun. Trees would have been nice. But mountains for a backdrop are a splendid sight. This was the court where she had learned to play.

Roy skipped and leaped and tossed his bear, its arms flopping like broken wings. He dived to catch him, rolling on the grass, coming up with Bob in his arms.

Abby ran too, dancing to the refrain, *the dearest wife imaginable*. On to the court with its cracked surface, weeds poking through. The baseline was so faint that you could barely see it. The net had a hole. But at least the net was up. And nobody around. The court was theirs.

She gave Roy a new can of Penn balls to open. He snapped back the lid, the rubbery air hissed out, and she inhaled.

"You're weird."

He grabbed a new yellow ball and pitched it toward the fence, where it rolled into the weeds bright as an Easter egg. Roy swished his racket wildly. "Throw me one. Throw me one." She did, and he popped it up and over the wall. He whiffed the next one.

Roy started to scream and jump, his usual tantrum. Abby stood and waited, and he calmed down enough to try the correct forehand grip, as if he were shaking hands with the racket. He frowned, but he tried. He hit the ball off the rim. Then he couldn't hit the ball at all.

He went over and slumped by the fence. "I can't do anything right. I stink at sports."

Abby sat down next to him. "Why is that?"

"The other kids are bigger. In soccer they push. I can't throw a basketball that high. I've never made a basket."

That was sad. "It is a big ball. Well, in tennis you don't have to be tall. Nobody pushes. And you get to hit lots of balls. In baseball you might hit one or two. Maybe none. Tennis is a game for your whole life. You do have the agile body for it, Roy. And you like to run."

"I have a tennis body? Really?"

"Yup. Don't know about the personality."

"Why not?"

Patience is the thing. It's not just about putting the ball away. A true tennis player likes to hit and hit. Hear the crisp pop of the ball. See it landing just inside the baseline. That would be heaven, hitting exactly where you want."

"There's no tennis in heaven. That's stupid."

"Oh yes, Roy. For some of us there would have to be. A court in the shade, new balls. A partner. And not being afraid of any shot."

"You're afraid of tennis?"

"Sure. Afraid to go to the net. Or I was. Then after losing enough times, I figured why not charge in? You can be afraid you'll forget how to hit a certain shot. But the worst fear is that you won't be able to play. Something will happen. So you go out and run and hit, and it's wonderful."

Roy jumped up. "I want to learn tennis."

"Great. We'll play doubles."

"I can learn it. I can. I can." Roy skipped out on the court, swinging his racket like a baseball bat.

All right, the volley. "Just hold your racket out."

He smacked one hard that she couldn't get. "You missed, you missed." Roy danced about deliriously.

But his ground strokes were something else. (How could anybody completely miss a tennis ball that many times?) Maybe he was too short for the racket. Too young to be doing this. But Roy kept trying.

"We could come back tomorrow," Abby said.

"One more. One more."

She went around the net and stood beside him. "Do you like the ball?"

He swung and missed. "I hate it."

"We'll stop."

"No, no."

She handed him the tennis ball, slightly dusty, but the fur was still crisp. "Here, hold it. Notice the seams." Roy eyed the ball suspiciously. He squeezed it. "Watch. Grip. Hit." She went back around the net.

Roy tried another forehand with a big loopy stroke, missing, but at least he didn't rush. A few more times. He was getting it.

Then after many tries, weary but relaxed, he released the racket head and met the ball with a perfect *whop* that sent it deep, briskly bounding up inside the baseline.

When Roy saw it go, that ball coming off his strings in this new way, he stopped moving to watch. He hugged his racket, squealing and leaping with his lean kid's body. "I did it. I did it. I hit it right."

258

"So how did it feel, hitting the sweet spot?" Abby asked on the way home to tell his mother.

"What's that?"

She drew a circle at the center of the strings. "It's the true place to hit. The ball goes out easy. The racket doesn't twist. The sweet spot is the heart of anything."

Few there are who find it, but it will change your life.

"I hit the sweet spot," Roy cried, bounding on ahead, running all the way home.

My wonderful wife. Hurry home—

37 Cow Camp

With the mountains behind them, she and Arthur headed for the desert, which stretches out from Utah towns any way you go. They were off to get Danny at the Far Star Ranch.

They passed the last of the alfalfa fields, the comforting, lanky cottonwoods, out to where the pinyon pines cling to the hills, then the land becomes a level gray, inhabited only by the patient sage. After that it's a long dry drive until the rocks turn red in southern Utah.

How she longed for the green of Virginia, its moist shade, the sudden drenching rains that bring vines up a trellis overnight. When you come from the west, you think that the east is concrete. No one tells you how lush it is, that Pittsburgh is a garden. Driving up the east coast to New York, Boston, it's foliage all along the interstate. Wild flowers grow in the median.

"Like it?" Arthur asked, looking out at the gray tongue of road going on forever.

"You know I hate the desert." It dried her brain. Maybe she lacked the imagination to make a playground of barren places, the way Don Quixote built castles in his mind out on the plain. But he never took a car trip with the family, did he, kids strangling each other in the back seat, while their parents say this is fun as they press the metal and count down those miles.

It did help to have a boyfriend in the car. Arthur stroked her knee. She whispered in his ear. "What is it you like out here?"

"Just riding along." He let the steering wheel go, and the pickup guided itself down the straight road. "I like a vista."

A vista to what? A valley spread with vegetation, a road circling up to a cliff where trees lean with the sea breeze. Those are vistas. A track to infinity with no exit is not. (And if *this* drive seemed long, imagine the return trip with Danny.) "So, tell me, what are your boy's other interests outside this cowboy thing?"

"Being a Marlboro guy?" Arthur chuckled. He thought that was just fine? Surely he'd smelled the cigarette smoke on his thirteen-year-old son. And Danny thought guns were neat. Cowboys collect arsenals of them.

"I'm sure he's doing more than smoking and wearing a holster." Let's see, what? "Cowboys fix fences, don't they? Feed the livestock. He'll learn about the different grasses."

"Danny is a lost kid, I know." Arthur looked out at the long road. "But he's a good boy. He'll be all right."

The sun had finally moved across the sky, dropping to the earth like an egg into a pan. Then comes the twilight, the desert's finest hour. The dry thoughts of afternoon are forgotten as the air takes on a glow, softly spreading pink across the dust and rocks and sage.

261

As they drove across this magical land, up ahead was an amazing sight. It was a hill of white sand, quite unlike the gray of the desert all around. How this was possible, she did not know.

They got out and walked through the sagebrush to the sandpile. No tire marks indicated delivery of the silt-like dirt. Not exactly white beach sand, but it was fine enough to make you want to go barefoot. They stepped down through the top warm layer to where it cooled your toes. Up they climbed, two people in the vast stillness of the desert.

There they stood, the sky deepening over the glowing land, as if a forgiving hand had touched a dimmer switch to soften the scorching day. It was one of those rare hushed moments of peace that make you wonder at all struggle. Chasing after a tennis ball and trying to hit it right. Straining with students so their writing might be clear, when all that we will leave behind is a name carved on a stone.

The gold band along the earth turned to flame. Then the color was gone as quickly as it came. The air began to cool. Soon more stars would come out than you could dream of on a city street. In the desert the stars go all the way to the ground.

She could not hate this. Maybe she could change and grow to like other things. One day she would embrace broccoli. Break into song along an icy walk. She and Danny would be friends.

Arthur's tan was gold in the dimming light, and his soft gray eyes had nothing in them to fear. They kissed for a long time on their white sand hill.

Afterward how lightly they made their way back to the truck, as if the weight of wondering about themselves had lifted. All would be well.

One teenage son was no reason to keep them apart. Naturally, he came first in his father's life. It would have been so for her. Arthur certainly was in a hurry though to get to his boy now. Luckily, policemen don't like being out here in the dark any more than speeders do.

Black night came, shrinking their world to the lighted slot in front of the headlights. She thought what a wonderful thing streetlights are. One of the treasures of civilized life. Bluish neon lights leaning over the freeway, shining on green and white signs announcing that a city is near. Street lamps of a colonial style glowing in the mist all along Shenandoah Street.

They turned off the highway onto a dirt road consisting of potholes. Bang, bang, bang. Teeth could be dislodged, car parts detached. A mere fifteen more miles of this, Arthur said, and they would be to cow camp.

"Cow camp?" Abby answered faintly. "What about the Far Star Ranch?" A bear rug spread before the fire. Western tunes sung by the Sons of the Pioneers.

Arthur reminded her that they'd been going to cow camp all along, never the headquarters of the Far Star Ranch. A cow camp, she learned, was where the cowboys stay overnight on the mountain when they are gathering the herd. Well, then. At least it should be terribly rustic.

Meanwhile, fifteen miles of slamming into gallon-size potholes was no breeze around the beltway.

The worst part was that Arthur seemed to be enjoying this. A truck passed them going the other way and came so close that it pinged their mirror with a gigantic *whirr*. Arthur just waved back at the driver. That's how lonely the desert is. Somebody nearly runs you off the road, and you think that he's your buddy.

"Hold on, Abby, we're almost there," Arthur said, patting her leg, this person she had considered marrying an hour ago.

At last the road narrowed in the headlights (although it did not become smooth), and Arthur got out to open a sagging wire gate. Weeds scratched the side of the pickup as they drove through, on up a hill to a white frame house with a dog on the porch. Excuse me, cow camp? This could be any run-down neighborhood. Where was the log cabin with a palomino tethered to the fence post, neighing softly into the velvet night?

Danny came out and stood on the porch. He was chewing something. Tobacco? Taller in cowboy boots, he leaned against the doorframe, not making a move toward his father.

Arthur went over and hugged his son. Danny's arms stayed limp. Fifteen miles of potholes for this? (Ah, but a potential stepmother better stay mute.) Either Danny was punishing Arthur for bringing a woman, or he was just a brat.

Danny sat between them on the way home.

"So, what did you like most about being a cowboy?"

"Everything."

"Did you have a favorite horse?"

"Nah."

"It must be nice riding out in the morning."

"Yeah."

This stimulating exchange moved Abby to share her own interests with Danny, and she told him how much she liked tennis.

"Sports suck."

Arthur did not leap in here to help the conversation along, although surely he could not think that a teacher desires a monologue. Maybe he was letting her and Danny get used to each other.

Never had a gas station looked so good. Out behind the restroom, Abby gulped a Dr. Pepper and conversed with herself. "How do I escape?" "Hitchhike home?"

She edged around the corner to check out the Gulf pumps with this hope in mind. But Arthur's pickup was the only vehicle in sight. Then she saw her chance, which had been there all along. The *back* of the truck. No matter how hard the steely floor, the fury of the sun beating down, that partitioned space could be hers.

Neither Arthur nor Danny uttered the least objection as she climbed up in the truck bed. Arthur never was one to tell a person what to do, something she liked about him very much. Danny probably hoped she would fly out of the truck bed like a loose dog as they sped along. Nevertheless, Abby hoisted herself up and lay back on the itchy blanket, breathing the sweet air of solitude.

Inside the cab Danny and his dad were talking now. She

265

couldn't read their lips. Just as well. Maybe when the three of them became a family, they could buy one of those old taxis with a glass wall sealing her off in the back. As her mother said, there are many ways to be happy.

So they rolled on down the road, where no physical jarring against her metal bed came close to the trauma of attempting conversation with a teenager. Abby thought about the pleasures of this trip, that moment with Arthur on the white sandpile. They would have other fine moments. You cannot expect perfect days.

And so, relax.

Soon they were home. The sun had stopped its burning, and the shade was deep.

That night Abby lay awake listening to the crickets through the open window, their pulse quick in the warm air. The good weather should continue for Tucker's wedding this weekend. He was so young, so excited. Maybe nervous, he said, but not afraid.

She might have slept then. But the moon came in the room, making a bright path across the floor leading to the closet door. No, this was not the time to read her mail, coming off a trip with Arthur.

Then again, it hadn't exactly been a romantic getaway for the two of them, had it. Fifteen miles of ruts in the road for that boy. A plugged-up toilet at cow camp.

Anyway, it was past midnight. A new day. Mail call.

She followed the moonlit path to her box of letters, their weight precious against her as she carried them back to bed. Today's message was a thick one, pages of hotel stationery that had come in a thrilling packet from overseas. It was a letter Stan wrote over several days back before they were married.

6:01 a.m.
It's a rainy day here in London that would be perfect for us to stay indoors. But I am without my love. Where are you? Last night the delegation attended a party and seemed to enjoy themselves in the smoky room. All I could think of was you. I put in a call across the Atlantic, but you were out somewhere. I know I can't expect you to stay home thinking of me every minute. But unreasonably I want that to be true.

The jute negotiations are stalled for the day. Someone would have wondered why I was smiling as I walked out on the wet street after a tedious meeting that got us nowhere. I was realizing how lucky I am to have you in my life.

I must confess something to you. I have always been afraid that I couldn't love anyone. The thought of continuing on with any woman gave a sense of panic. With you all that has changed. The only panic now would be if I could not spend my life with you.

I am giddy, joyful, grateful for this. You are the most wonderful woman on earth.

12:15 p.m.
Back at the hotel I thought there might be letter from you. I tried to reach you by phone again, and you were out. I hope you don't think I'm keeping track of you. But when I

can't contact you I begin to get a vise-like feeling around my heart as the minutes, hours, and days go by without being able to touch you. It is the feeling of being in an iron lung.

Let me reveal how sensitive I am about even the possibility of us ever separating—the inconceivable thought of you being with someone else. During the blue Monday before I left on this trip, you came into the den and asked me what was wrong. I apologized for being such a shithead. It was stupid jealousy over some guy who had called to play tennis with you while I was away. I got this frightened feeling. What if you found somebody else?

I have taken a drink to reduce the turmoil in my stomach because of our separation of two weeks and needing to see you so desperately. I would probably turn into a drunk trying to forget you if we were ever to part, which is something I will never let happen. That I know.

Rats, somebody is pounding on the door for me to go to a delegates meeting.

More later, my love—

38 *Rightness of Fit*

It was the day before Tucker and Natalie's wedding, with its last-minute fittings and worried glances at the sky, where even in Utah the clouds can go black. Elizabeth had made the wedding cake herself, tier upon tier of Tucker's favorite, devil's food. Natalie liked it too. Elizabeth also heroically attended to the details of the reception, which the mother of the bride said would give her hives.

The small yard took on a festive look with its green and white striped tent, secured to poles slanting deep enough in the ground so that no wind could tear them out. Tucker was up in the morning hauling folding chairs, whistling as he unloaded them from the truck. Any nervousness he might have felt did not show.

As Abby passed his room, she did hear him say on the phone, "Don't be scared, Nat." Tucker motioned her in, proudly displaying the wedding ring he was trying on, a turquoise band to match Natalie's. It is probably a good sign when a man wants to wear a ring. "Love you," he said as he hung up.

"Can I ask you something, Aunt Abby?" She found a spot on the bed, which Elizabeth had heaped with forty-five throw pillows once she acknowledged that her son would not be moving back.

Tucker put his head down on his skinny knees sticking out of cut-off jeans with frayed edges. His dreadlocks fell forward, those braids his mother could not undo. He wore a single gold earring, although several more holes went up his ear. Elizabeth suspected that other of his body parts were pierced as well, however none that she wished to discuss. Natalie wore a stud through her tongue.

"Maybe I shouldn't ask you this," Tuck said, still with his head down. "I mean, like, you know—"

"What?"

"Your divorce bummed you out."

"It did."

He looked up, afraid. "Nat is freaked out about divorce, I guess because of her parents doing it. They are pretty messed up. Her dad has been married three times. He gets dumped. Her mom hates marriage. She lives with guys. Nat dreads the thought of being like her. But she's scared it'll just happen, like if you've got cancer genes or radiation shit."

Abby smiled. "It's possible. What do I know? Wouldn't it be great if I could give you advice. Communicate. Compromise. But divorce is no accident either. Someone decides. One person, anyway, has to want it."

"I mean, Natalie, she really *hates* divorce."

"It is a death. Oh, Tuck. But I'm glad I didn't want to leave him. So glad for that. I can't see you ever wanting to leave either."

270

"Walk out on Nat? Whoa." Tuck swung back his braids, making them click. "Not her. She's the only one who thinks I have a brain."

"Sorry about that."

"Did I tell you I'm going back to school? The community college. Like where you teach."

"Good for you. And marriage usually helps."

"I'm going into physical therapy. For seniors. I know they're crotchety. Like this old guy I delivered groceries to. All he did was sit in his chair and clip coupons. But now they've got water aerobics. It doesn't have to be that way."

"I'm proud of you."

"Natalie's the one got me going. And being married and all, I can't be a slob." Tucker grinned. He had teeth. Braces gone. Straight white teeth. "People think it's no big deal getting married when you've been living together. Hey, man, tomorrow is my wedding day. I just wish my mom could chill. She knows we're going to split up."

"Nobody can know that." Except maybe the person getting married.

"Tucker?" Elizabeth called up the stairs. "Come help me move these chairs."

"OK." He jumped up, more attentive than Abby had seen him. However, as he went out, Tucker said in a lowered manly tone, "Natalie never bosses me. She's awesome."

"I like your woman."

When her sister was ready, Abby was going shopping with Elizabeth to find shoes for the wedding. Something to go with her low-cut black dress and still be sturdy enough to climb the hill to the cemetery.

Meanwhile, here was a window of time. Never travel without your reading material.

6:15 a.m.

Rome is such a romantic city, with couples kissing everywhere. I wish we could show them that Americans can be just as loving. And the many cats! Another reminder of you. They brush up against the legs of tourists and leap onto the monuments.

I wondered how it would be if you and I were standing here two thousand years ago. Even if we had met then, I believe we would have loved each other. I can imagine us slipping easily out of the loose-fitting garments of the day, although it might not have been acceptable to do so.

When I go into the cathedrals, filing by the flickering candles, I realize that I too believe in miracles, if not necessarily religious ones. Having you in my life is one of them. Maybe it did take a God to make this happen

With us there is a rightness of fit. That's the only way I can describe it. I would not have believed such a thing was possible if it hadn't happened to me.

I just stopped writing this letter to take a cold shower (for obvious reasons). Rather, a bath, as there is no shower here. Boy, is this tub small. It's barely larger than a beer barrel. We would have problems maneuvering in this one.

5:30 p.m.

I hurried to the hotel. A letter from you. This was going

to be a better evening than I thought.

I tore it open, and your pictures slid out. I rushed up to my room clutching them, heart pounding. I knew I was late for a dinner with our adviser, but I had to get a quick peek. I laughed with relief and exhilaration. Those pictures made me so high that I lost all tired feelings.

So now you've done it. All the effusive, mushy language I have been withholding is going to start gushing out. I don't care how excessive I sound. I must be with you always, Abby. Never doubt that.

I marvel at your strength, beauty, and determination. You are indeed a wonderful and extraordinary woman.

10:32 p.m.

Your letter kept me high all night at a dinner for our delegation, which turned out to be unexpectedly stimulating. Or maybe I was just so happy to be in love with you. I hope you will forgive my redundant use of the word love *for I can find none better to express my feelings. I am simply a man who adores you and cannot find the words to say how much.*

"Time to go shopping," Elizabeth called.

"Just a second."

OK. Abby folded away her letter and jumped up to accompany her dear sister, help her find what she needed for the all-important day.

She took Elizabeth's arm. "Everything's going to be fine."

"What are you talking about?"

"The wedding, the weather, your shoes."

They went to every shoe store in the mall, in and out, looking at plain black pumps, flats with round toes and with pointed ones, sandals with straps crisscrossing up the leg, clogs with chunky soles to make a person tall. "I'll decide. I will."

"Take your time," Abby answered from far away.

"Why are you in such a good mood? You hate shopping."

Abby strolled along, singing her song. They went back and got the first pair of sling-back pumps Elizabeth had tried on. Maybe not the easiest to walk in, but they should get her up the hill. And they showed off Elizabeth's legs magnificently.

"You really think so?"

"I've always said you have gorgeous legs."

On the way home Elizabeth stopped to pick up a prescription. Abby cheerfully waited in the car.

"Sure you won't be bored?"

"No problem."

6:30 a.m.

I was disturbed from a restless semi-sleep this morning by a call telling me my flight had been canceled. I hung up mortified at the thought of staying away from you another day and night, maybe two. I came as close to tears as I have in a long time.

If I should ever be parted from you indefinitely, Abby, I

274

really believe I might go mad. They would find this insane lost man, completely unable to function without his love. I have no doubt we will be happy together always. Marriage to you will be the most wonderful thing in the world.

I reached in my briefcase and uncovered your pictures. All I could feel was a massive swell of warmth consuming my body and mind. Boy, are you a beauty. Just wish I could see all of you and your long legs.

I realize one of the many reasons I love you is because you let me say it to you over and over again without it ever appearing routine.

10:30 p.m.

See, you are the last thing on my mind at night as well as the first thing in the morning. I changed rooms and in the process lost a tub and gained a shower that is only marginally more humid than a typical August day in Washington. But you and I would enjoy ourselves in any shower, I am sure.

"What's that you're reading?" Elizabeth asked as she got in the car. "Sorry I took so long."

"Actually, this is—"

"You can't believe how many people were waiting for prescriptions. All these senior drug addicts."

"And yours?"

"Valium. A gift to myself to get through this wedding."

"You'll be gaining a daughter."

"Oh please. Daughter-in-law. Not every woman is

thrilled about that."

Maybe this was true. All the nicer when it happens.

"See you tomorrow," Elizabeth said with a grimace as she let off Abby at their mother's place. "Thanks for shopping. You were patient."

"It'll be an amazing wedding. You'll see. Thank you for your sons. My nephews. They are terrific."

Elizabeth looked startled, as if this were a new idea. Then she nodded and did not deny it.

Abby went into a deliciously silent house.

Only one more night without my love. I can't see how I would ever last a month of negotiations without you. I have noticed one benefit of these trips—I quickly lose my appetite. All I want is you, Abby. See, you are a higher need than food.

I tried calling you earlier this evening, even though you will be in my arms soon. It was my only release for the building tension I feel without you.

When your line was busy every time, I guess I had one of those anxiety attacks, heart going tight. It was hard to breathe. Now the only feeble release to my pent-up need is to continue writing. How these marks on a paper could make me feel so close to you is a mystery. At least you will have tangible proof of my great love for you, not that it is something you need.

We are so lucky we have no barriers to being happy always. Neither of us got into damaging relationships out of loneliness or need before we met. Naturally, we had involve-

ments with other people. But we realized they weren't the real thing. We were able to wait for the right person.

Although I always expected that I would marry some-day, I never thought I would be so completely in love and so satisfied with anyone. Now it would seem impossible to continue on alone.

I cannot be without you ever again.

Midnight

By now the separation from you is nearly unbearable. My God, what would I do IF. If something should ever destroy our love. Surely I would lapse into a catatonic stupor, unwilling and unable to function on this earth.

The longer I am without you, the greater my anxiety grows. I feel as if a huge iron lung is encasing my body with ever-tightening pressure that can only be relieved by your presence.

8:10 a.m.

I just took my last walk through the Roman market without you. Would it be asking too much if I asked that it be my last walk ever without you?

Initially I found myself only counting days until I saw you again. Now it is hours.

I can't wait until we are married. It will be another new high with you. Marriage will also provide a calming effect, I am sure. It is comparable to completing a story. No matter how much you have read and enjoyed it, you will never be satisfied until you finish it.

Or a better analogy is that marriage is another chapter in our lives. Not the end of anything but the beginning of a new phase.

I will continue this letter on the plane. It is only hours now, my love—

39 A Wedding

Aspen Hills was a fine place to get married or buried. The cemetery stood on a rise near the canyon with Mount Shoshone behind, dressed in purple velvet and a necklace of white. Below, the valley shimmered in the heat, with the sparkle of traffic here and there out to the horizon where the lake lay silver in the sun.

Elizabeth in her low-cut black dress and sling-back pumps hurried up the gravel road ahead of the family, her arms full of flowers. As she stooped to place them near the spot where her son would vow to love another, she was the picture of a voluptuous widow.

The wedding guests good-naturedly climbed the hill, some women carrying their better shoes, their slim ankles rising like stems out of their bulky sneakers. One lady did persist in spike heels, balancing on her husband's arm, her patent leather toes disappearing in the dust.

Tucker and Natalie's friends came wearing hiking boots.

The nearby foothills were bleached weeds this time of year, making the green of the cemetery lawn the more vivid, moist to its edges from the perpetual care of the sprinkling system here.

Suddenly from up high came the sound of bagpipes, their pure penetrating notes causing people to look. Where? Where? There he was, the bagpiper lifting his knees sharply under his red-plaid skirt as he stepped between the tombstones.

Elizabeth, who had anticipated rock music on this day, looked up from her flower arranging with parted lips.

Jack's motorcycle answered below, arriving with lusty farts. He did a wheelie in the parking lot then started up the hillside until his bike was spinning in the dust. He got off, rubbed the toes of his boots on his pant legs, and made his way toward his wife.

Elizabeth had turned away from the sound of the detested bike and was stuffing flowers in a clay pot. Jack came up behind her and put his hands around her waist. She stayed rigid, staring away from him. Yet as the sweet notes of the bagpipe sounded across the cemetery, and the setting sun gave way to arms of shade, Elizabeth turned and rested her forehead on her husband's chest.

A minute later she was calling to Roy. "Come back here. You'll get all dirty." He was scrambling up the hill into the dusty weeds. With a whoop he turned, slid down in his dark adult-looking suit, and chased across the lawn to hop from grave to grave.

"Stop that." Elizabeth's face grew dark as she confronted her younger son, born to be her next trouble. "Abby, take him."

So she and Roy found a place to sit and watch the guests, on the lookout for Natalie's parents, who were forced to meet on this day. After leaving her husband, Mona had gone through several men. But to everyone's surprise, she had stayed with her current companion for over a year.

Natalie's father, Milton, got married soon after his divorce to a widow he met in his capacity at the funeral home. The woman's husband had died unexpectedly from a bee sting, and perhaps the shock propelled her into marriage too soon, for she left Milton a few months later. Doggedly he tried marriage again, this time to someone who had been divorced.

"That's her. That's got to be Natalie's mom," Roy whispered. The woman had Natalie's dark flashing eyes and proud demeanor. In a magenta dashiki, she was more flamboyant than her daughter. But there was something familiar in her walk. Regally she came, barely slowed by her task of propelling the wheelchair that contained her current companion. Chad had been a husky fellow when they met. Then almost immediately after he moved in with Mona, a mysterious disease had caused him to shrink. Natalie expected that her mother would leave Chad as she had the others. However, Mona seemed to thrive with this man. She stayed with him, she said, because she didn't have to.

Despite his altered size, the occupant of the wheelchair smiled cheerfully, rolling along as if he were in a parade. Chad guided his driver to a row of empty seats, where Mona parked him on the aisle, laughing at something he said as she sat down.

Tucker stood in front wearing his usual black jeans but with a white tuxedo today. And something else was radically different. His dreadlocks were gone. Tuck's reddish hair had been cut, combed back, and greased, still wavy though from being in braids. He had not given up his gold earring, which gleamed in the late afternoon sunlight as he turned to watch for Natalie.

Ten minutes went by, fifteen, and a nervous buzz started up among the wedding guests as they looked around for the bride. She might be having trouble with her dress. Maybe she'd forgotten something. Or she could have changed her mind. Folks looked this way and that, not knowing where a bride would come from out here.

Something in the trees moved, and out came Natalie's father, a tall, gangly man in black, from his bola tie to the cowboy boots poking out from his extra-long pants. His hair was jet black too. Plenty of hair, though not necessarily tamed for the occasion. A tuft sprouted up on his crown like a section of lawn the mower has missed.

Milton was followed by wife number three, young and forlorn in a flowered, waistless dress as she cast about for an empty seat. But you can't catch up to someone else's family, can you. A first wife, maybe. A second wife, never. A third wife, don't even try.

People turned to watch the father of the bride. All but Mona and her companion in the wheelchair, who chatted and laughed conspicuously.

Remembering his new wife, Milton went back to situate her in a folding chair. He gave her shoulder a pat and then headed across the lawn into a grove of aspen trees.

Everyone was watching. Surely something was wrong.

Finally, a cry went up, "Here she comes!" The bride emerged from her wilderness dressing room onto the cemetery lawn. Yet it was a Natalie the likes of which Tucker's family had not seen.

She who had only been sighted in sweats or jeans with a baggy top now glided in a fabulous wedding dress. Not cream-colored. Not eggshell. This one was pure white. Yards of skirt floated forth. Lacy sleeves extended to emphasize long, exquisite fingers. Most amazing was the astonishingly slim waist of the dress. Where did that come from? So this had been their Natalie all along, just hidden.

Tucker blinked his eyes. Natalie stepped onto the red carpet going between the chairs, looking only at him. No veil obscured her lovely, slender face, whose olive skin could abide the sun. Her dark hair was pulled back with a gardenia in it. Gradually she came, her pearl drop earrings trembling.

Milton, a foot taller than his only daughter, bent to hold out his arm, even though he seemed to be the one needing support. His big awkward step put him well ahead of her. Even when he self-consciously shortened his gait, he had difficulty matching her stride. Yet here they came, one more proud father giving away his daughter to the strains of Mendelssohn's wedding march, which boomed out of the bushes on cue.

The couple faced each other to say the vows that they had written. Tucker promised to listen to Natalie; she said she would not nag. The groom leaned to kiss his bride. But something was wrong with this picture. Milton was still in it. He stood there between the pair and wouldn't go away. Tuck barely got his chance before the father took his turn, kissing his daughter on the lips and hugging her as if he would never let her go.

All was quiet in the cemetery.

When Milton finally released his grip, the crowd applauded with a special vigor. But success was not to be his. As he turned to go, Milton tripped on the toe of his cowboy boot, lunging at the wheelchair in his way, narrowly missing it, and stumbling on down the aisle, barely staying on his feet. It must have been a long walk after that back to the empty chair by his young wife.

The guests then looked to the front, whistling and cheering "the new Mr. and Mrs. Tucker Thompson."

The reception as well exuded that gay air of relief which may be the most noticeable aspect of post-wedding celebrations.

Arthur had arrived, and he helped Abby keep the punch bowl filled. By now even the most reluctant guests were up and dancing under the green and white canopy on this warm night. Ready for rain, but it never came. Even Elizabeth looked pleased with the evening's events, perhaps surprised that no disaster had occurred. Milton danced with his daughter every chance he got, and Mona took Tucker for several spins around the small improvised dance floor, adeptly maneuvering around her ex.

Abby and Arthur danced as they never had in high school. It was easy being in his arms. Someone mentioned what a nice-looking couple they were. But tonight was no time to speak of their plans, was it. This was Tucker and Natalie's night, he at the age of twenty, she at twenty-three, marrying for the first time with all the hope that brings.

At last the couple waved their good-byes and slipped away to get ready for their honeymoon in Mexico.

One small drama was yet to take place. She and Arthur saw it. They stopped stacking the dessert plates to watch, as the band announced its final number.

Mona whispered something to her companion. He had been quite the center of attention, attracting guests to his wheelchair, those who didn't like to dance and would rather be humanitarian.

Across the yard Milton sat slumped on a bench by some bushes, looking into his drink. His wife had gone somewhere.

With a sweep of her dashiki, Mona strode across the dance floor, the gold thread in her open sleeves sparkling as she stepped off onto the grass, going over to where Milton sat. She reached out to him.

He looked up sharply. Then he slowly extended his hand. When he stood, he seemed taller than before. And he moved with a new grace as the two of them danced the last dance together.

40 *Dream Man*

He came toward her. She was not imagining this. He was coming from the bus stop, taking off his tie as he hurried home.

Abby went to meet him, of course she did, past the magnolia tree with its creamy bloom down in dark leaves, petals soft as skin.

Stan was smiling at her. He put his arm around her shoulders. "Are you OK?"

Many things came up in her to say, but she did not speak. Then those things didn't matter anymore. Troubles of the past, gone like something in a bad dream.

They came to their house on Shenandoah Street, where Dwayne was perched in the window as he always was, his tabby body filling it.

She and Stan were sitting on their white leather couch. He tossed out his tie with a red stripe in it. She recognized that tie. Dwayne hopped down from the window, making a thud—she heard the sound—and trotted over. The sun came in the room, warm on them.

Stan took her hand. She could feel the callous where he held his racket, the sharp edge of his skin. His eyes were blue. Those were Stan's eyes. "I am so sorry," he said. He turned the palm of her hand up and ran his finger along it. "But you knew I'd be back."

The old nausea, the fear of hoping came up in her. Then by some miracle it washed away, blessedly gone, leaving her cleaner than she had ever felt. A light came into her, filling her entire body.

"I hoped," she said, able to smile at him now. Stan looked glad. Extremely relieved. She realized then how difficult it must be for a person to come back.

Yet here he was. She always knew she would see him again. Stan held her close, so close that their hearts were touching, the way it had always been with them. How lucky that in her pain and her anger she hadn't spoiled it all. She might have cursed him, burned his precious letters. She had wanted him dead. Dead!

Now everything was new. You can become new again.

She and Stan were laughing at something, anything. Life was light, as it truly can be. They could go to the grocery store again. Go to the movies.

They stood out on their patio, the comforting heat of the pavement coming up in them. It was Virginia and green all around. The bent shadow nearby was the dogwood tree, growing up beside them, blooming all in white.

Abby woke up in her mother's basement, where the sun came through the window well, warm on the couch.

Even though the dream was gone, its sweetness stayed in her, all throughout her body.

It was time to get ready for Arthur. She would go to him. Go now.

She drove high in her father's Isuzu through the August light, past shadows slanting along the long green lawns. It was all very beautiful.

They went out for barbecued ribs. She had never tasted any more tender and delicious. The meat slipped sweetly off the bone. The potato skin was baked to crispy perfection, created to be a butter boat, and she used it as such. And in Utah restaurants they serve every kind of pie.

"I'm ready. Done with my baggage," she told Arthur.

He laughed at her. "OK." He did look pleased. She thought how great it would be to make a man happy.

"I can learn to be a stepmother. I'll just back off."

"You'll get to like each other." Arthur stroked her hand. "Things will get better."

"I'm sure your boy can be just fine. But don't you see? That's what we learn from a first marriage. Not to expect too much."

"You wanted more than I did." Arthur took a bite of potato with no butter on it, not even sour cream. Who could do that? Well, she liked him anyway.

"You must have had some expectations."

"I'm easy." Arthur drank his water, even though he had a glass of wine. Wine, water, juice. He was comfortable with it all. "I just hope you'll want to stick around."

Abby blinked at him. "You think I would leave someone after what happened to me? Arthur, Arthur. Surely you know me better than that. My worry is that you won't tell me when something bothers you. It's too scary when a man is positive all the time."

"What if nothing bothers me?"

"Oh please. At least tell me one thing you want in a wife."

Arthur looked around the restaurant, where a waitress carried a platter of ribs and onion rings and glasses of Coke along one arm. "I don't need somebody cooking for me." What? Abby had planned to be domestic this time, trying new recipes as never before. "I can eat a bag of chips," he said.

Abby had been known to subsist on that herself, quite a pleasant thing to do really, nibbling your dinner. Well, all right. Not all habits of single life must be abandoned. Maybe Arthur was onto something here: marriage without meals. They would live a carefree life. Survive on snacks. "All right," she answered, pleased with herself for being so flexible.

But she had to ask, "Is there nothing that would break your heart?"

"If something happened to Danny, sure. But I guess if it's a person's time to go, it is."

That type of fatalism had not been helpful in her life. Well, maybe she could learn (if she hadn't been ruined by how-to books). "You really weren't devastated when Isabel left?"

"It was bad. But not really. Our marriage never was that great."

"Would you ever have left her?" Abby pressed on.

"Nope."

What a comfort in that thought! It should help in every way. And surely she could change and live out here. Look to the mountains. Enjoy the delicious desserts. The sun shines every day.

She and Arthur said a tender goodnight, brimming with their future.

Only as Abby closed the door, feeling the cool ease of the knob, the swift click behind her bringing its rush of freedom, did she realize what Arthur had probably known all along.

What if? There she stood, knowing it was possible. Some morning in the spring, when the planes were flying east, she too could be sitting on a bed next to someone, saying, "I never meant for this to happen. It has nothing to do with you."

41 *Cat at My Window*

I doze in the sun. I can see again a cat who came to my window a long time ago. Her coat was gold in the sunlight as she came stepping through the grass with her white paws.

I leaped up to my basement window. The cat meandered on by. I chased around the room as if she were there, racing around the walls, going where she went.

She came another day, strolling by my window, rubbing against it. She looked in at me with her big eyes. My body was quivering.

I watched for her. Sometimes she lay down by the window and slept right there. I pressed against the glass, up next to her purring. Or maybe the sound was me. I did not sleep. I stared at her. I saw her eyes shut down and disappear in the gold stripes of her face. Her body lifted as she breathed. A whisker twitched, and her paw slapped it. She hiccuped in her sleep. Dreaming of tuna fish perhaps. Her ears were pink in the light.

One day she came limping. Had she been hit by the wheels of the highway? Kicked by a cruel foot? Did she get in a fight with another cat? *Grrr.* My hind end shook. I prepared to pounce, to ravish with my teeth. She licked the hurt paw, and it jerked away. Her nose had a dark scratch on it. Dirt clung to her. She wandered away.

I galloped around my enclosure, dashing up and stopping in front of walls. I looked for her. She did not come. I watched out in the grass for her stripes bouncing along. I could not see them.

I stayed longer at my dish. I stopped staring outside.

Then one day a shadow moved on the floor. I felt something up in the window behind me. The cat was back! She moved more slowly. Her coat was not as shiny as before. But it was her. There she was at my window again.

A purr started up in me, rattling through my body. I sprang up, knocking papers flying in the air, books smacking on the floor. I meowed. I waved my tail. I lay down beside her.

When she went away, I was still so excited I barely made it to my litter box.

All that was long ago.

Now I live up high where branches grow. A bird hops by, and I get agitated momentarily. My fur fluffs up. I growl. The creature flaps away, and I go back to sleep, sleeping peacefully.

I can still see the cat who came to my window once, a golden cat in the sunlight, stepping through the grass with her white paws.

42 *Mount Shoshone*

When you have come back from Wong San,
other mountains are nothing.
—from the Chinese

"Can we go on the fire watch, Aunt Abby? Please, please?" Roy blinked his highly expressive, big brown eyes.

"You'll be bored watching for smoke."

"I won't, I won't. We'll probably see a fire. I bet we will."

Well, grab him while he cared. Soon Roy would be a teenager and not want to speak to an adult again. She could do her packing later. "OK. Let's go."

The fire watch took place at the station in the canyon facing the back side of Mount Shoshone. Here the limestone cliffs rise steeply, and the glacier stays all year, supplying water for the towns below. The switchback trails going up cut through the foliage like comb marks. A waterfall from a distance is a mere white thread in rock. But if you look carefully, you can see it move.

Roy brought his Game Boy, and Abby had a book. But she couldn't keep her eyes on the page. They lifted to the mountain, where the Indian lovers lay chiseled against the

293

blue, his headdress at one end, her hair tumbling down the other. There for the ages. You could almost see them breathe.

"Aunt Abby, there's smoke. It's a fire." Roy jumped up and raced to the call box on the wall, which they had been warned not to use carelessly. "Look, over here." The hazy area where Roy pointed could easily be mistaken for smoke by someone seeking a fire. Yet the film across the canyon remained level. She reminded Roy that most forest fires are started by lightning. This was a peaceful summer day.

He went back to his game, disappointed.

And Abby thought how good an ordinary day is after you have had bad years.

When their watch was done, she and Roy decided to take a short hike. Just check out the main trail going up Mount Shoshone. Naturally, once they started, he begged to go the whole way. "You went to the top. You're always talking about that."

"And you will, Roy. But not today. It's eight miles up, and you'll need an early start. We'll just test out the trail."

Aspens lay twisted in their way, bent to the earth by last winter's snow. Then the path cleared and moved steeply up. In no time they looked back with pride at how far they had come. Cars inching along on the canyon road were toys. The Anderson dream home was a pile of sticks on the hillside.

Roy raced on ahead, showing that he could run uphill, his slim boy's body lost in Levi's that dropped off his hips. He wore his red baseball cap backward, the way kids do.

Abby caught up to him where the trail grew wide enough for two. They walked together. "You're a good kid."

"You don't know the bad thing I did."

"We all do bad things."

"Promise you won't tell?"

"Sure."

"You're the one I shouldn't tell." Roy broke from her, stumbling up the hill. "I did it to *his* pictures."

"What, Roy, what?"

He stopped and scowled, his pale face drawn with great seriousness. "Promise you won't be mad? It was *him*."

"Uncle Stan?"

Roy threw his arms around his head, covering his eyes and ears. "I'm not supposed to talk about him." He scampered on up the trail, turning at the switchback, out of sight.

"It's all right," she called. He didn't answer.

She heard a squeal up there. He must have seen something. It wasn't the sound of a person falling or being hurt. Roy stood on a rock. "I dropped my bear." He started to cry. "I'm going to get Bob. I've got to get him."

"Don't you dare," she called, sounding like a mother. Being an aunt was better, just having fun. "You stay right there." Why did he have to bring that damn bear along, anyway? Isn't nine too old to have a teddy bear?

Roy was sliding off the trail, going for Bob. "OK, wait. I'm coming with you." A rock bounced down the hill and cracked into the canyon. Then it was quiet on the mountainside.

"Roy?" she shouted. Her voice came back. She could not see him. "Don't you dare do anything crazy. It's just a teddy bear. We'll get you another one," she said, realizing that was a dumb idea.

She gazed into the ravine, where bushes were claws, tree trunks clubs. The bottom was rock. A body could easily be lost down there. By the time help came, it would be too late. She listened for the sound of moaning. She looked for a boy's red baseball hat.

"Roy?" she called. "Roy," she whispered.

Oh, God, oh, God. Not that. Please not him.

She ran down the trail, feet slamming the ground, her insides jamming against her ribs. The walls of the canyon, with their fabulous and familiar shapes, were sublime no more. Cruel stone. What had she been thinking, bringing that boy up here?

"Hi, Aunt Abby." She slid down on her butt, gripped a rock, and looked up. Roy was sitting on a ledge, swinging his legs. "I found my bear. I got Bob back." He waved a paw.

"Don't you move. You stay right there." She marched up the trail, turning sharply at the switchback, although her fury was modulating to a queasy gratitude. "You had me scared to death."

"Sorry," Roy said, hugging his bear.

He did hold onto her hand after that. "So, you want to know the bad thing I did?"

"Yes. Tell me what you did."

"I colored spiky hair on him in the family picture book."

296

"Uncle Stan."

"I didn't mean to. I couldn't stop."

She started to laugh. Roy watched her and then joined in. If there's a better sound than a kid's laughter on a mountainside, she didn't know what. They laughed together there.

"That's good." She stopped and wiped her eyes.

"My mom said to pretend that Uncle Stan was dead. She called him a dirty word. *Bastard.* But the black crayon spikes looked gross. So I got the scissors and cut off his head in the pictures."

"And he still wouldn't go away."

"I knew I was in trouble then. So I hid the picture album in the piano bench. Nobody plays that music anyway. My mom never does. Promise you won't tell?"

"I won't. But you know who will get blamed."

Roy stomped the ground. "Me. I'm the only kid."

"Tell them you were pretending Uncle Stan was dead."

"He was mean to you. You hate him."

Abby stopped on the path, where the shadows had come by now, but across the canyon the sun was bright. "You think that I *hate* Stan? Oh no, Roy," she said softly. "Can I tell you my secret?"

"Sure." His eyes were big.

"People don't like me talking about him. I'm supposed to be over that—like when they say you're too old for your teddy bear."

"I've had Bob for my whole life." Roy held up the bald bear with floppy arms.

"I like that about you." She rested her arm around Roy's

narrow shoulders, and they walked in silence for awhile. They stopped to look back up at the glacier, a graceful curve of white away from the sun, never to melt. "You'll hike to the top before long."

"Can we go next year? Will you come?"

"Don't know if I could make it."

"You could. You could."

"So, what do you remember about Uncle Stan?" Abby asked as they headed down the mountain. Roy hesitated, curling his fingers tight inside of hers. "Go ahead. Say anything."

"Uncle Stan was fun," he burst out. "That time we went out to Washington, and he took us to see the fireworks. I never saw so many people. He put me on his shoulders. Only Uncle Stan is a short guy."

"Yes, he is," she said. "Just right. And he tries harder on the tennis court, running all-out for every shot."

"You honestly like short guys?" Roy stood as tall as he could.

"I surely do. Why would I want a sore neck?" Abby answered, contorting herself as if she were facing up to kiss a giant.

Roy giggled. "Your friend Arthur isn't short. Are you going to marry him?"

"Probably not."

"He's nice." Roy patted his bear.

"He's very nice. We just don't care enough."

They were coming down by the waterfall. A rustling. Then rushing water, bigger and bigger. Thunder. "Would you marry somebody else?" Roy asked.

"Maybe. Sure." They entered the spray of the falls, letting it get them wet. "So, do you have a girlfriend, Roy?"

"Aunt Abby, I'm just a kid. I hate girls." He threw a rock in the pool at the bottom of the falls. "There's this girl who's after me. She calls me up. I told her I need my space."

"At the age of nine, I would say so. Maybe you always will. Not everyone should be married."

"I'm never getting married." Roy stepped back from the plunging water.

"Oh, but it's a fine thing to try."

She looked out across the darkening canyon to where the hills were gold. A smile came up in her for the great joy she'd had.

The earth grew warm as they came down into a meadow. There through the trees was the red roof of Deer Lodge. "Look. That's where Stan and I got married, on New Year's Day of the year you were born. The snow was as high as your head. Gigantic icicles glittered in the windows. My dress sparkled when I moved. They say it was below zero that night, but I never felt the cold.

"Stan was waiting in front of the lodge, so handsome in a black tuxedo, standing out against the snow.

"Some people cry at weddings. We looked at each other and laughed. Afterward, we crossed the bridge to the banquet hall, where the stream bubbles up out of ice. How does it do that? The path was lit with candles in brown paper bags. The flame inside them danced.

"A full moon came out, making the snow bright. It was the biggest moon I've ever seen. According to the scientific journals, it was the most luminous of the century.

"That's my secret, Roy, my thoughts that I'm supposed to hide. I'm reading Stan's letters from long ago. Once. I will read them once."

Roy skipped along beside her. "That's what you were doing in the root cellar. Your memorabilia." Smart kid, remembering the very word.

"I happen to have a letter with me now." Abby took a page of hotel stationary out of the back pocket of her jeans.

"I want to see. What does Uncle Stan say?"

And so she read.

Finally, we are in the air leaving Rome. Instead of days I can count the hours and at last the minutes until I see you.

I cannot stop writing. I must have some connection with you, as if you are my oxygen. So my letter continues. It will probably be the longest letter you'll ever get, if not the most literary.

For the last ten minutes, I tried to read a magazine, attempting to convince myself that I could focus on something else. It didn't work. The hotels in the travel ads only made me imagine being in such places with you.

We must marry soon. This current separation has given me an urgent need for that. Let me say it again. I would be honored if you would be mine always. If something were to happen to make that impossible, how bleak my life would be. I wouldn't want to live without you.

"Bleak, what is that?" Roy asked.

"Sad. Empty. Not fun at all."

"Wow."

In a few hours we will see each other again, God willing (a phrase I would never have used before). How wonderful, spectacular, exhilarating that you will be waiting for me. How terrible, dwindling, and death-like it would be if for some reason you were not in my life.

I have no reason for saying this, only that sometimes life's possibilities are so glorious and the future is so full of hope and warmth, a person can get afraid.

They are bringing the trays of food, so I will stop temporarily. I guess I better eat to sustain me for the joyful hours ahead.

Then I will return to my stumbling and repetitive words, which I know you will receive generously, as they come from my heart.

Be with me always, Abby—

Mary Allen Redd
(PhD, University of Maryland)
teaches English at
Utah State Valley College.
She lives in Provo
with her husband, a dog, and
a cat.